THE TRUTH DANCER

Stave V of V: Fire

L.R. Merriman

"Let her and Falsehood grapple;
who ever knew Truth put to the worse,
in a free and open encounter?"

— John Milton

Being the First Movement of

Spirit of Truth

THE TRUTH DANCER

Stave V of V: Fire

L.R. Merriman

Truth Point

This is a work of fiction. Names, characters, places, and incidents either are the product of the author's imagination or are used fictitiously. Any resemblance to actual persons, living or dead, events, or locales is entirely coincidental.

AI was used during the creation of this work to generate chapter header calligraphy and suggest editorial revisions under the direction and guidance of the author.

Published by Truth Point LLC
Sheridan, Wyoming
thetruth.dance

First edition, 2026

The Truth Dancer · Stave V of V

Library of Congress Control Number: 2026917288

ISBN: 979-8-9944334-8-5

10 9 8 7 6 5 4 3 2

rev. 574849b · 2026-07-26

Books in the

SPIRIT OF TRUTH

series

Movement I

THE TRUTH DANCER

STAVE I · EARTH

STAVE II · WATER

STAVE III · AIR

STAVE IV · SPIRIT

Stave V · Fire

Movement II

THE WILDS GIRL · FORTHCOMING

CONTENTS

Stave V

THAMARIA

thuh-MAIR-ee-uh /θə'mɛr.i.ə/

PRONUNCIATION GUIDE

Characters

Aerellyn
AIR-eh-lin /ˈɛər.ɛ.lɪn/

Aurvandiel
aur-VAN-dee-el /ɔrˈvæn.di.ɛl/

Elenden deArthis
EL-en-den deh-AR-this / ˈɛl.ɛn.dɛn dəˈɑr.θɪs/

Floré
flor-AY /flɔˈre/

Hadrian
HAY-dree-un /ˈheɪ.dri.ən/

Kells
KELZ /kɛlz/

Lün
LOON /luːn/

Melanthiel
meh-LAN-thee-el /mɛˈlæn.θi.ɛl/

Merauve
muhr-OV /mərˈɑv/

Niska
NIS-kah /ˈnɪs.kɑ/

Pakonaskow
pa-KOHN-as-kow /pəˈkoʊn.əs ˌkaʊ/

Sebastian
seh-BAS-chun /sɛˈbæs.tʃən/

Septain
sep-TAYN /sɛpˈteɪn/

Sorcha
SOR-cha /ˈsɔr.tʃə/

Therandien
ther-AN-dee-en /θɛˈræn.di.ɛn/

Theron
THAIR-un /ˈθɛr.ən/

Thulë
THOO-lay /ˈθuː.leɪ/

Tomás
toh-MASS /toʊˈmæs/

Vaylen
VAY-len /ˈveɪ.lɛn/

Places

Cindrel Vale
SIN-dril VAYL /ˈsɪn.drɪl veɪl/

Cobb
KOB /kɑb/

Drahan
DRAY-han /ˈdreɪ.hæn/

Kestrel
KES-trul /ˈkɛs.trəl/

Thamaria
thuh-MAIR-ee-uh /θəˈmɛr.i.ə/

Thane
THAYN /θeɪn/

Thellassian
the-LAS-ee-un /ðəˈlæs.i.ən/

Words & Terms

Argentil
AR-jen-teel /ˈɑr.dʒɛn.tiːl/

Arthis
AR-this /ˈɑr.θɪs/

Azurath
AZ-zhoor-ath /ˈæʒ.ʊrˌæθ/

deArthis
deh-AR-this /dəˈɑr.θɪs/

haraq
hah-RAHK /hɑˈrɑk/

Hilgeas
HIL-geez /ˈhɪl.ɡiːz/

Kaldren
KAHL-dren /ˈkɑl.drɛn/

kata
KA-ta /ˈkæ.tə/

Kervani
ker-VAN-ee /kərˈvæn.i/

Kon-dah
KOHN-dah /ˈkoʊn.dɑ/

Lok'tem
LOHK-tem /ˈloʊk.tɛm/

Orissan
oh-REES-un /oʊˈriːs.ən/

Qiran
ki-RAHN /kɪˈrɑn/

Shiranath
SHEER-uh-nath /ˈʃiːr.əˌnæθ/

Tachet
TA-chit /ˈtæ.tʃɪt/

Thamarian
thuh-MAIR-ee-un /θəˈmɛr.i.ən/

Val'dren
VAHL-dren /ˈvɑl.drɛn/

Valdris
VAL-dris /ˈvæl.drɪs/

STAVE V

Chapter 62

Reunion

I focused on counting steps, trailing my left hand along the wall, reading the familiar landmarks in the stone's texture. Jonathan's hand rested on my shoulder, his grip steady. His breath came even behind me. The turns came as naturally as breathing: left at the first junction past the barred gate, straight past the passage where *Azurath* still glowed faint above the forbidden stair, right where the ceiling dipped low enough to brush my hair.

We met no one.

That mercy alone made me whisper thanks as we walked. Master Limerick's instructions were specific: *Do not greet anyone on the way.* The thought of slipping past Brother Martín or Edwin in the dark and offering nothing but silence... My throat tightened. I hadn't realized how many people I would be leaving without farewell until the catacombs gave me time to count them.

The passages stretched longer than I remembered. Or perhaps my mind, knowing this was farewell, insisted on extending each step.

Scant light outlined the cobbler's exit at the top of a narrow stair—moonlight leaking through shuttered windows in the shop above. I climbed the steps and felt beside the doorframe for the catch, fingers searching longer than they should have. I hadn't triggered the mechanism last time.

"Trouble?" Jonathan's voice held a smile.

"The catch is... there." I pressed, felt it give. "Been a while since I used this exit."

The door swung open onto a storeroom thick with the smell of leather and boot polish. Shapes resolved as my eyes adjusted—shelves of finished shoes, lasts arranged in rows, a workbench covered with scraps and awls left mid-work.

I hesitated at the threshold.

Will I be able to get back in?

Would there be a Spirit School to return to? Would the Broken Anchor's basement still hum with morning chores and evening fellowship when I next walked these streets?

I pressed two fingers to my heart and stepped through; Jonathan followed. The door closed behind us with a soft click. Locked now, from the inside.

I had no key.

Haven's streets lay quiet in the autumn dark.

The moon hung three-quarters full, its light silvering the cobblestones and casting long shadows from eaves and awning poles. Our breath misted in the cold—winter was coming, and the night carried its advance scouts in the frost that rimmed the puddles between the stones.

We moved quickly, keeping to the edges of the thoroughfares where the shadows ran deepest. Jonathan matched my pace without complaint, though I caught him glancing skyward more than once.

We heard the market before we saw it.

Even at this hour—especially at this hour—Haven's market square hummed with commerce of the sort that preferred darkness. Braziers flickered at scattered stalls where vendors sold things best left unnamed. Figures clustered in doorways, their conversations falling silent as we passed. The air smelled of woodsmoke and cheap wine and something sweeter that I didn't want to identify.

A woman stepped into our path. Her dress hung low at the shoulder.

"Where are you boys hurrying off to so late?" Her voice carried honey and calculation in equal measure. "Looking for somewhere warm to—"

Jonathan's hand caught my elbow and pulled me past without breaking stride.

The woman's laughter followed us into the night, fading as we left the market's glow for darker roads beyond the walls.

The dirt road south unwound before us, pale in the moonlight, rutted from cart wheels and hooves. The buildings thinned, then vanished. Farmland opened on either side—fields gone dormant for the winter, their stubble silver with frost. The pack pressed heavy against my shoulders, heavier than I'd expected. Master Limerick had said there were supplies enough for both of us. I hadn't considered what "enough" might weigh.

Jonathan walked beside me now that the road allowed it, his eyes lifting skyward at intervals. He raised his arm, fist clenched at full extension toward the western horizon where the moon sat. Stacked his other fist above it. Then lowered both.

"What are you doing?"

"Measuring time. I read that the Sandril travel mostly at night, navigating by the stars—but I never learned the constellations well enough." He repeated the gesture. "The moon's easier. A fist and a half of movement is roughly an hour. Master Limerick said two hours south before we stop."

"And?"

"We're about halfway." He smiled, but the expression held weariness beneath its warmth. "Let's keep moving."

The adrenaline that had propelled us through the catacombs began to fade, leaving only questions in its wake. Where was Limerick now? Had the soldiers believed whatever story he'd prepared? Were they searching the house, the garden, the gate to the catacombs?

"You're thinking loud enough to wake the dead."

"Am I?"

"Your breathing changed. And you started walking faster." He adjusted his pack strap, then let out a long breath. "I told Sorcha I wouldn't leave without saying goodbye. Then did exactly that."

I said nothing.

"She'll forgive me eventually," Jonathan continued. "I'll write from Ember. She'll understand. She knows what it costs to leave without goodbye. She's done it herself."

Walking helped. The questions kept circling, but some of their edges had dulled.

Jonathan called a halt when the moon had traveled three fists since we'd left Haven.

"Here," he said, pointing toward a stand of evergreens that marked a border between two fields. The trees rose dark against the stars—firs, I thought, their branches climbing in neat whorls. "That should do."

We left the road and picked our way across the frozen stubble. I swung my pack down at the edge of the trees, grateful to be free of its weight while Jonathan gathered deadfall from beneath the outer branches.

"I nearly set my cloak on fire trying to warm up under a pine once. The pitch caught like lamp oil." He arranged stones in a rough ring, then nodded toward the firs above us. "These branches should be high enough. And thank the Spirit there's no snow yet."

I worked my pack's buckles, leather stiff with cold, straps unfamiliar. When the main compartment finally opened, moonlight fell across its contents.

A dark green felt case. Beneath it, a small drawstring pouch—flint and steel, tinder wrapped in oilskin. I set it beside Jonathan and kept searching. Down low were the bedrolls, tightly rolled. A change of clothes. A waterskin. But there, wrapped in clean linen—

I knew that smell.

◁

The cloth came away to reveal biscuits, their tops golden-brown, their scent rising into the night air. Still warmer than the surrounding cold. Beside them, wedges of hard cheese and strips of dried meat.

My throat tightened. Mistress Cathal had known, or at least suspected. The fussing over us at the kitchen table, the repeated insistence that we eat more—she had seen our departure coming before we had. I imagined her now: greeting the Imperial soldiers at the door with that imperturbable expression, offering tea while we fled through tunnels beneath her feet. No doubt grumbling over the inconvenience while quietly priding herself on accommodating them.

The fire caught on Jonathan's third attempt. Small flames climbed through the arranged wood, painting our clearing in warm light.

We ate without speaking much. The biscuits were perfect—tender within, crisp without. The cheese broke cleanly. The meat rewarded patience. Mistress Cathal's cooking had never tasted so precious.

When the food was gone, I reached for the green felt case.

"Jonathan." I held it up. "Thank you. For this."

"Let's hear it." He smiled and nodded. "That's thanks enough."

The case unfolded like a flower blooming—three sections of polished wood. The brass collars caught the flames as I assembled them, each piece twisting into the next with a soft squeak. Assembled, the instrument stretched nearly twice the length of Tobias' mountain ash pipe.

I raised it to my lips, found the angle, and split my breath across the edge.

The first note came uncertain—this instrument required different technique from a simple pipe. But the second note found its center, and the third, and then I was playing.

No song at first. Just fragments. Phrases that rose and fell like breathing, like firelight on stone. The sideflute's voice was richer than I remembered, resonant in the cold air.

Then, without deciding to, I found the opening notes of something that had no name. A melody built from the ache of departure—the hard work of soup kitchens and the confusion of politics I didn't understand. The sacrifice of masters who gave themselves to a city that hated them.

▽

The mystery of blue symbols glowing in the dark. Limerick's fierce embrace and the sound of laughter on mornings when the world seemed simple.

Haven.

I was playing Haven.

Not the city of merchants, thieves, and constables who'd thrown me in a cell. But the other Haven—the one that hid beneath the surface like the catacombs themselves. The Haven that fed the poor and sang in silver caverns and held light in its cupped hands against the gathering dark.

The melody wound toward silence.

Jonathan's sigh broke the stillness. He'd arranged his bedroll near the fire, his head pillowed on his pack, his eyes reflecting flame.

"I missed this," he said.

I drew the cloth through each section before disassembling them, brass collars releasing with soft clicks. The felt pockets received each piece in turn, and I smoothed the case closed and wrapped the strap securely before tucking it beside my bedroll.

"So did I."

That first morning, we spread the pack's contents across the frosty grass and took proper inventory.

Master Limerick had packed for a journey, not an escape. Oats wrapped in oilcloth—enough for seven or eight hot breakfasts if we stretched them. A small tin of salt. Dried apples. The cheese and meat we hadn't finished the night before. A coil of thin rope. Two knives: one for food, one that wasn't. Flint and steel. A compass that Jonathan pocketed immediately.

Beneath the practical supplies, I found a small lacquered box sealed with wax. The characters on its lid were Qiran.

"Tea?" Jonathan took it from my hands and inhaled, turning it toward the morning light. "This is fine work. The box looks Southern provincial, but the artwork is all Qiran—see how the mountains are stylized?" He passed it back.

I turned the box in my hands. The lacquer was deep red, almost black, with a pattern of mountains picked out in gold. Someone selected this with care: someone whose kindness had always required an interpreter, whose corrections I'd heard as contempt, whose patience I'd mistaken for disdain.

This box needed no translation. The gift said what the words couldn't.

I tucked it carefully beside the bedrolls.

Deeper still, my fingers found parchment. A letter, thick and folded, addressed in Master Limerick's hand: *Roman*.

I drew it out—and nearly dropped it.

The working on the seal hit like a slap. My vision swam. The letter seemed suddenly fascinating, desperately important, the most interesting thing I ever held. I needed to open it. Needed to read what was inside. Needed to—

"El?" Jonathan's voice came from somewhere distant. "Toss me the oats?"

I blinked. Forced my eyes away from the seal. The compulsion released like a hand unclenching from my throat. I shoved it back into the pack without looking at it again. My hands were shaking.

Jonathan watched me with sharp eyes. "Something wrong?"

"I found some correspondence addressed to Master Roman. There's some enchantment on it." I swallowed. "Definitely Master Limerick's work. Different, but—maybe some kind of test. Or protection." I cinched the pack closed. "I'm not going to find out which."

We redistributed the weight between us, though not by much. Jonathan's own pack bulged with books and manuscripts—the fruits of his months with Elder Master Hadrian.

"If your pipes weighed five times as much," he said when I remarked on it, "would you leave them behind?"

Fair enough.

We fell into our old rhythms quickly. I woke first most mornings, coaxing the fire back from its overnight embers while Jonathan slept a few minutes longer. Then forms: I cycled through the schools—Earth's grounded stances, Air's flowing sequences, Water's circular movements, Spirit's open-armed vulnerabilities.

Jonathan occasionally joined me for Water forms—his technique was better than mine, actually. His years at the monastery showed in the smooth transitions between stances.

"Your weight's too far forward," he said on the third morning, watching me struggle through *Bending Kelp*. "Here—" He demonstrated, sinking his hips back while his arms swept the opposite direction. "The counterbalance comes from your center, not your shoulders. Imagine holding a staff."

I tried again. Better.

Spirit forms he practiced alongside me most often, though his versions differed slightly from what Brother Martín had taught. The same shapes, the same vulnerability—but the rhythm varied, as if the forms had been passed down through different lineages and slowly diverged.

He cooked while I made tea from the lacquered box—dark leaves that steeped into something slightly bitter, with an aftertaste like smoke and something floral I couldn't name. Then we walked.

Those first days, we traded stories. I told him about Haven: the catacombs, the *Azurath* glowing above forbidden doors, the masters who had watched over me in the dark. My time lost beneath the city. The council. Master Feng's brutal instruction and the morning we'd wept during our final sparring.

Jonathan listened the way he always did—completely, without interruption, holding his questions until I'd found the shape of what I needed to say.

"The writing above the stone doors," he asked when I'd finished describing my dream-wandering through the catacombs. "The *Azurath*. Could you read any of it?"

"When I was dreaming, I could read everything. Understand it, even." I kicked a stone from the path. "But I only cared about one word. One name."

"Melanthiel."

I nodded.

Jonathan walked on in silence, his brow furrowed the way it did when he was working through a problem.

"You need to learn Temple notation," he said finally. "If you're going to keep encountering Singer script, you should at least know how the sounds work. Even if you can't read the meaning, you could speak what you see; at least remember it well enough to record it."

I asked about Waterfall. About Willem.

"He and Seline asked permission to leave not two days before I set out for Haven." Jonathan smiled. "Going to seek her father's blessing before the snows made travel too hard. 'Do things properly,' Willem said. He was practically glowing when we parted."

"They're getting married?"

"If her father agrees. And knowing Willem..." Jonathan shook his head. "The man could charm winter into spring if he set his mind to it."

The days blurred together. Walk. Rest. Walk. Make camp. Lessons by firelight.

On our third evening, Jonathan selected a branch from the fire—its end still glowing ember-orange—and crouched beside a patch of bare earth. Where the hot tip touched the ground, it left marks that smoldered faintly, each stroke holding its light for a heartbeat before fading to char.

"The phonetic system," he explained, drawing a symbol that flickered like a captive star. "Two parts to every written sound. A character for the consonant—the bones of a word." He tapped the smoldering shape. "And marks around it for the vowel—the breath that gives it voice. You could write any word in any language if you knew enough of them."

He drew a character that looked like a bird's footprint pressed into mud—the consonant, he said. The 'r' sound. Then he touched the ember to a point beside the character, leaving a small open circle.

"That mark makes it 'ar.' The opening of *Aurvandiel*." He brushed the earth clean and drew the consonant again, this time ringing five open circles around it, evenly spaced. "Five positions. Five open sounds."

He spoke each one, touching the corresponding circle—*ee, ay, aw, oh, oo*—front to back of the mouth, tense and projected, the sequence opening and then closing as his finger moved. I knew those sounds. I'd heard them cycling through the passages beneath Haven, distant and strange—and again, up close, when Septain's singers tuned their voices before the first note of true song.

"Combine this with the consonant for 'r', and this is how you'd start to write reed, ray, raw, road, root..."

"Dots for the quieter cousins—*ih, eh, a, uh, uu*." Jonathan pressed the ember firmly at the topmost position, turning the circle into a filled point. "Circle here sings *ee*. Dot here gives you *ih*. Same position, less projection." He demonstrated rib, red, rat, run, rook.

"When one sound slides into another, you draw the journey. So for the sound *ow* like now, draw from the dot *a* to the circle *oo*." He drew a swooping line between the two positions.

Another character followed—curved like a river unsure of its course. Jonathan drew an open circle in the bottom left, ember-bright against the night. "This is 'on.' Listen." He said the names slowly, stressing the second syllable: "*Ar-VON-dee-el. Mel-ON-thee-el. Thair-ON-dee-en.*" He looked up. "It's in every dragon name we've found. Wherever it is used, the stress of the name falls on it."

"The same sound in every name?"

Jonathan nodded. "The same symbol. Sometimes with a modifier, but yes. Elder Master Hadrian believes the word 'dragon' itself may predate the splitting of tongues—inherited whole into every language from the oldest."

Each evening brought new lessons, the ember-traced symbols burning orange against my vision long after the light faded—a warmer echo of the blue *Azurath* that lit the catacombs. Each day's walking became review—Jonathan quizzing me on sounds, correcting my pronunciation, wandering into tangents about linguistic connections he and Hadrian had discovered.

"Thamarian doesn't have this sound," he said one afternoon as we walked, demonstrating something that emerged as a breathy hiss around his tongue—air escaping around the sides rather than over the top. "But it's common in Orissan. They position their tongue for an 'l' but blow air around the edges." He tried it again, the sound strange and ancient. "The Qiran use the standard 'l', which only deepens the hatred between the peoples. Orissan purists hear every ordinary 'l' as evidence of cultural contamination—proof that the speaker has let foreign influence corrupt the sacred word."

I practiced until my mouth ached. Several of the sounds felt strange, like speaking a language my throat had forgotten it knew.

On the fifth evening, Jonathan changed his approach. He scratched familiar words into the dirt—Thamarian words I knew by heart—but written in Temple notation.

"Read this," he said.

I studied the symbols. Sounded them out slowly, feeling my way through each character. "Eh... len... den." I looked up. "That's my name."

"Again. Faster."

"Elenden."

"Good." He wrote another. "This one."

"Joh... na... than." I grinned. "Jonathan."

"Now this." A longer sequence.

I worked through it sound by sound, the symbols becoming less alien with each attempt. "Ehl... kahn... reed." I frowned, sounded it again. "El can read."

Jonathan laughed. "Barely."

Day by day, the landscape changed around us. The farms gave way to scrubland, then to something drier still. Short twisted trees replaced the firs and oaks. Tall pale grasses bent in the wind. Yucca plants thrust their spear-like leaves toward the sky, and the earth shifted from brown to rust-red, broken by outcroppings of exposed stone that looked like old blood.

On the sixth evening, Jonathan told me to listen.

I heard it before I understood what I was hearing: a low, constant voice beneath the wind. Not quite a roar. More like breathing. The sound of water moving with patient purpose—a cousin to the endless cascade that had formed Waterfall Monastery's backdrop, but deeper. Slower. Closer to the sound of the Thellassian river.

"The Drahan," Jonathan said. "We'll reach it tomorrow. Cross it, and we'll be at Ember Monastery by nightfall."

He should have been pleased. Instead, his jaw was tight, his eyes fixed on the darkening horizon.

"What should I expect?" I asked. "Master Roman threw a die at my head when we first met. I don't think I impressed him."

A ghost of a smile crossed Jonathan's face. "Roman's not the problem. His people are." The smile faded. "Three years back, Master Limerick sent me here to shore up my histories. Fire School keeps the oldest records—they've been more careful than most about preserving what the Empire would rather forget." He fed a branch to the fire. "I spent most of my time shepherding."

I glanced at him. "Wait. Tending sheep?"

"Ember keeps flocks on the hills above the river. Part of their self-sufficiency, but also—" He smiled, and something in it suggested genuine fondness. "Fire Schools teach governance. Leadership. And there's no better teacher than a flock that doesn't care about your rank or your arguments. You learn to read the land, anticipate where the herd will drift, position yourself to guide without forcing." He shrugged. "Leading sheep and people aren't so different. Both require seeing the whole while tending the one. Both punish impatience."

That sounded like something Old Henrick, my father's land steward, would say. "You liked it."

"I did." The smile faded. "But there was a history teacher there. Summa." Jonathan spoke the name like something that tasted sour. "He had... Imperial sympathies. We argued. Often. He supported the Empire's decision to close the northern mines in favor of sea trade from the southern nations, primarily the Kaldren."

"And you disagreed."

"The Kaldren depend on slave labor." Jonathan's jaw tightened. "Summa knew that. He worked to justify it as less risk to our own people. Cheaper goods, different lives—that was the arithmetic to him."

The fire crackled. Somewhere in the darkness, an owl called.

"My mother was a mining assessor for the Empire," Jonathan continued, quieter now. "Did I ever tell you that? Taught Sorcha and me to read the earth before we could read words." He paused. "When the northern mines closed, the Empire offered her a position in Kaldren. Managing their interests there. She thought it would be temporary. A few months. Maybe a year."

"I was ten. Sorcha was eight." His voice had gone distant. "Six months after she left, one of the Kaldren warlords raided the mine. Took the Imperial staff as hostages. Demanded ransom."

He selected a long stick and reached it into the fire to rotate a log, sending sparks spiraling upward.

"The Empire refused to pay. Instead, they offered the tribe the same trade terms they'd given the previous warlord—the ones who'd sold them the route in the first place." Jonathan's hands had gone still on his knees. "Cheaper to replace the staff than to set a precedent. The tribe accepted. The hostages were never heard from again."

Jonathan's face was turned toward the fire, but his eyes saw something far away—a ten-year-old boy reading dispatches, cross-referencing reports, trying to find his mother in the Empire's careful arithmetic of acceptable losses.

"I spent years researching it," he said quietly. "Wrote to every official who might know something. Filed requests through proper channels. The Empire's records are thorough; unfortunately, so are their silences." He turned the stick in his hands. "Sorcha and I ended up at a foundling house. Eventually found our way to the monasteries."

"I was furious. At the Kaldren. At the Empire. At Summa. At everyone who could weigh lives against coins and find them wanting." He snapped the stick in half, tossing both pieces into the fire. "I said things to Brother Summa I shouldn't have. Things that can't be unsaid."

"You're still angry at the Empire."

He was quiet for a long moment. "Summa said something, near the end. Before I left." The firelight caught the line of his jaw. "He said the Empire doesn't have a heart to harden or a conscience to sear. Only people do. That my anger was wasted on institutions—I should direct it at the men who made the choices and took the actions. The ones who hid behind Imperial machinery to avoid the weight of what they'd done."

"What did you say?"

"I told him he was one of them." Jonathan's voice was flat. "That his clever philosophy was just another way of hiding behind skirts. That he could parse blame however he liked—but if he could defend the Empire, he was no different from the men who let my mother die."

The fire popped. Sparks rose and scattered.

"There was some truth to what he said, though." Jonathan grabbed another stick and began stripping bark from it with his thumbnail. "Took me years to see it. The Empire is just a word for the machinery. Somewhere, someone decided my mother's life cost more to save than to lose. A person. With a name I'll probably never know." He shook his head. "I'm angry at *him*. Whoever he was. And if he was following orders, whoever *gave* the orders. And if those orders came from policy, whoever *wrote* that policy on down the line." His crooked teeth showed briefly—not quite a smile. "I still disagree with him, but Summa was just trying to help me aim."

I rested my hand on his shoulder.

"I'm sorry," I said. "About your mother. About all of it." The words felt inadequate, but I pressed on. "And I know it's selfish to say, but—I'm grateful your path brought you to the monasteries. Grateful it brought you to Waterfall when I needed a friend." I squeezed his shoulder. "I wish you'd found her. I wish things had been different. But I can't wish away our meeting."

Jonathan didn't respond. But two of his fingers rose to touch his heart for a moment.

We sat in silence while the fire burned low. The Drahan's voice carried across the distance.

Finally, I reached for my sideflute.

"Would you like to hear the Kindling Song?" I asked.

Jonathan looked up. Something relaxed in his expression—not releasing the grief itself, but acknowledging the limits of it.

"Yes," he said. "I would."

I assembled the sideflute by firelight, brass collars gleaming. Found my breath. Split it across the edge.

The first notes rose into the darkness—and the sparks from our dying fire seemed to brighten as they drifted through the notes. Coincidence, probably. Wind shifting. But I played on, and the embers glowed, and the sparks climbed higher.

I played it through once. Then again, slower, letting each phrase breathe.

When I finished, the fire had burned to embers, but those embers pulsed with surprising warmth. The stars blazed overhead, ancient and indifferent and beautiful.

Jonathan's eyes were closed. His breathing had steadied.

I packed the sideflute away quietly and banked the coals with more dry wood. The embers glowed beneath their blanket of ash as I pulled my bedroll closer to the warmth.

Chapter 63

Countenance

Merauve's eyes snapped open. His arms were already moving—hands rising to clear whatever pressed against his face.

He threw off the covering. Drew Tachet. Stabbed through the fabric before his heart could complete its startled syncopation.

The blade punched through wool with a muffled *thock*. He sliced sideways in the same motion—a thread of blanket spiraling to the stone floor—then froze in the crouch he'd assumed without thought, weight balanced on the balls of his feet, the stiletto extended toward whatever threat had touched him while he slept.

Nothing.

The tower room held only silence and the dying gold of afternoon light. Embers pulsed in the hearth. Shadows pooled in familiar corners.

And Elenden sat across the small table, hands folded in his lap, watching.

The blanket. Merauve's gaze dropped to the wool tangled at his feet—dark grey, rough-woven, unremarkable except for the fresh hole Tachet had carved through its center. He recognized it. The blanket from Elenden's bed.

"I apologize for not waking you." Elenden's voice held no trace of alarm at the violence just witnessed. That infuriating serenity. "It was clear you needed rest."

Merauve straightened slowly, the blade still naked in his hand. His mind raced backward through the fog of unexpected sleep—testimony about the cobbler's shop, the route through the catacombs, the journey south… and then nothing. He had fallen asleep. In the prisoner's chamber. During an interrogation.

The entire exchange had been nearly silent. Even now, the guards beyond the door showed no sign of having heard. Small mercies.

He sheathed Tachet and felt his coat pocket in the same motion.

There. The map's folded edge pressed against his palm. Safe.

"Your testimony possesses remarkable qualities," Merauve said, each word delivered dry as desert bones. "I haven't slept so well in weeks."

He turned before Elenden could offer that gesture of dismissal.

The guards snapped to attention as he emerged. Their eyes found the blanket still clutched in his off hand, tracked the new hole in its center, asked no questions.

"Send for a replacement blanket," Merauve said. He did not elaborate. "It may be delivered with the evening meal."

"Sir."

"No one enters that chamber. No one. The protocols remain." He held the senior guard's gaze until acknowledgment flickered there. "Especially not Jerome."

"Understood, sir."

Merauve descended. Lamplight was beginning to bloom against the gathering dusk, the distant sounds of evening activity drifting up from the courtyard below. He located an orderly in the keep's main passage and delivered instructions in clipped sentences: a message to Major Thorne regarding intelligence that suggested their white-robed mutual acquaintance might arrive tomorrow; a simple dinner for the prisoner, one dish rather than the customary three; his own meal delivered to his quarters.

The orderly departed at double-time. Merauve continued toward the northwest corner of the grounds.

The fire had burned low in his absence, coals glowing beneath ash like half-closed eyes. Merauve fed it two logs from the stack, watched the flames catch and climb, then shed his coat and hung it on its hook.

He withdrew the map from the coat pocket and spread it across his writing desk, smoothing the creases flat. He consulted his notes alongside it. Additional maps. Cross-references. The Drahan's width at that particular bend. *Here. More west than south.* Seven days on foot from Haven, traveling with the boy Jonathan. Every detail aligned. Every landmark matched. There, where the river's blue line bulged: *Ember Monastery.*

The last True Fire School in Thamaria.

He began composing the report in his mind before setting pen to parchment. The formal salutations came first—*High Inquisitor Sirius, in service to His Imperial Majesty*—followed by the careful construction of intelligence.

Known to practitioners as Ember Monastery, the facility occupies one of the larger eyots where the Drahan River widens approximately two days' travel south-southeast of Fortress Kestrel...

The pen moved. Ink flowed. Merauve wrote with the precision that had earned him his posting—each phrase weighted, each detail selected for maximum impact with minimum exposure. He confessed that personal corroboration of the location remained outstanding, but emphasized that the source had proven reliable in previous verifications.

I am confident the High Inquisitor will wish to know immediately...

A knock interrupted his composition.

"Enter."

Merauve's hand moved as he spoke—sliding a blank sheet across the half-finished report before the orderly's eyes could find the page. The man entered carrying a tray: covered dishes, bread wrapped in cloth, and two bottles cradled in the crook of his arm.

"Dinner service, sir." The orderly set the tray on the side table, then presented the bottles for inspection. "Chef sends his regards. The Val'dren red, or the Brunello from the southern merchants?"

"The Brunello." Merauve kept his voice indifferent, though the choice was anything but. The southern vintage had been aging in confiscated barrels for years before falling into Imperial hands—a wine meant for celebrations, for victories.

The orderly arranged the dishes—lifting covers to release steam, positioning the bread within easy reach, setting the bottle down. He stepped back, awaiting dismissal.

Merauve's hand rose to wave him away.

Actually.

"Open it. Pour yourself a taste and tell me whether it needs decanting."

The orderly's eyebrows rose a fraction—surprise at being consulted, perhaps, or nervousness. He produced a small knife from his belt, cut the seal, and worked the cork free. Poured a careful measure into a glass. Held it to the firelight, swirled it once, and drank.

Merauve watched. Not the wine—the man. The movement of his throat as he swallowed. The color in his cheeks. The steadiness of his hands as he lowered the glass.

"There's some sediment, sir." The orderly cleared his throat. "Decanting would serve it well. The tannins have softened nicely—it's ready to drink."

"Then decant it."

The orderly complied, pouring in a thin stream, tilting the bottle to keep the sediment undisturbed. Merauve busied himself with other correspondence while the man worked, though his attention remained divided—counting time, watching from the corner of his eye for trembling hands, for perspiration, for any pallor that preceded collapse.

Nothing.

The orderly set the full decanter beside Merauve's cup and stepped back, awaiting further instruction.

"That will be all."

The man departed with a quick bow. He probably thought he'd passed some test. In a sense, he had.

Merauve waited until footsteps faded beyond the door, then removed the covering sheet and continued his report.

When the final sentence was complete, he reviewed the whole once more. Checked the ciphers—the particular arrangements of phrasing that would signal authenticity to Sirius' clerks. Satisfied, he set the report aside to dry and turned his attention to the wax.

The sealing kit occupied a drawer to the right of his inkwell—an assortment of sticks in various colors, each serving its specific purpose. Undyed for routine correspondence. Red for sensitive Inquisition business.

And there, shorter than the others, its surface bearing a faint shimmer that caught the candlelight strangely: Imperial purple.

The color reserved for communications of the highest sensitivity. The composition remained a closely guarded secret—some alchemical formula passed down through Imperial channels for over a century. What was known: the wax blanched white under heat, returning to purple only as it cooled. Attempting to lift such a seal without the proper solvent left unmistakable evidence of tampering. Unauthorized opening carried the death penalty—not as threat but as established fact, enforced without exception across the Empire's breadth. Even provincial governors thought twice before breaking purple seals.

Merauve held the stick over the candle flame, watching the wax soften. Purple beaded at the stick's end, blanched to bone-white as it liquefied, then fell—one drop, two, three—pooling on the folded letter's seam in a pale circle that seemed to glow against the parchment.

He reversed Tachet in his grip.

The pommel bore his personal cipher—a detail he rarely shared, never displayed. The ironwood cap concealed a seal plate no larger than his thumbnail: the Inquisition's geometric patterns nested around his own mark, cut so fine the lines were invisible until pressed into wax. He had commissioned it shortly after selecting Tachet's name, paid a master engraver a month's salary for the work, and spoken of it to no one.

He pressed the pommel into the molten surface and held it there, counting heartbeats. One. Two. Three. Four. Five.

When he lifted the blade, the wax had already begun its transformation—white fading to lavender, deepening toward purple as the seal cooled around the edges. His cipher emerged in sharp relief.

Anyone with proper clearance would recognize the sender. Anyone without would face execution for examining it too closely.

He set the sealed letter aside and rose from the desk.

The lodestone waited on the shelf behind him—rough iron ore serving as paperweight for regional intelligence materials accumulated since his first month at Kestrel and grown during this interrogation. Unremarkable. Functional. The sort of object that attracted no attention precisely because it served so obvious a purpose.

Merauve carried it to his desk. Then, carefully—the orderlies cleaned thoroughly, but precaution cost nothing—he knelt.

The underside of the desk was shadow and old wood, its grain running in patterns his fingers knew by touch. He reached back along the support beam until—*there*—the subtle depression where the lodestone's weight belonged. He positioned the ore carefully, adjusting by fractions until he felt the magnetic pull take hold.

Snick.

The sound was barely audible—a metal pin sliding into position somewhere within the desk's hidden architecture. Merauve withdrew his hand, rose, and turned his attention to the locked drawer on the desk's right side.

The key was not on his person. He crossed to the corner where the ceiling beam met the wall, its ornamental molding carved with the geometric flourishes common to well-appointed outbuildings of the era. He stepped onto the chest that served as his boot-storage, reached up, and felt along the beam's upper edge until his fingers found cold metal.

Let them search his chambers. Let them find the key, eventually, and open the drawer. They would discover sensitive correspondence, private observations, papers damning enough to suggest they had found his secrets. A honeypot. A sacrifice to satisfy the curious.

The real treasure required knowing about the lodestone.

He inserted the key into the lock and turned.

The drawer slid open. But alongside the drawer, moving in concert with it, came what had appeared to be part of the wooden edifice—a panel that matched the desk's exterior so precisely that even careful examination would reveal nothing. Behind it lay a compartment barely larger than a man's two fists pressed together.

Inside: correspondence too sensitive to trust to ordinary security. Notes in Merauve's own hand documenting observations he would never commit to official reports. A folded square of rice paper, yellowed with age, bearing Master Chen's precise brushwork. Chen had pressed it into his palm the morning the Imperial soldiers came—the last thing his teacher ever gave him, and the only thing Merauve had kept from that life. He traced the tally marks with his thumb, as he had done a hundred times. Each one a face.

And there, resting atop the accumulated papers: a simple silver ring with a blue-grey stone.

Merauve added the sealed letter to the compartment, positioning it beside the ring. Two pieces of leverage. Two currencies he might trade when the moment demanded.

He closed the drawer. Turned the key. Then knelt again, reaching beneath the desk to shift the lodestone from its magnetic seat.

Snick.

The pin withdrew. The hidden mechanism disengaged. The drawer was merely a drawer again—solid wood and ordinary brass fittings, harboring nothing more interesting than old intelligence summaries.

Merauve rose, returned the lodestone to its shelf, and replaced the key in its hiding place among the beam's carved flourishes. Only then did he turn to the Brunello.

He poured a measure from the decanter and watched the wine in the firelight—deep garnet shading toward brown at the edges. The first sip confirmed what the orderly had promised: age had softened the tannins, revealing layers of leather and dried cherry and something almost like smoke.

He carried his glass to the window and watched the last light fade from the western sky. Tomorrow, Cassius would arrive. Tomorrow, the game would shift again, pieces rearranging on a board whose edges he still couldn't see.

But today, he had done what could be done. Merauve drained his glass and prepared for bed.

He would sleep well tonight. He had earned it.

A crow's raucous cry shattered the morning stillness—harsh, insistent. The herald possessed none of its predecessor's musicality, only volume, and seemed intent on announcing its presence to the entire fortress.

Merauve opened his eyes to grey light and the unfamiliar sensation of having slept deeply and well.

He stretched, each muscle awakening in sequence. The previous day's tensions had unwound in the night. Cassius would arrive today, and Merauve was ready.

He welcomed the cold plunge, counting heartbeats beneath the surface before emerging sharp and awake. Tachet whispered its quiet song against his jaw.

He dressed without hurry. The practice leathers. Supple brown hide, worn soft at the elbows and shoulders from years of use. He worked each buckle in sequence: the gambeson first, its quilted linen carrying the scent of cedar from the chest where it wintered; then the jerkin, its leather cool against his forearms before warming to his skin. The weight settled across his shoulders like an old master's hand.

He caught his reflection in the window glass—dark hair still damp from the plunge, jaw clean, eyes clear. The man who looked back seemed younger than he had in weeks.

Frost silvered the grass between the shooting positions, each blade rigid with a crown of ice that would surrender to the climbing sun within the hour. Already the air had begun to thicken where cold met warming stone—faint ribbons of mist rising from the earthen berms, softening the distant targets. Merauve's boots crunched across the frozen ground, the sound sharp and satisfying in the morning stillness. He breathed deep: woodsmoke from the kitchens, wet earth, the clean bite of autumn making way for winter.

He selected a longbow from the armory rack. The wood was cold beneath his fingers—yew, well-seasoned, its grain running clean from grip to tip. He braced the lower limb against his instep, bent the bow across his thigh, and slipped the string's loop into its notch. He tested the draw—smooth, the tension building evenly—and found it acceptable.

He was not alone.

Alena stood at the range's far end, loosing arrows with steady rhythm. She'd chosen the middle target—fifty paces—the sort of distance that let muscle memory do its work without demanding full concentration. Her grouping clustered tight, three fingers' width from the heart. Probably less.

Merauve took position and began. Breathe in, draw, exhale halfway, hold, release. Center. Low. Just left. Center.

"Inquisitor." Alena acknowledged him without breaking rhythm. Another arrow flew. Another struck home.

"Scout." He loosed his own shaft, watching it punch through the target's center ring. "Your aim remains true."

"Kind of you, sir." Alena's eyes stayed on the target. "The spiders provided motivation. Nothing like nearly dying to sharpen one's focus."

They shot in silence. Alena's accuracy impressed—she aimed with her whole body, not just her arms. Economy of motion. No wasted effort.

"A wager," Merauve said as he retrieved his arrows. "Three shots. Farthest target."

Alena's eyebrows rose. The target he indicated stood at the range's extreme edge. "Stakes, sir?"

"Satisfaction."

"That will do." She moved to the line, arrow nocked.

Her first shot: outer ring. Her second: inner ring, two fingers from center. Her third flew true—but the morning air was denser than instinct expected, the frost still gripping the ground. The arrow dropped at the last, burying itself in the grass a hand's width before the target.

She lowered her bow. No excuses offered.

Merauve took position. Drew. The target seemed impossibly small.

His first arrow: inner ring. Close to her second—maybe a hand's breadth further. He adjusted his stance, risking the reset. His second: a thumb's width from the bull's-eye.

The wager was already won. But one shot remained.

He drew. Held. Let his breath settle.

The arrow struck the target's heart.

"Well struck, sir." Genuine respect. "Where did you train?"

"Windspire." The word emerged before he could consider whether to share it. "Though not long."

Alena's head tilted—recognition, perhaps, of a shared history she hadn't expected. But she only nodded, asking nothing further.

Merauve appreciated the restraint. Air School taught her well.

He returned his borrowed bow to the rack and crossed the courtyard while the frost still held.

In his quarters, banked coals still glowed. He stripped the practice leathers and dressed with care—the deep purple uniform, silver threading catching the light. The pin at his throat positioned just so.

The officers' hall awaited.

His table stood ready in the corner: fresh wildflowers—late asters and a sprig of something the frost hadn't quite finished. Morning reports folded beside his place setting. Chair angled to command the room's entrances. He took his seat and tapped twice against his teacup.

Steam rose as he unfolded the intelligence briefings. The tea was perfect—hot, strong. He considered the offered sugar, then nodded.

Most of the reports held nothing new. Patrol summaries of continued Val'dren movement. Quartermaster requisitions. But one page slowed his hand: corroborated sightings of Oceanic vessels raiding the

Southern Provinces, three separate attacks in as many weeks. Kaldren? He read it twice, filed it away for later consideration, and moved on.

Movement at the edge of his vision. The entrance. Merauve did not look up.

Jerome stood in the doorway, scanning. His gaze found Merauve's table, held, dropped. The junior officer turned and retreated without entering, shoulders tight.

Good.

Merauve returned to his reports as his breakfast arrived: eggs over-easy, their yolks gleaming beneath the lamplight, nested atop wilted spinach and thick-cut ham that carried the faint sweetness of sugar cure. He ate without haste. The plan had crystallized during archery.

He would not wait for Cassius like some anxious courtier. His letter to Sirius would go out today. If Cassius arrived when promised, he would still receive the intelligence first. But the margin would be thinner. Merauve was done playing supplicant.

He finished his breakfast, returned to his quarters, and retrieved the purple-sealed letter.

Second bell would sound within the quarter hour—the courier's scheduled departure. Merauve had timed it precisely. A letter delivered too early might sit in the dispatch office, vulnerable to curious eyes or convenient delays. A letter handed directly to a mounted courier, moments before departure, went nowhere but the road.

He crossed the courtyard as the sun climbed above the eastern wall. The courier station occupied the far corner, and there—already checking his girth straps—the duty courier stood preparing his rounds. A weathered man, lean from saddle-hours.

"Inquisitor." The courier straightened. His eyes found the purple seal, and his posture shifted—respect shading toward wariness.

"This travels with you today. High Inquisitor Sirius, at the capital. Priority routing."

The courier accepted with both hands. "Understood, sir. It will be at the relay station by nightfall."

"See that it is."

The threat needed no elaboration. The courier tucked the letter into his dispatch case and mounted. Merauve watched him ride through the south gate, dust rising in his wake. When the man had dwindled to a speck against the road, he drew out his tobacco pouch.

He had done it. Cassius would arrive to find Merauve prepared, positioned, holding cards the Lightbringer couldn't guess. Ember Monastery's location was already racing toward Sirius. The ring remained in the hidden drawer—leverage for negotiations yet to come.

He rolled the tobacco, struck his flint, drew the first satisfying breath.

"Sir!"

An orderly pelted across the courtyard, boots raising dust. The boy skidded to a halt several paces away, chest heaving.

Merauve drew again on his tobacco, exhaled slowly. "Catch your breath."

The orderly gulped air. His face was red—exertion and something else.

"Now. Your message."

"A visitor, sir. Just arrived through the north gate. Asked for you specifically."

"Did you obtain his name and business?"

The orderly's face fell. He shook his head.

"I see." Merauve let the disappointment show. "And what *exactly* did this visitor say?"

The orderly swallowed. "He said—" A pause to recall. " 'Fetch the ranking Inquisitor of this backwoods outpost and return at once.' " Another swallow. "And when I hesitated, he added, 'Don't tell me he's gone again.' "

"I told him you were here, sir. Was that—should I not have—"

"When did this exchange occur?"

"Not five minutes past, sir. I checked the tower first, as is your habit."

Five minutes. Merauve glanced toward the south gate, though the courier had long since vanished from sight. The letter was already beyond the first bend. Already beyond recall.

◁

If Cassius objected to the timing, let him explain to Sirius why a Lightbringer believed himself entitled to intelligence before a High Inquisitor.

Merauve drew on his tobacco and let the smoke curl slow. He checked his coat pocket for reassurance.

"Take me to him."

Chapter 64

The Turn

The orderly set a pace calculated to within a hairsbreadth—quick enough to convey urgency, measured enough to avoid the appearance of making an Inquisitor hurry. Merauve followed without comment, though he noted the effort.

Their route cut through the dueling yard. The pavilions had stood empty for weeks, their shaded benches awaiting spectacles that weather or circumstance postponed. Merauve's boots whispered through grass gone the color of old parchment.

They emerged from the pavilions' shadow, and Merauve saw them.

Two figures stood at the yard's far edge where the path curved toward the stables. One wore white—that distinctive white that seemed to gather light rather than merely reflect it. Cassius stood with his feet wide apart, one hand hooked over his sword belt, the other resting on the hilt. The weapon itself drew the eye: mother-of-pearl scales adorned the grip, and set within the pommel, a pearl the size of a robin's egg caught the morning sun like a captive moon.

Jerome stood before him, head bobbing in eager agreement. As Merauve watched, the junior interrogator shook his head to some question—emphatic denial—then nodded vigorously to whatever followed.

Cassius' gaze lifted. Found Merauve across the faded grass. The smile came first—wide, warm. Then the hand, raised in greeting like an old friend.

Jerome followed his master's attention. Whatever he read in that glance sent him retreating toward the stables, gathering the reins of Cassius' horse as he went. He glanced back once—uncertain whether he'd been dismissed or spared.

The orderly read Cassius' raised hand as license and vanished. Merauve continued his approach. Unhurried. The crunching grass gave way to the soft clip of cobblestone beneath his boots. He noted that Cassius did not move to meet him—merely waited, watching his horse depart, then withdrew a folded parchment from his cloak and studied it with apparent interest. Only when Merauve had closed to five paces did the Lightbringer tuck the document away.

"Inquisitor Merauve." The smile remained fixed in place. "We meet again. I confess no small relief at finding you present—I had begun to wonder if you'd departed on another diplomatic excursion."

Merauve drew on his tobacco and released the smoke in a slow stream. Cassius was taller than he remembered. "Lightbringer. I'm pleased you arrived according to your stated schedule."

Cassius' chin lifted a degree. The smile held. The brightness in his eyes did not.

"Jerome informs me the prisoner still lives." The warmth in his voice had cooled by several degrees.

"There are aspects of his testimony that require verification." Merauve saw Cassius' jaw tighten and continued before the interruption could spark. "Not least of which is the location of Ember Monastery."

Merauve carefully reached into his coat pocket and withdrew a folded map.

Cassius' expression shifted—subtle, but Merauve had spent a career reading faces. Interest. Hunger, quickly suppressed. The Lightbringer accepted the parchment, unable to keep his eyes off it, unfolding it to reveal Merauve's careful annotations.

"It seemed imprudent," Merauve continued, "to drop the curtain before we'd seen the final act."

Cassius examined the map in silence. His finger traced the river's path, paused at the marked location, moved on to the surrounding terrain. When he looked up, any charm had left his voice.

"Who else knows of this?"

Merauve had survived too long in the Inquisition's shadow hierarchy to miss the implications. There were stories told about the Imperial

Palace's defenses—how the workers who constructed its hidden mechanisms received generous compensation delivered to their families, but never returned home themselves. Some knowledge was too dangerous to share. Some knowledge was too dangerous to possess.

If Cassius could read truths from blood and steel, lying seemed unwise.

"As of this moment," Merauve said carefully, "only you and I."

The brown of Cassius' eyes went lightless—flat and deep as a well with no bottom. One corner of his mouth curled, the smile curdling toward something else. His hands shifted on the pearl-adorned hilt. His gaze flicked to the tower where Elenden waited, held there a breath too long, then returned to Merauve.

"However," Merauve added, examining his tobacco with studied disinterest, "a courier rides even now bearing notification of these findings to High Inquisitor Sirius."

Cassius' hands stilled. "When?"

"Second bell this morning. Not a quarter hour before your arrival." Merauve ground the tobacco out under his heel. "The dispatch will take several days to reach him. Sufficient time to corroborate the testimony yourself, should you choose."

Silence stretched between them. Cassius' fingers drummed against his sword's hilt—an irritated rhythm.

"You speak of prudence," the Lightbringer said at last, "yet you have not followed my primary directive." His voice had gone soft, almost gentle, as if explaining something obvious to a child. "Ambition and initiative I can accommodate. Even appreciate. But subversion..."

"The location is yours first." Merauve met his gaze without flinching. "As requested."

The honorific *my lord* had risen to his tongue. He swallowed the unwelcome suggestion.

Cassius studied him for a long moment. Then something softened around his eyes—a decision made. The smile returned, broader than before, and when Cassius reached out to clap his shoulder, Merauve almost believed it.

"True." The word came out laughing. "And I have you to thank for that."

The change was so complete, so instantaneous, that Merauve felt drawn into its wake despite his better judgment. Cassius' hand remained on his shoulder, familiar as an old comrade's.

"I won't have much time." The Lightbringer's voice had dropped, confidential now. "I'll need a fresh horse—something bred for hard riding—and supplies sufficient for the journey. I must also speak with Major Thorne to assess Fortress Kestrel's potential role in any necessary raids. Walk with me."

He was already moving, guiding Merauve alongside him toward the main keep. People materialized in their path as though summoned: an orderly who straightened at Cassius' approach, a guardsman who opened a door before they reached it, a page who appeared with water and received instructions to requisition a courier's horse with breathless attention. They flew into and out of his orbit, each one lingering a moment longer than necessary. Cassius dispensed attention like alms—a word here, a hand on a shoulder there—sending one man for supplies, another to the stables with specifications for the tack, a third to inform Major Thorne that the Lightbringer would be honored to share intelligence with him or his senior scout at their earliest convenience.

Merauve walked beside him, observing, cataloging. Something itched at the back of his mind—a certainty that he had become a prop in some performance. Cassius would pause abruptly in a corridor, nearly causing Merauve to stumble into him, then throw an arm around his shoulders and turn him down an adjacent passage as if they were old friends sharing secrets.

They were nearly at the Major's offices when a panting orderly intercepted them with news that Major Thorne and Captain Morris would see the Lightbringer immediately.

Merauve seized the opportunity. "I'll leave you to your meeting."

"Of course." Cassius released his shoulder, stepping back. "Inquisitor, you have my thanks. And the thanks of your Emperor. We'll verify your intelligence and provide a report before High Inquisitor Sirius arrives." He pressed a hand to his chest. "You have my word."

Merauve turned to go.

"Inquisitor."

He stopped. Cassius had not moved. Had, in fact, gone perfectly still.

"On my return," the Lightbringer said, "we must discuss your reward and your... dispatches."

The smile remained. Cassius even winked—a gesture of shared conspiracy, of secret understanding.

But beneath the warmth, something else waited. Something that made Merauve suddenly conscious of every shadow in the corridor, every doorway at his back, every step between himself and the sunlight outside.

He managed a nod. Turned. Walked away at a pace that was, he hoped, neither too quick nor too slow.

Behind him, he heard Cassius greeting Major Thorne. Merauve had his own visit to make.

Merauve's stride slowed as he neared the tower—habit, or something harder to name. Not today. Cassius would notice his absence. Would draw conclusions. He shook his head and continued past.

The stables bustled with more activity than the mid-morning hour warranted: grooms called to one another across the hay-scattered aisle, hooves stamped against straw, leather creaked as tack was hurried from hooks to waiting hands. Merauve paused at the entrance, letting his eyes adjust to the dimmer light.

He found what he sought in the third stall from the back.

Cassius' mare stood with her head low, nostrils still flared from exertion. Sweat had dried in white crusts along her neck and flanks, the salt patterns mapping the hard miles she'd carried her rider. Her coat—once a handsome dappled grey—lay matted and dull. Dark patches marked where the saddle had rubbed. Her breath came slow and labored, each exhale a visible effort, her eyelids drooped to half-mast.

Jerome stood at her side, curry comb in hand, working at the dried sweat with short, mechanical strokes. His technique was adequate—serviceable, even—but his attention kept drifting to the saddlebags draped over the stall's partition.

Merauve stepped into the shadow of an empty stall and waited.

The mare accepted Jerome's ministrations without enthusiasm. Too exhausted to protest, her tail hanging limp, her ears neither forward nor back. When Jerome moved to check her hooves, she shifted her weight slowly. He managed to lift the near foreleg, glanced at the shoe, and set it down without attempting the others.

Jerome set down the hoof pick and glanced toward the stable entrance. Then toward the tack room. Finding no observers, he reached for the saddlebag.

The buckle gave easily. Jerome's hand disappeared inside, emerged, disappeared again. His fingers closed around something that caught the light strangely—a medallion on a chain, its surface worked with geometric patterns that seemed to shift and twist even in the stable's dim interior.

Jerome held it up, turning it slowly. The designs bent in ways that defied the metal's flat surface, creating depths that shouldn't exist. His lips parted. His eyes went distant, unfocused, as if reading something written in the medallion's impossible angles.

Merauve kept his gaze fixed on Jerome's face, carefully avoiding the sigil itself, and stepped forward. His boots made no sound on the scattered straw.

"Find something interesting, Junior Interrogator?"

Jerome's whole body convulsed. The medallion slipped from his fingers, disappearing into the straw at his feet. The mare, startled by his sudden movement, shifted and stamped—then subsided, too weary to sustain alarm.

"I—" Jerome's voice cracked. His eyes showed white around the edges as he spun to face Merauve. "Inquisitor. I didn't—I was only—"

"I suspect our visitor will want his possessions returned." Merauve let his gaze drop to the scattered straw where the medallion had fallen. "Intact."

Jerome dropped to his knees, hands scrabbling through the bedding. He found the chain first, then the medallion, holding it at arm's length as though it might bite. His movements as he returned it to the saddlebag were hurried—fingers fumbling to brush hay from the chain's links before shoving it back where it belonged.

He straightened with the bags over his shoulder, bracing himself against the stall's wooden partition. Some color had returned to his face, along with a defensive set to his jaw.

"The Lightbringer asked me to care for his horse and ensure his belongings were properly transferred." The words came too quickly. "I was inventorying the contents." A breath. A gathering of wounded dignity. "All seems to be in order."

Merauve said nothing. He moved past Jerome to the mare's side, running a hand along her neck. The muscles beneath his palm trembled with fatigue. He lifted her lip, checking the color of her gums—pale, though not dangerously so. Her water bucket sat untouched in the corner.

"She'll need mash, not hay," Merauve said, still examining the animal. "Warm water with bran. The grain can wait until tomorrow." His fingers found a spot on her withers where the hair had rubbed away entirely, leaving raw pink skin beneath. "And salve for these saddle sores."

"The Lightbringer's errands require haste." Jerome's voice had steadied, finding familiar ground in justification. "Better a lame horse than a fallen empire."

Somewhere in the back of Merauve's mind, he wondered what Elenden might say to that.

Merauve turned to face him. "The horse might disagree."

He let the silence stretch, watching Jerome's defiance thaw into discomfort. Then he drew Tachet.

Jerome flinched. His back pressed flat against the stall partition.

But Merauve only crouched beside the mare's off foreleg—one Jerome hadn't bothered to lift—and braced the hoof against his knee. The shoe was loose: one nail working free of the hoof wall, another bent at an angle that would lame her within a day's ride. He worked Tachet's point beneath the bent nail and levered it straight, the metal squealing faintly as it yielded.

"Better." He released the hoof and rose, cleaning the blade against his sleeve before sheathing it. "Ensure the farrier sees her. That nail would have her crippled eventually. Our guest seems to care little for the beasts that bear him."

Jerome's throat moved. He clutched the saddlebags closer to his chest.

"Now." Merauve folded his arms. "Tell me of your conversation with him."

"I don't—" Jerome stopped. Started again. "He asked whether the True still lived. I told him he did." His eyes slid sideways, finding the far wall suddenly fascinating. "Nothing more."

"Nothing more." Merauve let the words hang. "So you neglected to mention your failed attempt to poison me?"

"That was an accident." The defensive edge returned. "I've already told you. The herbs were meant—I didn't know you would—" He drew a ragged breath. "I've done everything asked of me. Your caseload has been flawless this past moon. Full confessions, proper documentation, every sentence appropriate to the crime. I've taken different routes through the fortress. Eaten at different hours. Stayed out of your sight as requested."

His voice cracked on the final words. When he spoke again, it was barely above a whisper.

"Why do you hate me?"

Merauve studied him—the trembling hands, the sheen of sweat at his temples. Not unlike the mare's own salt-crusted flanks. A man caught between masters, uncertain which way to turn.

The recognition was unwelcome. Merauve stood in the same position—weighing Cassius against Sirius, measuring which loyalty might cost him less. The only difference was that Jerome let his fear show.

"I don't hate you." Merauve kept his voice level. "I don't think about you." His gaze swept the mare's neglected condition. "I hate incompetence. Waste." Back to Jerome. "Disloyalty."

"I have only ever been loyal to the Empire."

The words landed in the straw and died there. Merauve had spoken similar ones himself. Loyalty to the Empire. A phrase capacious enough to justify almost anything. The mare shifted her weight, straw rustling beneath her hooves.

Merauve let the silence answer for him. Then he nodded toward the saddlebags still clutched against Jerome's chest.

"Follow through on your commitments." He stepped closer, dropping his voice. "Yet mark him. Every meeting while he remains at Kestrel. Every conversation. Every word you can capture. You will record it. You will remember it. You will report it to me."

Jerome's shoulders squared. A soldier receiving orders. A task he could understand.

"Written," Merauve added.

Jerome's shoulders curved inward again. He had expected restoration. This was merely reprieve.

Merauve held his gaze until the younger man looked away. "High Inquisitor Sirius will arrive within a seven. Perhaps a ten. I expect absolute loyalty. Exclusive loyalty." He paused. "Is that clear?"

"Your confessions this past moon have not gone unnoticed. You've been placed in circumstances beyond your control or expertise." Merauve let that settle. "Succeed in this, and I will write your commendation to full Interrogator myself."

Jerome nodded. The motion was quick, eager.

Merauve turned and walked toward the stable entrance. The morning light fell harsh across the threshold, making him squint after the dimness within. He wondered, briefly, what Cassius had promised—and whether parchment and rank could compete with whatever dark currency the Lightbringer dealt in.

Near the tack room, Scout Naman stood arguing with one of the stable hands. Their voices carried clearly in the morning air.

"—a courier's horse, he said. Fast and fresh, ready within the hour—"

"The courier already rode out at second bell. We've nothing prepared for—"

"Not *the* courier. A fresh horse fast enough to deliver an urgent rider. Those were the orders."

Merauve passed them without remark. Behind him, he heard Jerome's footsteps moving toward the keep, the saddlebags thumping softly against his hip.

The morning sun felt thin on his face. Cassius would ride for Ember Monastery today, on a fresh horse that hadn't yet learned to fear him.

Merauve's hand found his tobacco pouch. Empty. His gaze drifted to the tower's upper windows—a flicker of movement there, or perhaps just light on glass.

He turned toward his quarters instead.

The air in his quarters was blessedly still. Merauve shed his coat, hanging it on its customary hook, then moved to the sideboard. The Val'dren red stood where he'd left it—a working wine, dry and undemanding, suited to hours of concentration rather than celebration. He poured a small measure—enough to taste, not enough to dull—and set the glass aside while he turned his attention to the tobacco box by the window.

The carved lid opened to reveal his stock of rolling leaf, layered between sheets of oiled cloth to preserve moisture. He lifted each leaf in turn, testing pliability between thumb and forefinger, holding the better specimens to the light to check for tears or blemishes. Three he set aside as too brittle—good for filling tobacco. The rest he arranged in his pouch, layering them so the stems aligned, the leaves nested without crushing.

But he did not roll. Did not light.

Instead, he carried his wine to the desk and turned his attention to the correspondence that had accumulated during his morning's diversions. Interrogation schedules for the coming month. A junior interrogator's request to investigate suspected corruption in Haven's mayoral office—the young man had included three pages of circumstantial evidence and breathless speculation about "implications reaching the highest levels." Merauve had seen dozens of such requests. Every junior believed they'd stumbled onto the conspiracy that would make their career. Most discovered only that powerful men had powerful friends, and that zeal without discretion ended careers more often than it advanced them. He set the request aside. Outright denial dignified the inquiry—practically invited the next. Better to lose the pages beneath the quarter's routine traffic, until delay and silence taught its own rebuke.

Merauve initialed, annotated, set aside. The wine opened slowly, its tannins softening as he worked. He permitted himself small sips between documents, letting the vintage reward each completed task.

A commotion reached him before the hour had turned. Hooves on cobblestone. Voices calling across the courtyard. Merauve's pen hesitated above a supply manifest.

He could remain here. Continue his work. Let Cassius stage his exit without audience.

The thought spoiled even as it aired. Hiding in his chambers while the Lightbringer performed for the fortress—that was the behavior of a coward. A man who ceded the field before the battle began.

He set down his pen, retrieved his coat, and stepped into the afternoon light.

The courtyard had transformed into theater.

Cassius stood at its center beside a fresh-saddled courier's horse—a grey gelding with clean lines and eager carriage, nothing like the salt-crusted mare now recovering in the stables. The Lightbringer's white robes caught the autumn sun. His pearl-adorned sword hung at his hip, and his bearing suggested a man about to ride into legend.

People had gathered. Not summoned—drawn. Orderlies paused mid-errand. Guards drifted from their posts just far enough to watch without abandoning duty. Even the kitchen staff found reasons to linger near the well, their attention fixed on the figure in white.

Merauve positioned himself in the shadow of the eastern colonnade, where he could observe without participating in the spectacle.

"—and should the Spirit grant us fortune," Cassius was saying, his voice pitched to carry, "I shall return bearing intelligence of vital importance to the Empire." He swept his gaze across the assembled faces, bestowing his attention like a priest his blessings. "A traitor hides within our midst—one who has evaded Imperial justice for far too long. I ride to confirm our suspicions and bring an accounting."

Information I supplied, Merauve thought. *Intelligence I extracted. And now he wears it like a trophy.*

A young guard—barely more than a boy—stepped forward to hold the gelding's bridle while Cassius made final adjustments to his saddle-bags. The Lightbringer paused to clasp the youth's shoulder, murmuring something that made the boy flush with pride.

Not everyone had gathered to worship.

Major Thorne stood near the stable entrance, arms crossed, weight on his heels. His jaw was set, his eyes narrow—the same expression he wore last spring when a patrol lost to whiteout conditions was found three days too late, frozen in a ravine a mile from safety. As Merauve watched, Thorne's gaze swept the courtyard and found him in the shadows.

The Major nodded once. A small gesture, easily missed. Then his attention returned to Cassius. He did not applaud. Did not smile.

Cassius mounted. The grey gelding danced beneath him, sensing the energy of the moment, and the Lightbringer gentled it with a hand.

"Spirit willing," he called, raising one hand in benediction, "I ride to bring light where darkness has festered too long."

He turned the horse in a slow circle—letting the crowd drink in the image—before pointing it toward the south gate. The crowd parted before him like water before a prow. Hooves rang against cobblestone—a measured canter, dignified rather than urgent, allowing sufficient time for admiration.

Merauve watched until horse and rider passed through the gate, until the white robes diminished to a pale smear against the southern road, until even that faded into distance and dust. He exhaled.

His gaze swept the dispersing crowd—guards returning to posts, staff resuming interrupted tasks, the ordinary rhythms of fortress life reasserting themselves. Near the western barracks, partially concealed by a water trough, Jerome stood with a small journal open in his hands.

The junior interrogator's pen moved in quick strokes. His attention remained fixed on the gate where Cassius had vanished, his lips moving slightly as if rehearsing words for later transcription.

The boy was following orders, at least.

Merauve turned and walked back to his quarters. He had his own work to do.

The afternoon stretched into evening as Merauve bent over his desk, surrounded by the detritus of planning.

Maps spread across every available surface. Troop deployment schedules. Courier routes and their expected timing. His own notes, accumulated over weeks of testimony, cross-referenced with Imperial intelligence reports that predated Elenden's arrival. He had drawn lines between documents, created webs of possibility that sprawled across parchment like spider silk.

What if Sirius promoted him? He sketched the implications—new posting, expanded authority, the personnel he would request for his staff. Names appeared on his list, were crossed out, replaced. The logistics of transition. The opportunities for placing trusted operatives in key positions. What if Sirius dismissed his contributions?

What if Cassius' masters proved more generous than Imperial advancement? Another page, another set of calculations. The Lightbringers operated outside normal chains of command. Their resources remained opaque, their true objectives unclear. Joining them meant abandoning the structures he understood for power whose shape he could only guess at.

A knock interrupted him.

"Enter."

An orderly appeared, arms laden with additional correspondence. "Evening dispatches, sir. And the kitchen inquired about your dinner preferences."

Merauve gestured toward a clear corner of the desk. "Set them there. I'll sort them myself." He considered the question of food—his stomach had begun making suggestions he'd been ignoring. "Something light. A salad of autumn greens, if the kitchen has them. Bitter leaves, with whatever spiced fruits remain from the harvest. Dried fruit if not. Oil and vinegar, nothing heavy." He paused. "And tea. I'll be working late."

"Yes, sir."

The orderly departed. Merauve turned to the new stack and found, near the top, a folded page bearing Jerome's cramped handwriting.

The report was thorough. Times noted to the quarter-bell. Locations precise. Every person Cassius had spoken with, every instruction he had issued in theatrical prose. Jerome had even recorded the Lightbringer's exact words about a traitor hiding within their midst—words that would read rather different in official files than they had sounded in the courtyard.

Yet for all its detail, the report offered nothing Merauve hadn't already guessed. No glimpse behind the mask. Just the public face of a man who understood exactly how much to reveal.

Cassius should reach Ember Monastery the day after tomorrow. A hundred people could not live in community without leaving signs—smoke, livestock, the traffic of supply carts. Yet Imperial patrols had ridden that region for years and reported nothing. Either the monastery's concealment bordered on miraculous, or someone had been looking the other way. After verification, Cassius would return to Kestrel.

Upon his return, the Lightbringer would expect Merauve to follow through. The True's death, delivered as promised.

The simplest path, in most ways. A single thrust of Tachet, properly placed. He *could* bring Elenden before a Virtue Trial instead—the formal process would delay execution, create opportunities for appeal or intervention. But either way, Elenden's death was the door to Cassius' good graces.

Unless Cassius' good graces were worth no more than his horses.

If the Lightbringer collected tools and disposed of them when they dulled, what made Merauve believe he would prove the exception?

His pen hesitated over the parchment.

Merauve set Jerome's report aside and leaned back in his chair.

What wasn't he seeing?

Hope had little standing on a battlefield. Strategies failed not from error, but from insufficient imagination—from the refusal to picture disaster in detail. He could not merely prepare for what he wanted. He must prepare for what he could not afford to be surprised by.

He had done the easy work of planning for Cassius' favor and his wrath. For Sirius' approval and his censure. For promotion and for ruin.

He had not planned for outcomes where Elenden survived.

He pulled fresh parchment toward him and began to write.

Contingency: Relocation. A route through the northern passes, timing aligned with patrol gaps. The scouting team was stretched thin—tracking Val'dren movements to the south while monitoring the traveling folk's gathering to the north. Windows of opportunity existed. A supply cache, planted in advance, could sustain two travelers. The forged identity papers in his locked drawer, prepared for emergencies that had never materialized—those would need modification, but the bones were sound.

Contingency: Concealment. The fortress contained spaces that saw irregular inspection. The old grain stores, largely abandoned since the new silos were constructed. The collapsed section of the eastern wall, deemed too expensive to repair and simply sealed off. Places where a man might be hidden, if one were willing to accept considerable risk.

Contingency: Deception. A body, properly prepared, could satisfy cursory inspection. Merauve knew the theory—had employed it once before with the aid of Physick Grendle, in circumstances he preferred not to recall. The morgue held unclaimed dead from the autumn fever. With appropriate disfigurement, appropriate staging...

The scenarios multiplied beneath his pen. Each contingency spawned complications; each complication demanded solutions; each solution revealed new vulnerabilities that required their own contingencies. His hand moved faster, annotations crowding the margins, arrows connecting disparate pages. The candles burned low. His dinner arrived and sat wilting as he worked, eventually consumed without attention. The tea grew bitter in its pot.

He did not notice.

Contingency: Misdirection. If Cassius could be drawn away on false intelligence— *Contingency: Alliance.* Thorne's quiet nod in the courtyard suggested possibilities, Maudy the serving girl— *Contingency: Leverage.* The ring in the hidden drawer, Aerellyn's location—

Merauve stopped writing.

He sat back and examined the scattered pages. The handwriting grew increasingly hurried toward the bottom of each sheet. Ink smudges marked where his hand had moved before the previous line dried. The plans themselves were intricate, creative, *inspired.*

He had not felt this engaged since—

The recognition spread through him like the first sip of strong spirits—a warmth in his chest, a sharpening at the edges of his vision. His pulse quickened. His hands, usually so still, wanted to keep moving.

—since three families huddled in lantern-shadow in Master Chen's cellar. He had believed in things, then.

Merauve shook his head to clear the memory.

The truth remained. These were not plans for managing an asset. They were plans for saving a life. Somewhere between the first contingency and the dozenth, the exercise had stopped being theoretical.

Somewhere between the dipping and the dripping, the well and the waiting page, his hand exposed what his heart had hidden. He did not want Elenden to die.

Merauve had perhaps four days—five at most—before his hand was forced.

He gathered his scattered notes, organizing the more sensitive pages into a folder that he locked in his desk's hidden compartment. Then he extinguished the lights, one by one, and prepared for whatever sleep might come.

In the darkness, his thoughts drifted to the tower room where Elenden waited. Sleeping now, perhaps. Or sitting at the window as he so often did, watching stars wheel across the autumn sky—seeking what signs, Merauve could not guess.

Four days.

He was nineteen when the soldiers came for Master Chen. Nineteen, and so certain he had accounted for everything—every patrol rotation, every informant's loyalty, every gap in the Empire's attention. He had mapped the patterns for years.

He had not seen the new sergeant. Had not accounted for the guardsman's fever that morning, the replacement who walked an unfamiliar route with sharp eyes.

He would not make that mistake again.

Chapter 65

Ember Monastery

Merauve's eyelids lifted in the darkness. Eagerly—as though something within him had finished its work in the night and demanded consciousness to admire. He lay still, cataloging this unfamiliar sensation.

He had made a decision.

The thought brought a conspiratorial smile to his lips. There was a certain satisfaction in the prospect of keeping Elenden alive, not least because Cassius desperately wanted him dead. Merauve recognized the pettiness of the impulse, but he did not reject it.

Beside the bed, Tachet hung on its mount, its wicked length smiling alongside him.

"Let's try this again, shall we?"

"Sir, I could—"

"That won't be necessary."

The orderly retreated. Merauve lifted the tray himself, balancing the porridge and bread and sliced pears.

He nodded at the guards and drew back the bolt.

Elenden stood at the window, silhouetted against grey morning light. When he turned, his gaze found Merauve's face and held there, the look of a man who had opened a familiar door and found a stranger's house beyond it.

Merauve set the tray on the small table and began arranging the meal. The porridge steamed. The bread's crust crumbled slightly as he positioned it. He was aware of Elenden watching him—aware, too, of the warmth spreading through his chest. The satisfaction of rescuing something fragile from frost. A flower pressed between pages before winter could claim it. A fish returned to water before its gills ceased their working.

He was too proud to preen. But he savored the secret all the same.

"You were gone yesterday." Elenden's voice came quiet, wondering. "Yet here you stand twice as present."

Merauve's hands stilled on the honey pot. He looked up to find those sea-blue eyes waiting.

Various responses presented themselves. Denial. Deflection. The old masks, ready to hand.

Instead, Merauve raised his index finger and pointed it at Elenden.

The young man's eyebrows lifted. Then his expression softened—surprise folding into recognition, recognition blooming into a small smile that held simple gladness.

Merauve indicated the chair with a lift of his chin.

"Ember Monastery," he said. "You were just arrived."

Jonathan led me down a narrow path that wound through bare autumn fields toward the Drahan's edge. The river's voice grew louder as we walked—a deep, serious sound—the kind that made you measure your footing. Autumn mist hung low over the water, and the far bank—if there was a far bank—dissolved into grey before I could guess the distance.

Before we reached the bank, an older man emerged from between two leaning willows. His hair was thick, greying at the temples from what might once have been dark brown. He moved with the careful steps of someone whose body had been arguing with him for years and had mostly won.

"Adam!" Jonathan's face lit. He closed the distance quickly and embraced the man, who returned it with surprising vigor for someone who walked the way he did. Jonathan stepped back; though the man made no sound in response, his hands answered in quick, easy signs that spoke their own language.

Jonathan turned to me, grinning. "Elenden, this is Silent Adam. One of Ember's finest."

I opened my mouth, then closed it. Heat crept up my neck. "I don't... I'm sorry, I don't know handspeak."

Both of them laughed—Jonathan's voice bright, Adam's breathy but no less genuine. His shoulders shook, green eyes crinkling, and his hand waved dismissively before tapping his ear, then pointing at me.

"He can hear you just fine," Jonathan said. "Better than most, actually. He just can't speak back."

"I'm honored to meet you, sir."

Adam's weathered face creased into a smile. He gestured for us to follow, already turning toward the river.

The Drahan ran brown where we approached, sediment kicked up by the eyot's presence upstream to the south. Adam reached the bank and, without ceremony, removed his shoes. He tucked them under one arm, hiked his robes above his knees with the other, and stepped directly into the river.

I glanced at Jonathan.

His grin widened. "Watch."

Adam waded forward—one step, two, three—until he stood knee-deep in the middle of the current. The water flowed around him, but his footing remained sure. Steady. As if he walked on solid ground hidden just beneath the surface.

"They call it the ghost bridge," Jonathan said, already unlacing his own boots. "Weighted rope lattice, maybe two or three feet down. Can't see it through the murk, but it's there. Has to be tensioned from the other side, or the slats just hang loose and the current carries them."

▷

I stared at the brown water, then at Adam's bowed legs walking through the middle of it.

"You're serious."

"Very." He tugged at a stubborn knot. "Arms free for balance. Adam will take the packs."

I glanced at the older man with his tottering gait. But Adam simply held out his hands. I surrendered my travel pack. Jonathan did the same. Adam accepted both without apparent strain, settling one on each shoulder, then turned and waded back into the current as if the additional weight meant nothing.

The late autumn air bit at my bare feet. Jonathan was already stepping in, arms spread wide, grinning.

The first step onto the submerged bridge sent a numbing cold up around my ankle. The second found mossy rope beneath my toes, slick and treacherous. My arms windmilled. My weight shifted too far against the current. For one breathless moment I was certain I'd pitch face-first into the Drahan.

Jonathan's hand caught my elbow. "Easy. Small steps. Feel for the slats."

I found my balance again, breathing hard. On the far bank, Adam waited with both packs set on dry ground, his feet somehow already dry, as though the river had agreed not to inconvenience him.

Step by careful step, I made it across. My legs trembled by the time I reached solid ground—more from tension than exertion.

Adam reached behind a moss-covered rock and pulled something I couldn't quite see. Nothing visible changed, but Jonathan nodded.

"Bridge is slack now. Anyone trying to follow would just find rope pulled sideways by the current. Uncrossable without knowing the mechanism."

I looked back at the muddy river. "Clever."

The eyot was larger than I'd expected—less island, more hidden country. Trees grew thick on the eastern edge, their roots drinking deep from the Drahan. But beyond them, the land rose and varied in ways that caught me off guard. Rocky outcroppings jutted from browning

▷

fields. Rounded boulders twice a man's height clustered together like families. The terrain rolled and dipped, reminding me achingly of the moors back home.

As the land flattened, shepherds tended small flocks in the fields, the sheep rooting for whatever morsels remained before winter claimed them. We passed close enough to one flock that I could see their thick coats, already grown in against the cold.

The wind gusted sharp across the open ground, and I envied those sheep their wool.

"Were you out here?" I asked Jonathan. "When you first came?"

"Every third day." He said it without complaint. "If I wasn't in class, I was with the flocks. Dawn to dusk."

I watched a young shepherd—couldn't have been older than fifteen—guide a ewe back toward the others with a gentle tap of his crook. "Will I be joining them?"

"That's for Master Roman to decide." Jonathan's tone suggested he genuinely didn't know.

What struck me, though, was the shepherds' response to Adam. Every one we passed stopped their work. Straightened. Bowed low. Adam walked on as if he noticed nothing, his slow and sideways stride unchanged, but I saw how their eyes followed him. How they waited until he'd passed before resuming their tasks.

"Who is he?" I asked quietly.

"One of the Elder Masters," Jonathan said. "Like Hadrian at Waterfall—someone who's earned his seat at the table. Ember Monastery calls them 'Watchers.' "

Adam led us toward a rising rocky hill, its face more cliff than slope. As we approached, I spotted iron doors set directly into the stone—massive things, dark with age, flanked by two guards in monastery robes with red armbands. Swords hung at their hips.

The guards opened the doors for Adam without question.

Beyond them, the mountain opened into a great hall that belonged to an older age.

The walls were dark granite, cut clean and fitted without mortar—each block seated so precisely that a knife blade couldn't find the seams. Copper crowned every doorway, beaten into patterns of flame and vine. Bronze molding traced the joints where wall met ceiling, where column met floor—functional seams transformed into art. Sconces of wrought iron held torches along the walls, each one unique, each one shaped by a different hand across what must have been generations of smiths.

The ceiling vaulted high overhead, held in an arch no mountain shaped on its own. Shafts cut at angles through the rock caught the sun and scattered it across the floor in pale gold bars—and everywhere that light touched metal, the hall seemed to breathe with warmth.

At the center, a fire roared in an iron grate adorned with bronze tetrahedrons. The smoke rose straight and true into a chimney cut through living rock, while fresh air breathed up from channels in the floor. The flames burned almost white at their heart.

Tapestries hung between the sconces—old enough that their colors had deepened rather than faded. But my eyes kept returning to the copper, the bronze, the iron. Every piece bore the marks of hand-forging.

Adam gestured us toward the fire, then disappeared through a side passage.

"He's gone to tell Master Roman we're here," Jonathan said, already holding his hands out to the flames. "Make yourself comfortable. This might take a bit."

I joined him, relishing the heat. My feet were still numb from the river crossing.

"When I was here before," Jonathan said, "it took Adam nearly a quarter bell just to find Master Roman. The monastery goes deep—more structured than Haven, not as old, though." He nodded toward a sconce shaped like a curling fern. "Ember started as a copper mine. Centuries ago, before the Monastery. The veins run rich—copper, tin, traces of silver. Everything metal you see here, they forged themselves. The bronze is their own alloy. Some of the older brothers have spent forty years at the anvil. They say the forge-heat gets into your bones."

He gazed up at the vaulted ceiling, the light shafts, the branching corridors. "Lots of passages, though. Lots of places to—"

Silent Adam appeared directly behind us.

I jumped. Jonathan laughed, though his eyes widened too.

The older man's face remained serene. He gestured with one broad hand: *Follow*.

"Double meaning in the name," I muttered as we gathered our things.

Jonathan's grin returned. "Oh, absolutely."

Stone corridors stretched away from the great hall, lit by torches that cast dancing shadows. Every dozen paces, angled shafts pierced the ceiling—each no wider than a hand—catching whatever daylight remained and threading it down into the depths. The effect was strange: torchlight and sunlight mingling, warm and cool, as if the mountain couldn't decide whether to welcome visitors or swallow them. Adam led us through several turns, each passage looking much like the last, until we reached a heavy wooden door.

He knocked once, then entered without waiting for response. We followed.

Master Roman's office was smaller than I expected. Shelves lined three walls, crammed with books and scrolls and loose parchment that seemed moments away from avalanche. A desk dominated the center—dark wood, scarred and smooth, covered with more papers held down by jagged black stones, glossy and knife-edged. In one corner, an iron brazier no larger than a washbasin held a bed of coals that glowed the same white-orange I'd seen in the great hall's fire. Heat radiated from it in steady waves, warming the stone chamber without smoke or sound.

Behind it sat Master Roman.

His skin was that same sunbaked clay I remembered, his beard cropped close and threaded with more iron-grey than I had noticed before—though perhaps I simply hadn't been looking. The widow's peak made his face seem carved for rendering judgment, just as it had in the council chamber at Mountain Monastery. But here, in the lamplight, I saw something I had missed then: the shape of his features recalled Pakonaskow—the same nose built for profile on a coin, high and hooked but pressed flat at the crown, the same deep-set eyes beneath heavy brows, though Roman's burned a shade lighter—amber where Papa's had been umber.

He was writing something, each stroke of the pen a small verdict rendered in ink. Deep red robes soaked in the lamplight. On his desk, amid the chaos of papers, a curved sword rested in a worn leather scabbard—close enough to reach without rising.

Adam closed the door behind us but remained inside.

Master Roman looked up. Saw Jonathan. His face broke into a smile that transformed his severe features.

Then his gaze shifted to me.

The joy drained from his face like flame from a doused forge—that sudden hiss, that curl of steam, that absolute extinguishing. His eyes flicked to Adam for a moment, then Jonathan, before returning to me.

"Jonathan, Adam: why have you brought a noble in sheep's clothing among my flock?"

Rather than answer, I reached into my pack and withdrew Master Limerick's letter, careful to hold the seal away from me.

I held the letter out toward Master Roman. Arm extended. Waiting.

His eyebrows rose. He made no move to take it for several seconds, then his hand lifted—not reaching, but granting permission. I crossed the remaining distance and placed the letter in his palm, then stepped back quickly, relieved to have it gone.

Roman broke the seal and read.

I watched his face, remembering Master Senna's observation: *Even silence is its own language.* Roman made no effort to hide his expressions—but that didn't mean I could read them. Surprise, certainly. His brow furrowed at something near the middle of the first page. Then consideration, his eyes lifting briefly to study me before returning to the text. Near the end, something stirred that might have been amusement—or alarm.

When he finished, he returned to the beginning and read it again. More slowly this time. His finger traced a passage near the bottom, lingering there.

The silence stretched. I took my cue from Jonathan, who stood still and quiet beside me. I studied the room to avoid staring—the curved sword on Roman's desk, the chaos of papers held down by those stones, the lamp casting warm light across surfaces worn smooth by years of use. His pen lay where he'd set it, ink drying on whatever he'd been writing when we arrived. Silent Adam waited quietly by the door. The brazier crackled. Somewhere deeper in the mountain, I thought I could hear metal ring against metal—the forges.

Finally, Master Roman pressed his eyes closed beneath those heavy brows and pinched the bridge of his long nose.

"When I was young—" Roman leaned back in his chair and steepled his fingers. "—there were men in my country who called themselves lords. Petty tyrants serving their appetites and calling it law." His voice had gone flat. "They taxed the harvest until children starved. They took sons for soldiers and daughters for worse. And when the people cried out for justice, these *lords* explained that order required sacrifice. That stability demanded obedience. That questioning authority was itself a crime."

His fingers drummed once against the desk, then stilled.

"I fled north rather than be counted among them. Rather than become what they were." He looked at me. "But a man is not his title. Nor his blood. Neither the sins nor the virtues of those who came before him." He glanced at Jonathan. "We must not allow small men to cast big shadows. Wouldn't you agree, Jonathan?"

Jonathan's posture shifted—something passing between them that I couldn't read. "Yes, Master."

Roman sighed and set the letter aside.

"Limerick begs tempering. Hadrian urges protection. Kairn counsels patience. Senna..." He paused, something flickering at the corner of his mouth. "Senna was clever enough to hedge her praise." He tapped the letter once with two fingers. "My friends all see something in you that escapes me, and so I must trust to friendship rather than wisdom here. Very well. Let me outline a practical challenge."

"Traditionally, first-ranks from outside Ember would join a dedicated cohort—history in their first term, economics in their second, law and political theory thereafter. But we have taken fewer visiting students in recent years." He looked directly at me. "There is no mixed cohort with a sole history focus for you to join."

Silent Adam's hands moved in quick shapes. Roman watched, then barked a short laugh and pointed two fingers back at him.

"True. If there's one lesson from studying history, it's that men refuse to learn the lessons it teaches. Too few have the humility to learn from the mistakes of others." He nodded toward Jonathan. "We also lack one on economics for Jonathan to continue his studies."

He rose and moved to a slate board mounted on the wall, chalk already in hand.

"Fire School studies Justice—what it demands, how it fails, under what conditions good people thrive. How men lead. How they are led. The structures that make civilization possible and the corruptions that undermine it." He drew a shape on the board: four points connected by six lines. A tetrahedron, rendered flat. "The tetrahedron is our sign. Four vertices. Four faces. The geometry of flame." He turned to face us. "To teach governance, we practice it."

He tapped the apex. "Students begin in *hearths*. Four members, like the tetrahedron's vertices—one second-rank at the apex, three first-ranks forming the base." His chalk traced the triangular foundation. "The name is deliberate. The hearth is where justice is first learned. Or first violated. Four around a fire, small enough for genuine fellowship. Small enough that dross cannot hide."

He stepped back, surveying his work. "Upon reaching second rank, those who prove worthy become guides for their own hearths. Three first-ranks beneath their care." He paused. "Advancement comes by trial, not tenure. Merit alone determines the pace—and the trials are voluntary. A student may remain at first rank for years if they choose. Some never attempt advancement at all."

"What becomes of them?" I asked.

Roman's expression didn't change. "They go home when they're ready—after a year, or two, or five. A village that sends us a promising son and receives back a trained mind has gained something valuable. Stewards. Advisors. Men and women who understand how justice functions, even if they lack the gift of leadership." His gaze moved briefly to Silent Adam. "Others remain here. The mines need laborers. The forges need skilled hands. The flocks need shepherds. The flame forges and tempers—but it is the hearth-stones that hold the heat. The monastery could not survive without those who serve in ways no curriculum measures."

He drew a larger structure now—three tetrahedrons arranged around a central point. "Third-ranks who pass their trials lead *kindreds*. Three hearths united beneath one guide. Twelve students, thirteen with their leader."

A structure emerged on the slate: a tree growing downward, roots spreading into branches.

"The number is no accident," Roman said quietly. "Twelve around one. The same pattern you'll find in older things than monasteries."

"And the fourth-ranks?" Jonathan asked.

"Each fourth-rank leads three kindreds. Only four hold this rank at any time—one hundred and twenty students beneath their combined authority." Roman set down the chalk and faced us. "We are selective about admissions. More selective still about advancement. Fire refines what it does not consume. Better to test many and train few than to graduate leaders unfit for the weight they'll carry."

"Each year, the Watch selects one fourth-rank to join their number. The role is lifelong—whether they remain at Ember or scatter to the corners of the world, they belong to the Watch still, and may return to speak in it." His eyes found mine. "The Watch governs the school. Masters serve as judges when disputes arise, but we do not rule. We arbitrate. Any arrangement for your studies will require their approval. I can recommend, but I cannot compel."

"What will you recommend?" Jonathan asked.

Roman's gaze moved between us. "That you form a hearth of two. Irregular, but not unprecedented. Jonathan knows our ways, our histories, our arguments. He can—"

Movement at the edge of my vision. Silent Adam's hands were shaping words—quick, emphatic gestures that interrupted whatever Roman had been about to say.

Roman's eyebrows rose. He responded in the same silent language, fingers forming shapes I couldn't follow. Adam nodded once.

"It seems," Roman said slowly, "that Silent Adam has volunteered to join your hearth."

Adam's eyes crinkled. His hands moved again.

Roman almost smiled. "He says the young keep him from growing too settled in his ways. We will still petition the Watch for guidance on a second-rank to round out the four—" He glanced at Adam, who raised a single finger in confirmation. "—and which kindred you'll join. But I believe we have a way forward."

He gathered the letter and folded it carefully, tucking it into his robes.

"For now, Jonathan and Adam will orient you. Occupy yourselves as befits you. Should you lack imagination, Adam will know what needs doing." He paused. "The Watch meets in three days—they'll decide then." His expression hardened. "Until that time, I suggest you govern yourselves well. Those who inherit authority are not often trusted by those who earned it. Some will be looking for reasons to deny a lordling."

"I understand," I said.

"Do you?" Roman's eyes held mine. He moved back toward his desk, lowering himself into his chair. "Show us what manner of man you are. The Watch will judge accordingly."

Silent Adam opened the door. The audience was over.

Jonathan touched my elbow, guiding me toward the exit. But at the threshold, I paused.

"Master Roman."

He looked up from his papers.

"Thank you."

"Don't thank me yet," he said. "The Watch hasn't ruled."

Adam's weathered hand found my shoulder, gentle but firm. I let him guide me into the corridor. The wooden doors swung closed behind us, and the latch fell into place like the soft thunk of a gavel.

Chapter 66

Hearth

Silent Adam consulted with a brother who passed us in the corridor—a young man with jet-black hair and a harried look. He gave Jonathan and me a skeptical glance, then responded to Adam in handspeak, bowed, and departed.

Adam led us into the mountain.

The room he brought us to was small—bunks built into opposing walls of the bare chamber. The stone felt faintly warm beneath my fingers—like Melanthiel's caves—and as with her room, where I expected darkness, I found light.

A shaft no wider than two fists had been cut through the rock above the doorway, angling upward into the mountain. Its interior gleamed—lined with beaten bronze, each plate fitted to the next and polished bright. Light entered somewhere far above and bounced down through the channel, reaching us as warm amber.

"Light channels," Jonathan said, noticing my attention. "Ember's founders learned the technique from miners who needed to work deep veins without risking fire."

I traced the shaft's bronze lip with one finger. The metal was cool.

"Three hearths share each channel," he continued. "The main shaft runs from the surface, then branches where it reaches the living quarters. Easier to maintain—the brothers can polish the trunk without too much trouble. The final branches are short enough to reach." He glanced at the fading glow. "You can tell how recently it's been done by how bright the light falls."

I pressed my palm flat against the wall. "The stones are warm."

"Bronze pipes," Jonathan said. "They run from cisterns heated by the forges, up through the stone, then back down. The water carries the heat; the bronze shares it with the rock." He rapped his knuckles against the wall. "Ember sits above old mine shafts—the brothers converted them into a circulation system."

Adam's hands moved in quick shapes.

"We may have to move once the Watch rules," Jonathan translated, "but this will do for now. We'll share a washroom with the rest of the kindred—hot water there too."

I pressed each mattress while they continued their silent conversation. The lower one was stuffed with wool—it gave under my hand like risen dough. The upper was thinner, its frame closer to the stone. I set my pack on the upper bunk and sat on its edge, feeling the firm resistance beneath me. Better.

Adam looked toward me as Jonathan gestured something, but he made no other motion I could read.

When we'd finished settling our few belongings, Adam lowered himself onto a low stool near the door. His hands moved again—slower this time, more deliberate.

"He says he should confess something," Jonathan said. "He volunteered to join our hearth partly to satisfy his curiosity." A pause while Adam's hands continued their shapes. Jonathan's brow furrowed. "Two Spirit Brothers, one who has..." He hesitated, watching Adam repeat a sign. "I'm not sure I understand."

Adam tried different gestures—one hand drawn flat across his vision like a horizon, then two fingers near his eyes closing to a point, then spreading wide.

"Half-sight?" Jonathan tried.

Adam pointed.

Jonathan and I exchanged a glance. Not True sight, Master Limerick had said.

I met Adam's eyes.

"I hope we don't disappoint," I said.

His shoulders shook with silent laughter.

A knock came at our door—a brother delivering three bowls of stew on a wooden tray, along with a small loaf of dark bread. The smell arrived before I saw the food: rich broth, herbs, and something else. Something that made my nose tingle with memory.

"Finally," Jonathan said, accepting the tray. "I've missed these spices."

We settled cross-legged on the floor, the bowls balanced on our knees. Adam moved more slowly than we did, his hip setting the terms of each step, but he made no complaint.

I lifted the first spoonful to my lips. The broth was good—lamb, I thought, with root vegetables soft enough to fall apart. But beneath the familiar flavors ran a sharp, almost medicinal heat that spread across my tongue and climbed toward my sinuses.

"*Haraq*," I said.

Adam's hand shot up, finger extended toward me.

"You know it?" Jonathan asked, surprised.

"The Val'dren season everything with it." I took another bite, letting the heat build. "I made the mistake of rubbing my eye after cutting it once. Thought I'd gone blind."

Adam smiled broadly. His hands shaped something quick.

"He says that's how everyone learns," Jonathan translated. "The burn is a more effective teacher than any warning."

We ate in comfortable silence for a time. The stew warmed me from the inside, pushing back the chill that had snuck into my bones during the river crossing. Through the light channel above the door, the amber glow was beginning to fade—afternoon giving way to evening somewhere on the mountain's surface.

I watched Adam's hands rest motionless in his lap and made a decision.

"Adam," I said. He looked up. "Will you teach me handspeak?"

His expression shifted. He nodded once, slow and solemn, as though I'd asked him to carry something heavier than it appeared.

"He says it's harder than it looks," Jonathan said, translating the signs that followed. "There are several dialects. Few learn to sign. Many see, but few truly listen with their eyes." Adam's hands moved again. "He'll teach you: first to listen, then to speak."

Like Air School. I said nothing.

Adam held my gaze for a long moment. Then his hands began to move.

Our first lesson started with what lay before us. Adam pointed to the bowl, then shaped a sign—two hands curved as if holding something round, then a sliding motion along the sides. *Bowl.* He pointed to the stew, made a different shape—hand cupped but fingers rippling like liquid, then a quick scooping motion toward the mouth. *Stew* or *Soup* depending on the ripples. The bread. The bunk. The walls. Each object received its name, and I repeated the shapes with clumsy fingers while Jonathan corrected my form.

"Your wrist is too stiff," he said. "These words flow. Watch Adam's hands—see how the signs connect? You're chopping each one apart."

I tried again. Better, but still wrong.

Adam caught my attention. His hands moved in a longer phrase, and Jonathan laughed—a bright sound.

"He says your handspeak is like his walking." Jonathan grinned.

The lesson continued as the light faded. Adam was thorough—he insisted on teaching the grammar beneath the nouns—the way signs modified each other, the difference between a statement and a question. My fingers fought me—flute work had trained them to cover and release. They wanted to move in sequence and combination, less in nuance. I learned three ways to sign bread, each more subtle than the last. My eyes burned from watching so intently.

But something was taking root. By the time dusk had claimed the light channel, I could follow one or two simple phrases without Jonathan's translation. *Eat more. Tomorrow work.*

Jonathan leaned back against the warm stone wall, stretching his legs out before him.

"I was never part of a hearth before," he said quietly. "When I came to Ember the first time, I studied alone. Attended lectures. Read in the library." He glanced at Adam. "I didn't mind; I figured I could learn faster on my own."

Adam shook his head slowly. In the gathering darkness, his hands were fading from view, but Jonathan had positioned himself where the last grey light still touched Adam's fingers.

What followed came through Jonathan's voice, but the words belonged to Adam:

"Hearths are the only true way to learn Justice. Not from books. Not from lectures. From *life shared*—meals taken together, arguments weathered, laughter, burdens carried in common." Jonathan paused, watching Adam's hands. "The classroom teaches theory. The hearth teaches truth."

Adam's fingers kept moving, and Jonathan kept speaking:

"The Empire forgets this. It forgets its purpose."

"What is its purpose?" I asked.

Adam's answer came through Jonathan in a softer voice:

"To protect the hearth. Nothing more. The Empire exists to preserve the ordinary happiness of ordinary people—a husband and wife talking by their fire, friends sharing a meal, a man reading in his own room, a mother singing her child to sleep. These small moments are civilization's purpose. When government serves them, it fulfills its charge. When it forgets them—when it grows jealous of the loyalties it cannot command—it becomes a destroyer of the very thing it was made to protect."

Adam leaned forward. Even in the darkness, I could feel the intensity of his attention.

"The family was first," Jonathan said. "Before kingdoms, before empires, before law codes and standing armies and tax collectors. The hearth-fire burned before any throne was raised. It has rights older than any crown." His voice caught something of Adam's conviction. "The Empire is merely a collection of hearths. Its sole purpose is to safeguard their flourishing—not to replace them, not to redirect their loyalties, not to insert itself between parent and child or husband and wife or brother and brother."

The darkness in our small room was nearly complete. I could no longer see Adam's hands at all—only the faint gleam of his eyes.

"This is why we study Justice here," Jonathan said, and I knew Adam must still be signing, though I could not see it. "Not to build empires. Not to train governors who demand obedience. We study Justice to understand what feeds the hearth, and what structures undermine its fire." A long pause. "The hearth is the proper focus. Warmth. The smallest unit for life. The place where justice is first learned or first betrayed. Get the hearth right, and the kingdom follows. Neglect the hearth, and no laws can save you."

Silence settled over us.

I looked at our small chamber—the bunks, a stool, three bowls emptied of stew. Three people together for mere hours, already sharing food and philosophy in the dark.

A hearth.

Adam's hands moved again, but I couldn't make out any shapes. He stopped. Tried once more. Stopped.

Then he rose from his stool, slowly, and moved toward the door. When he opened it, torchlight from the corridor spilled across his arms. He turned back to us and signed in the borrowed light.

"He says he can only speak where there is light to see," Jonathan said quietly. "He's going to wash before bed."

Adam stepped out. His footsteps faded down the corridor.

I sat on the edge of my bunk, fingers mimicking what they'd just been taught. I couldn't see them well. The torchlight from the hall still reached through the half-open door, but it would not last. Jonathan would close it soon or the sconces would gutter. When Adam returned, the darkness would still be here—and without the light, his voice would be extinguished. He would lie down in silence.

Every night, the same small death. Was it lonely?

I remembered Redcloud—sitting on that split-rail fence that first free afternoon.

I heard his footsteps returning. That slow, careful gait.

I crossed to my pack. My fingers found it by touch.

"Adam."

He paused at the threshold, silhouetted against the corridor's glow. I scrambled down from my bunk and pressed Tobias' gift—the rowan pipe—into his hands.

His fingers explored the instrument—learning its shape, its weight, the placement of holes along its length. In the darkness, I couldn't see his face, but I felt his stillness. His confusion.

"A voice that doesn't need light," I said.

I felt through my pack again and drew out Jonathan's gift—the three-sectioned sideflute. I assembled it by feel, brass collars finding their seats, cork gripping cork. Then I raised it to my lips and played a simple scale. The notes climbed and fell in the small stone room, clear as water.

I watched Adam raise the pipe. His first attempt produced nothing—just breath escaping without catching. For a moment I feared his lungs wouldn't have the wind to sound it, something mechanical with his throat. But the second found something—his chest tightened, and a thin wavering tone emerged and died almost instantly. The third held. A note. Rough-edged, uncertain, but real. I could feel as much as hear it—the pipe's voice and something beneath it, a low vibration from Adam's chest that seemed to steady the breath into sound.

I guided his fingers to the proper holes, showing him by touch what I couldn't show by sight. Another note emerged. Then another. Not music—not yet. Just raw sound, the material from which music could be made.

"You teach me your language," I said, smiling, "and I'll teach you mine."

Adam's hand found my shoulder. He gripped it once—firmly, a promise sealed without words.

As I turned and left for the washroom, I heard him raise the pipe to his lips again, testing, exploring.

Jonathan waited until later that night, after I'd climbed to the upper bunk's thin mattress. The stone wall radiated warmth against my side, heat borrowed from forges burning somewhere below.

His voice came soft in the darkness:
"That was well done, El."

Adam insisted our hearth drop the titles—not Master, not Elder Master, not even Silent Adam. Just Adam. When Jonathan tried "sir" the first morning, Adam's hands cut the air and held a closed fist in what needed no translation.

Breakfast arrived on the same wooden tray as dinner—porridge this time, thick with oats, a single egg apiece nestled in a hollow carved into the wood. We took our places on the floor, bowls balanced on knees. Adam explained through Jonathan that hearths took their morning and evening meals together, but kindreds gathered for a more formal dinner every seventh day. A rhythm of intimacy and community, private and shared.

"We don't have an assigned kindred yet," Jonathan added, watching Adam's hands.

I followed their exchange as best I could, hunting for shapes I recognized. Most slipped past too quickly. But when a pause opened, I lifted my hands and signed what I hoped was a question: *Today work?*

Adam's face creased with something like delight. His hands moved in response—too fast, too complex. I caught only fragments.

Jonathan translated, grinning. "Your handspeak is terrible, but your courage isn't." Then his face sobered. "He says yes. He wants to give the Watch no excuse to dismiss us. The easiest way to contribute—the work that needs no training—" He paused, watching Adam's hands continue. "Mining support. Loading and hauling spoil and slag."

"Spoil?"

"Waste rock. What's left after they extract ore and coal." Jonathan's nose wrinkled. "Slag is worse. Forge leftovers. Glassy grit and ash, whatever didn't burn clean."

Adam's hands moved again, and this time I caught the shape for *hearth*.

▷

"All hearths work as one," Jonathan said. "No one goes into the mine alone."

Adam rose and retrieved something from a shelf near the door—lengths of rust-colored cloth. He held one up and demonstrated: unwinding, wrapping, then folding it into a triangle, positioning the point to drape down over his nose and mouth, wrapping the ends behind his head and tying them firm. When he finished, only his eyes showed above the fabric.

His hands shaped words for Jonathan: "The deep places make dust. Slag grit, coal black, stone powder. Still best to breathe through your nose, but this keeps most of it out."

He helped us wrap our own with our spirit binding cloth. When I drew a strong breath, the fabric pressed against my lips, warm and close.

I guessed then, why so many at Ember learned handspeak.

Three days blurred into a single ache.

The first morning we hauled slag from outside the forge pits—climbing down iron ladders into heat that pressed against us like a living thing, filling wooden barrows with glass-sharp remnants while sweat carved tracks through the dust on our arms. Adam worked beside us. His wide stance looked whole when bracing a barrow, and his massive shoulders drove the shovel so easily he'd filled and lifted one before Jonathan and I were half done with ours.

The second day brought coal sorting—tedious hours in a shed near the mine entrance, fingers blackening as I learned to see the difference between grades.

"Not charcoal," Jonathan said, correcting me. "Charcoal's made from wood—burns clean but fast. This is mined. Buried forest, pressed into stone." He hefted a jagged chunk, its surface glinting like darkened glass. "Burns hotter and longer. You couldn't run a forge like this on charcoal—you'd strip the mountainside bare in a few seasons."

Good coal was dense, bright where it fractured. Lesser coal was lighter, dull and crumbling. Mixed in with both was stone that had slipped through the first sorting. My hands remembered the motion long after my mind had wandered.

The third day we descended deep into the tunnels.

The cold hit first—wet stone, water seeping through seams, the weight of the mountain pressing down. My chest tightened before my mind caught up. Haven's catacombs lived in my body still—the absolute dark, the stone closing in. I made myself keep walking. We loaded waste rock into carts that ran on iron rails, then pushed them toward the daylight where our breath fogged. Our wrappings grew heavy with moisture and grit.

Down in the tunnels, I noticed a brother in blue.

He moved ahead of the work crews, pausing at junctions, crouching in alcoves where the air sat still. His wrappings were sky-pale against the darkness.

Adam raised a hand and stopped our barrow. He walked toward the blue-wrapped brother, and I watched their hands move in greeting. The brother pointed down the left passage, held up three fingers. Adam nodded and returned.

"Air tester," Jonathan explained through translation, watching the figure settle into stillness at a low passage, head tilted as if listening to something beneath hearing. "Water School trained. They sense what we can't—bad air that gathers in pockets. If he signals us back, we go back."

"Like a canary," I said.

"Except the canary dies to warn you." Jonathan's eyes went back to the blue-wrapped brother, still crouched in that low passage. "Adam says they're highly honored here."

We worked until the blue-wrapped brother raised his hand—a simple gesture, palm out, that sent us climbing toward the surface. I never learned if he'd sensed something wrong or simply judged we'd been down long enough.

Topside, the cold bit sharp after the tunnels' chill, but I welcomed it. We lowered our wrappings and let the wind scour the sweat from our faces.

"Where does all this go?" I asked, nodding toward the laden barrow.

"Windbreaks," Jonathan said. "The sheep shelter on the leeward side during storms."

In the distance, I could see where older spoil heaps had become part of the landscape—artificial ridges running along the high ground above the Drahan. The oldest of them had begun to green, stubborn grasses claiming what the miners abandoned.

Evenings, I peeled my wrappings away and saw the day's labor recorded in grey-black stains—the shape of my breath, the outline of what I hadn't inhaled. The hot water in the washroom became the closest thing to prayer I knew. I stood beneath it until my skin flushed red, watching coal dust and stone grit spiral down the drain.

Then music.

Jonathan pored over texts he had brought while Adam waited in our small room with the rowan pipe, his eyes bright as though the day's labor had never touched him. I assembled my sideflute with fingers that ached from gripping shovel handles, and we began again where we'd left off.

Adam hummed when he played. Not a melody—not quite. A low, steady drone from somewhere deep in his chest, the way a mother might hum without thinking while she rocks a child. His throat couldn't form words, but it could hold a sound—barely audible beneath the pipe's voice, felt more than heard. It seemed a small thing—just how his breath worked, the natural resonance of air passing through a throat that had forgotten how to speak but remembered how to sing. I didn't bring it up.

He was not good. The humming didn't help—that low vibration from his chest divided his breath between throat and pipe, so the tone thinned and wavered where it should have held. His fingers found wrong holes more often than right ones. The mountain ash could sing so sweetly; but under his breath, it produced sounds I hadn't known wood could make. Something between a whistle and a wound. I was grateful for the stone walls between us and the corridor.

But he *tried.* Night after night, the same phrases, the same patient repetition. And somewhere in his fumbling, I heard what I must have sounded like to Tobias—graceless, earnest, refusing to stop.

I glanced at Jonathan, bent over his books, pretending not to hear. He had endured months of my clumsy beginnings without complaint. I understood that grace a little better now.

I played the phrase. He echoed it, badly. I played it again. Closer this time. Again.

Do it perfect. The memory of Master Feng brought a smile to my lips.

"Your fingering is terrible," I told him, "but your courage isn't."

Adam smiled, shook his head, and raised the pipe to try again.

By the third night, he could hold a child's melody through to the end. He lowered the pipe and his face broke into a broad smile.

I crashed into my bunk each night like a stone. Dreamless. Complete.

I hadn't thought about the Watch in days. Hadn't worried about their ruling, whether Ember would keep me or cast me out. The labor had burned away everything but the next task, the next breath, the next ache. I found I didn't care what they decided. Part of me—the part too tired to lie—hoped they would send us away.

The knock came before dawn had filtered through the light channel—two sharp raps, then the door swung open without waiting for an answer.

"El?"

△

Every muscle in my body protested as I turned. I rubbed my eyes against the corridor's lamplight and felt my shoulders trembling with even that small effort.

Copper hair—the color of autumn leaves. I knew that hair—

"Sebastian?"

He stood in the doorway, wearing the same grin I remembered from kitchen duty and survival lessons and smuggled pastries in the infirmary back at Mountain Monastery. He was taller, or I remembered him smaller. His shoulders had broadened. The boy who'd scrubbed pots beside me had become someone else while I wasn't watching. His eyes, though—those hadn't changed. They found mine and held, like a dare.

"Look at you." Sebastian crossed the room in two strides and pulled me into an embrace that made my sore muscles sing. "Last time I saw you, you were hobbling on a crutch. Now you're—" He held me at arm's length, studying my face. "You've grown."

"So have you." My voice came out rough with sleep. "What are you doing here?"

Sebastian blinked. Then that laugh I'd nearly forgotten. "I got through geometry. Stayed for applied mathematics—leadership track. Brother Matthias wasn't gentle about it, but he got the job done." His grin widened. "This is my home. The better question is: what are *you* doing here?"

"I'm to be part of a hearth. At least for the next few months, if the Watch allows it." I gestured toward the bunks. "Sebastian, this is Jonathan. And Adam."

Jonathan had risen to sitting, hair disheveled, watching our reunion with sleepy bemusement. Adam was navigating from his bed to the stool near the door.

Sebastian turned toward Adam. I caught the moment his feet shifted together—the beginning of a bow—and the moment he remembered he wasn't supposed to anymore.

Adam winked.

Sebastian's smile returned, easier now. "I had to see it for myself. The kindred spent half of yesterday's meal talking about Silent Adam and the two Spirit Brothers putting the other hearths to shame laboring in the tunnels." He shook his head. "I suspected, but I feared to hope. And I thought it best if I delivered the news personally."

"What news?"

"You're to join my kindred."

The words landed strangely. Somewhere in the exhaustion of the past three days, I'd made peace with rejection—had practically welcomed it. That weary apathy dissolved now.

"I wondered if they'd let us remain a hearth of three." Jonathan sat up straighter and rubbed his eyes.

"You misunderstand." Sebastian's grin slid sideways. "The Watch refused to allow a—how did they put it?—'rudderless hearth.' The analogy made no sense to me." He glanced at Adam. "Apparently *someone* refused to serve as guide."

Adam smiled proudly, but made no sign.

"Most of the discussion centered on who should serve as your fourth until some second-rank volunteered."

Jonathan's crooked smile emerged. "Let's hope he's not a slave driver like Adam."

Sebastian winced, but covered it quickly with a laugh that filled the small room. "No one works as hard as Adam." He cleared his throat. Squared his shoulders. "I passed my trials for second rank, El."

Jonathan cocked his head, eyes flicking to Adam for confirmation of what he was beginning to suspect.

Sebastian drew himself up in mock formality and offered a sweeping bow. "*I* am to serve as your guide."

"Fine," I said, after a beat. "I suppose you can stay."

His eyebrows rose.

"But you can't have my bunk." I kept my face straight.

"And you can't practice your flute at night," Jonathan added.

I broke.

Sebastian gave a quizzical look but no one elaborated. "Very well. I accept the terms." He raised a questioning eyebrow toward Adam. "I believe we'll be following the regular classes today—" Adam made a flat open hand, lifting the palm slightly: *of course, at your pleasure.* "Together. I'll be back shortly with breakfast."

He disappeared into the corridor. I barely had time to splash water on my face and wrap my bindings before he returned, balancing a tray laden with porridge, bread, and—I caught the sharp scent—*baraq*-spiced eggs.

We settled cross-legged on the floor as we had every meal since arriving. The room felt fuller now. Complete.

Sebastian distributed the food, then looked at each of us in turn—Jonathan, Adam, me.

"Come," he said. "I've stories of my own, but I suspect yours are stranger. There should be no secrets among hearths. Tell me everything."

▽

Chapter 67

Government

Jonathan and I exchanged a look that didn't belong at a breakfast table. Even Adam shifted on his stool, his lined face suddenly interested in the porridge.

Sebastian's eyes moved between us.

"It seems *everything* may have to wait." He lifted his bowl and blew across the surface. "Start with how you met?"

Jonathan seized the safer ground. "I came to Waterfall Monastery chasing a reference in Kaelen's Compendium—a footnote about what caused the second founding that sent me halfway across the continent." He grinned. "The library didn't disappoint. Neither did the company."

I let him talk. It was easier to listen than to measure what could be said. Jonathan had a gift for narrative—he could sketch the shape of our friendship without touching the sharp edges.

"...Elder Master Hadrian had him using a walking stick instead of a crutch. First time I'd seen that approach. Kendel—one of the healers—didn't think much of it either. But his ankle knit faster than any of them expected..."

My attention drifted. Not from boredom—from vigilance. Every sentence Jonathan spoke, I weighed against the secrets it might brush. The decision to perform at the Summer Exhibitions. The orphans we'd rescued.

"...so we escorted him to the capital for the Summer Exhibitions..."

The coded warnings, the blue fire, the flight north. I heard only fragments now, my mind running ahead to dangerous ground. The *Shiranath*. Melanthiel's cave. How much would Sebastian guess from what was left unsaid?

Movement caught my eye. Adam was watching me.

His green eyes held mine without apology. Then, quick as a sparrow tucking her wings, he winked. *Half-sight* he had said... I wondered how much Adam knew—or guessed.

"...and that's how I came upon him at Haven while visiting my sister," Jonathan was saying, his narrative winding toward the present. The bowls sat empty now, porridge scraped clean, bread reduced to crumbs.

Sebastian raised a hand. "Forgive me." He stood and crossed to the light channel, studying it with more attention than it deserved.

He glanced at Adam, who was already rising. "We'll be late to class."

Jonathan reached for his pack and produced a leather-bound journal and stylus. Sebastian's eyebrows rose.

"The rooms will have wax tablets."

Jonathan shrugged and tucked the journal under his arm. "I prefer something more permanent."

Sebastian considered this, then nodded. "Fair enough."

We gathered ourselves and followed him into the corridor, leaving empty bowls and unfinished stories behind.

The corridor climbed through several turns before opening onto the great hall we'd entered on our first day. Sebastian led us past the central hearth—its fire crackling, heat washing over us—toward an arched passage.

The classroom beyond was beautifully carved, tiered like an amphitheater, with stone benches falling in concentric arcs toward a speaking floor. Light fell from shafts cut high in the vaulted ceiling—the same bronze-lined channels as our sleeping quarters, but wider here, arranged in a ring near the apex. They threw broad bars of gold across the stone, catching the dust motes that swirled like distant tumbling stars.

"What happens when it rains?" I asked.

Sebastian glanced up. "The light channels have baffles. Rainwater drains to cisterns below." He gestured toward a bench in the third tier. "We'll sit together as a hearth." My legs still ached from the mines, and a bench felt like mercy after three days of barrows.

Students filtered in around us—a mix of ages. Some looked younger than me; others had grey threading their beards. Silent Adam drew a few glances as we settled into place, though no one seemed shocked to see him sitting among students.

"Can this room hold the whole school?" I whispered.

"With Masters and all, it's tight, but yes. It's the biggest room here." Sebastian kept his voice low as more students arrived. "We won't see that today—just three kindreds."

"Governance will handle mostly political theory and statecraft this semester," Sebastian added. "You should be glad. Last semester was law." He shuddered.

The schedule followed a four-day rotation, Sebastian explained as more students arrived. One day for governance—the Fire School's specialty. One day for general education and swords. One day dedicated to the virtue Justice, and one day for labor. He caught my expression and grinned. "Don't worry; you won't be sorting coal *all* week."

"What's tomorrow?"

"For us, generals. Mathematics, sciences, rhetoric, philosophy, then weapons training. Those will have smaller groups, different levels. You won't stick with the hearth—you'll join cohorts matched to your ability." He glanced at Jonathan. "We'll need to quiz you on placement. Figure out where you belong."

Before I could ask more, the room fell quiet.

A man entered from a lower door—rotund, red-faced, moving with a bustling energy that belied his size. His robes strained at the middle, and he carried a leather satchel bulging with scrolls. He laid it aside on his desk. Something about him reminded me of Lord Carrick: large in presence, boisterous in manner, impossible to ignore.

"Brother Gentian," Sebastian murmured.

Gentian reached the speaking floor and turned to face the tiers. His eyes swept the room once, then fixed on some middle distance as if addressing the air.

"We were discussing two general philosophies regarding the government of men," he announced. "Who can recall me one?"

Nearly every hand rose. Gentian pointed to a smaller lad in the front row.

"Systems as solutions," the boy recited. "It is not the fault of man but the fault of systems that leads to injustice. Fix the systems, fix the problems."

"Excellent. And the other?"

He selected an eager boy near us. "Systems as tradeoffs!" The boy's voice rang off the stone, and he flushed slightly at its volume. "Man is not true. Systems composed by broken men to govern broken men will always have tradeoffs, not solutions."

"Quite right, quite right." Gentian fished something from the satchel on his desk—a handful of roasted nuts—and popped one into his mouth. "Today we focus on the former. The perfect state." He paced as he chewed. "Set aside your assumptions. For the duration of this class, assume men are neither true nor untrue—simply misled. Our task is to lead them straight. How might we begin? How have others attempted this in the past?"

He didn't wait for answers.

"The Orissan across the eastern seas believe that if the state is to be its guardian, then the state should be its caregiver as soon as possible. At birth, an assessor measures the physical aspects of the child—skin tone, bone structure. Before the child is weaned, government representatives will have visited multiple times. An appropriate cohort is assigned based on physical characteristics, and the child is removed from the parents to be raised by the state. Throughout the remainder of their childhood they are re-measured and re-sorted: eye color at one year, temperament at two, aptitude at five—each assessment narrowing the cohort until the child's role is fixed."

A murmur rippled through the tiers. Gentian raised a hand.

"I present, not advocate. Listen before you judge." He resumed pacing. "Through a prescribed series of segregations and assessments, each child is arranged into what the Orissan call a 'perfect match'—a cohort with a singular role. Their merchant class is drawn from those with lighter skin pigmentation—presumably to better align with foreign traders. They are allowed and encouraged to wear patterned clothing. They learn languages and mathematics sufficient for ledger keeping, light logistics for supply. Never economics. Economics belongs to the governor class. These children hear only music in the Lydian and Ionian modes—bright, optimistic, suited to commerce."

He paused to let that settle.

"Their warrior class is raised on the Dorian mode—martial, disciplined; pain without collapse—and permitted Phrygian for controlled fury." His voice took on an edge. "A musician caught playing Lydian to a soldier loses his hands. The soldier who listened loses his ears. Each caste hears only the music that shapes them for their role, wears only fabrics suited to their station, learns only histories appropriate to their function."

"The Orissan believe this creates harmony. Every person selected, shaped, molded, and measured. Every person in their perfect place, doing their perfect work. No wasted potential." Gentian spread his hands. "One of their sages is quoted as saying:

Every seed thrives in its proper field.
Leave men free, and they will not be equal;
force them equal, and they will not be free.
We trade a false freedom for a true harmony:
planting each where he will flourish,
sparing him the sorrow of a wrong soil.

And before you dismiss it—their empire has endured a thousand years if you ignore the Qiran schism. Longer than ours."

Someone coughed. The sound had nowhere to hide among all the stone.

"The Kaldren," Gentian continued, "take a very different view. You can reliably guess an Orissan's station just by looking at them. The Kaldren, by contrast, believe birthright is the supreme indication of status. Born to slaves? You are a slave and deserve a slave's station. Born to lords? You are a lord and deserve a lord's station."

He held up a finger.

"But—and this is crucial—you do not reach what they call the *Lok'tem* until you are thirteen. The term has no clean translation—something between 'the Bloom' and 'the Becoming.' Until then, children are *kail*: unformed, unsorted, good for nothing. A lord's child and a slave's child are equally nothing. They may eat together, sleep together, learn nothing of station. The Kaldren believe you cannot know what a plant will become until it grows tall enough to show its leaves. Only at thirteen does the sorting begin—only then does a person exist. Notice the break. They believe the person is like a seed, born to be a particular role in society, but society itself does not recognize that role until *Lok'tem*."

"While the Orissan separate their scholars from their warriors, the Kaldren consider only their lords worthy of any study—be it warfare, arts, or governance. As lord, you *are* the scholar, warrior, and government of your tribe, all in one. Everyone else serves as the lord requires..."

The examples grew bizarre. One nation trusted its citizens to govern themselves entirely; another forbade citizens from owning property. Gentian claimed a historian named Pell had documented a community where no person was considered above another, where the people gathered and voted on every matter of import. They'd been conquered and enslaved within a generation—but the practice had existed.

Gentian clapped his hands once.

"Break into kindreds. Discuss these approaches to perfecting the state. What is the best division of men from men, if any? And at what age, if any, should our perfected government begin to shape its citizens?"

The room stirred. Sebastian touched my elbow and guided us toward a cluster forming nearby.

This was my first time meeting the kindred—two other hearths joined with ours under a third-rank named Kane. He had to be close to twenty, with a calm bearing that reminded me of Fiske back at Mountain Monastery. Sebastian introduced our hearth; the others nodded politely before Kane called us to order.

The discussion that followed surprised me with its energy.

"I can't believe the Orissan think like that." The speaker had a thick western accent and fingers stained with coal dust or ink. "They treat people like ore—sort by color and purity to determine purpose?"

"Carry that analogy further and they may have some logic." An older student leaned forward—dark skin, darker eyebrows, the kind of face that looked like it had been thinking longer than most of us had been alive. "You can fashion a sword from any ore, but not all ore makes for good swords."

"The Kaldren aren't any better." A boy with a northern accent shook his head. "Orissan judge by skin, Kaldren by stock. They're like horse breeders—all that matters is bloodline. Wrong sire and you're a cart-horse, if you're lucky."

"Plants, ore, and horses aside," said someone else, "I think some education should be mandatory. No one wants the soldiers defending them to be fools."

"Well, no one wants their rulers to be cowards either. Should combat training be mandatory?"

"Who says men should even *have* rulers?" The northern boy leaned forward. "What about that group Gentian mentioned—the ones who voted on everything?"

"The ones the Kaldren enslaved?" A younger boy to his right elbowed him. "Yes, Tam. Clearly the perfect government."

Tam flushed but didn't back down. "They were conquered, not wrong. Those aren't the same thing."

Kane let the discussion flow, intervening only when voices grew too heated or when someone hadn't spoken in too long. The discussion drew me in despite my intentions to observe. It wasn't long before I was defending positions I wasn't sure I held, questioning assumptions I'd never examined. It reminded me of Redcloud.

After a time, Brother Gentian's voice cut through the discussions.

"Kindreds, return to your seats. Let us learn from one another."

The reconvening took on a different energy. Representatives from each kindred shared their conclusions—or their disagreements. Gentian listened, challenged, pushed. When best should a perfect state begin its governance? Should it assign roles? By what characteristics—birth, physical traits, demonstrated ability?

No consensus emerged. I suspected none was meant to.

The day flew past. History interspersed with foreign ways of viewing the world and focused discourse. I had no sooner marveled that people could think a particular way than Gentian introduced a completely different system.

By the time Gentian dismissed us, my mind felt stretched in directions I hadn't known it could bend. Some of them left me uneasy—my thoughts kept sliding off them like water from oiled leather, refusing to hold onto them a moment longer than necessary.

Over dinner, the hearth continued the conversation.

"I've always held the view that men are equal in value, if not equal in ability." Sebastian passed the mutton.

"No disagreement from me on that; but it raises the question: which abilities can be trained?" Jonathan accepted the plate. "Which are inherited? Which are… inherent? Can *anyone* serve as emperor after they're taught good leadership the way a smith learns his craft?"

Adam shifted impatiently on his stool, then signed something.

"He asks whether an old man like him could become a musician," Jonathan translated, a smile tugging at his mouth.

I blinked. "I don't see why not."

Adam's hands moved again.

"He says: not without training." Jonathan's smile broke into a grin.

The table fell quiet. Adam's eyes were twinkling.

"After dinner," I said. "We'll start after dinner."

Adam inclined his head. But when we'd cleared the bowls and I reached for my sideflute to demonstrate a phrase, he shook his head and held up his hands.

Handspeak first, he signed. *Teach only handspeak.*

"You want the instructions in handspeak?"

He nodded firmly. *All handspeak.*

It would have been infinitely easier to simply play the phrases myself—repeat them on the sideflute until his tone matched, his rhythm steadied, his breath found the right places. But Adam signed his questions, and I had no choice but to answer in kind.

I shaped a sign for *breath* and *short*. Mimed the motion. Adam tried the note, failed, and his hands formed a question I didn't understand. I looked to Jonathan.

"He says distance can be 'short,' but breath is different. Breathing needs to be 'shallow' or 'fast,' not 'short,' " Jonathan said.

fast, I signed, withholding a sigh.

Adam tried again. Closer.

The light channel dimmed. Sebastian had long since retreated to his bunk with a book, but he hadn't stopped listening.

"He wants to know if the third phrase is supposed to be choppy like that," Sebastian called without looking up. "Honestly, El. The sign means *detached*. I'm pretty sure that's the third time he's shown it to you."

I signed my thanks and turned back to Adam. His eyes were bright despite the failing light.

Neither of us would quit first.

Jonathan and Sebastian held a mock vote in the style of the Pellian communes and declared us both impossible. Training was thereby suspended for the evening.

Adam set down the pipe and signed something I should have remembered.

"Again?" I guessed.

He shook his head, repeated the sign more slowly.

Tomorrow.

I smiled despite my exhaustion. I signed *Yes.*

Because I had an idea. Adam didn't need to learn my language to learn music—and maybe I didn't need to master his. There was an older language, one that lived on paper instead of hands or breath. I would teach him to read it.

"What's true, gentlemen."

Sebastian's voice cut through the warm darkness. Light spilled briefly from the corridor as the door opened and closed, followed by the soft clink of bowls being arranged on stone.

"It's early," Jonathan mumbled from the bunk below me.

"If they can keep us up half the night with flute practice, I can wake us up early for assessments." Sebastian's grin was audible. "I need to report your placements in generals before first bell. We can eat while we talk."

I climbed down and stretched. My body had gone too long without morning forms—and to my surprise, it missed them. When had that changed? The absence felt like forgetting to eat. I resolved to ask Sebastian about katas sometime. The light channel above the door showed only the faintest grey—dawn was close but hadn't yet committed. Adam was already seated on his stool, accepting a bowl from Sebastian with a nod of thanks.

We settled into our usual positions on the floor. Porridge again, sweetened with honey, and the sharp scent of *haraq* rising from sliced eggs. I took a bite and let the heat spread across my tongue while Sebastian began.

"Simple questions to gauge your level. Jonathan and Adam, I could use your help." He gestured with his spoon. "Mathematics first. If a merchant buys cloth at three coppers per yard and sells it at five, what's his profit on twenty yards?"

I used the excuse of chewing to delay my answer. "Forty coppers."

"Good. Now—the diagonal of a rectangle with sides measuring three spans and four spans. How long?"

The question sent me back to Brother Matthias' classroom: chalk dust hanging in cold mountain light, his voice pronouncing my ignorance. I felt heat rise in my cheeks.

"Something over four spans," I said. "Four and... half a span? A bit more?"

Sebastian's eyebrows rose. He glanced at Jonathan.

"Five spans," Jonathan said gently. "The classic triangle ratio—three, four, five."

Of course it was. Brother Matthias had spent a whole class talking about it.

More questions followed. I spent more time circling the answers than landing on them—sometimes I would recognize patterns without remembering formulas, but most often I was lost. When Sebastian asked me to calculate how many sheep could graze a triangular pasture given its dimensions, I looked deep into my porridge and didn't bother offering a guess.

Sebastian and Jonathan exchanged a look. Adam's hands moved—a sign I didn't catch.

"Level one for mathematics," Sebastian concluded. All three of them nodded.

Rhetoric proved easier. Between bites of egg and porridge, they posed logical fallacies for me to identify, asked me to construct arguments, tested whether I could spot the weakness in a poorly reasoned claim. Fletch's lessons had carved these patterns deep.

"Easily level three," Sebastian decided, scraping the last of his porridge. "Lucky timing—they don't cover languages until spring term."

Sciences and philosophy fell somewhere between—I knew enough to follow discussions but not enough to lead them. Sebastian studied me for a moment, then asked which level I thought I could manage.

"Level one," I said. "For both."

"You could probably handle level two in philosophy."

"It will give me room to breathe. If mathematics gives me trouble."

Sebastian nodded slowly. "Fair enough. I agree."

We finished our meal as the first true amber began filtering through the light channel. Sebastian gathered the empty bowls and stacked them near the door.

"I'll show you where your classrooms are. We meet back at the great hearth before martial training."

The words sent an excitement spinning through my chest. Martial training. *Swords.*

Each school claimed its weapons. Earth taught hammers and axes—courage and commitment made steel. Water trained with staff and spear—redirection, flow, shaping an opponent's force as often as meeting it. Air favored bow and dagger—precision at distance, economy up close. Spirit studied empty hands—*the martial art*—the correction arrived in Master Feng's voice, and I smiled for it.

But the sword belonged to Fire. Justice's blade, they called it—a weapon that could defend or attack, parry or thrust, demanding balance between aggression and restraint. I had watched from windows and doorframes as my brothers worked through forms in the training yard back home. The ring of practice steel was a music I was never invited to play.

I would have been nine or ten—old enough to understand the sequences Corrin was learning, young enough to believe that understanding meant I could participate. I had crept to the edge of the yard, bare feet silent on the flagstones, and watched our master-at-arms, Garrick, guide my brother through a defensive form. When Corrin fumbled the footwork, I called out a correction before I could stop myself.

The silence that followed lasted three heartbeats.

Garrick turned to face me. He was built like a stripped oak, all dense muscle and scarred hands from decades of bladework. His eyes found mine without anger—which somehow made it worse.

"Young Master Elenden." He rested his weighted practice sword point-down against the flagstones, both hands folded over the pommel. "Come to teach the sword, have you?"

I gulped. Hope and terror warred in my chest. "No sir. Come to learn it."

His gaze moved over me once, head to foot, and whatever it found, his face kept to itself. "A swordsman learns humility first, balance second. You'll not touch a blade until you can walk properly." He gestured toward a water barrel at the yard's edge. "You want to help? Fetch water for your brother. Keep his throat wet and the dust down. Watch and learn."

I fetched water exactly twice. Then I returned to the moors and avoided the training yard. It hurt less to run wild across the heather than to stand at the edge of something I couldn't enter.

The memory faded as Sebastian led us through corridors past the great hall. Light fell from the channels above, striping the stone floors like the ribs of the mountain.

"Level one philosophy here," Sebastian said, pointing. "Science will be across the hall. Level three rhetoric at the end—they've combined it with grammar this term." He paused at an intersection where bronze shafts threw crossing shadows. "Level one mathematics is up those stairs. Meet back at the central hearth at afternoon bells."

The morning passed quickly. Classes moved from topic to topic at each bell; I felt like a stone skipping the surface of deep things. But my placement in the first levels made the curriculum manageable.

Mathematics was my final class of the morning. I climbed the stairs with dread rising in my stomach like cold water, but something strange happened.

The same math Brother Matthias taught—the same ratios, the same relationships, the same principles he had presented as condemnation—landed differently when spoken by a different voice. Brother Daren was a thin man with short brown hair parted neatly to one side and a habit of drawing pictures alongside his equations. Where Matthias had demanded, Daren invited. Where Matthias had pronounced, Daren wondered. Matthias had served Sebastian well enough. But I wasn't Sebastian.

The relationships of lengths, angles, and shapes hadn't changed. But somehow, hearing it explained as discovery rather than verdict, the numbers began to make a kind of sense. Not friendly yet, but at least no longer hostile.

When the bell released us, I descended the stairs feeling lighter than I had climbed them.

Our hearth gathered at the entrance fire. Jonathan looked thoughtful; Adam's eyes were expectant.

"How was math?" Jonathan asked.

"It wasn't terrible..." I admitted. Any success—however small—felt like a gift.

"Ready for martial training?" Sebastian's grin had taken on an edge.

"I've been ready since I was nine."

Jonathan glanced at me, curious, but I didn't elaborate.

Sebastian's grin widened. "Then I should warn you—you won't be touching a sword this term."

"What?"

He affected a voice higher than his own, rough with mock authority: "You'll not touch a blade until you can walk properly."

I stared at him. His words were an echo across years.

Adam's shoulders shook.

"You'll be with Sister Harken," Sebastian continued, savoring my expression. "Level one is footwork and balance." He clapped a hand on my shoulder. "And not much else."

"We'll suffer together," Jonathan added.

Sebastian and Adam departed for their advanced classes while Jonathan and I made our way toward the training halls on the eyot's southern end.

"Level one can't be as bad as Sebastian made it sound," I said.

The path wound between dormant pastures where sheep huddled against the cold, their breath rising in small clouds. Frost and flurries had silvered the grass last night, and our boots left dark trails where they broke through the crust. The air smelled like wet wool.

Jonathan's crooked smile emerged. "I dunno. He doesn't seem like the type to exaggerate."

He wasn't.

Chapter 68

Pride

We followed a scatter of students across the fields—red-wrapped figures from other kindreds, their breath pluming as they walked. The training hall stood at the eyot's southern end, a long structure of dressed stone with a peaked roof designed to shed snow. Smoke rose from vents at either end where braziers fought back the winter cold.

Inside, the wooden floors had been polished by use until they gleamed like honey. Tall windows of thick, bubbled glass cast pale squares across the practice space. Against the far wall stood a rack of practice swords, their wooden lengths arranged in neat rows. My eyes found them immediately.

The instructor stood beside the rack, her back to us as she drew one of the swords. She tested its balance with two quick cuts—diagonal, then horizontal—followed by a tight circle that brought the point back to center. Her lip curled. Without ceremony, she tossed the sword into the nearest brazier.

The wood caught quickly, flames licking up the blade's length. No one in the room so much as flinched.

She was the first female instructor I had seen at Ember. Her arms, bare below rolled sleeves, looked ropy, with old scars tracing pale lines across brown skin. Her iron-grey hair was pulled back so tight it seemed to stretch her face. Her red wrappings had faded to the color of old brick, and her eyes swept the room like a general surveying troops she knew would disappoint her.

She spotted our unfamiliar faces—two breaths of assessment, no more. "Back row." Her voice could have carried across a battlefield. My mind took too long to register it as a command. "Now."

We hurried.

"I am Sister Harken." The name landed like a hammer on an anvil. "You are here because you have never held a sword, or because you have held one so poorly you must unlearn it. It makes no difference to me. We begin from nothing either way."

She began to pace, every step deliberate—yet, impossibly, silent.

"This term, you will not touch a blade."

My eyes drifted to the practice swords against the wall. Close enough to see the different sizes and shapes. Oak and ash, most likely, their edges rounded for safety but shaped to teach proper form. Weighted... close enough to—

"You will learn to stand." Sister Harken's voice didn't rise, but I felt it snap my attention back like a hand on my chin. Her eyes had found mine. She blinked her dismissal. "To breathe. To shift your weight without losing your center."

She planted her feet and took a wide stance.

"Copy this. Hold it until I say otherwise."

The stance was simple enough. My body knew how to settle into stillness—years of truth dancing had taught me that much. Sister Harken didn't know me. She saw only another first-year with eager eyes.

Let her watch, I thought. *Let her see.*

It couldn't be as bad as Sebastian made it out.

My thighs were trembling before I'd counted thirty heartbeats; I told myself I was still sore from hauling rock.

"Now slide the left foot forward. Like this."

Sister Harken demonstrated a small movement that somehow changed everything about the stance. Weight shifted. Balance chased after. The trembling in my legs found new places to burn.

The two dozen students attempted to follow. Most did not.

"Hold."

She began walking through the rows, her gaze cataloging every error. When she found one, two fingers struck the offending spot—a hip riding too high, a knee angled wrong, a heel foolish enough to bear weight that belonged on the ball of the foot. The touched student peeled away to the wall, where a different kind of suffering waited: starting with a low squat that had to be held until she said otherwise.

Jonathan was tapped out after the second instruction. His face showed no frustration as he joined the growing line at the wall. I watched him sink into the squat, his back straight against the stone, and felt a flash of guilt for being glad it wasn't me.

Not yet anyway, I told myself. *Stay focused.*

Sister Harken's instructions grew more elaborate. Slide the right foot to match. Turn the hips. Drop the shoulders. Each adjustment felt like stacking stones on an already-fragile tower. My legs screamed. Sweat gathered at my temples despite the winter chill pressing through the windows.

More students fell away. The wall grew crowded.

When only five of us remained, Sister Harken's lip twitched. She dragged a leather-wrapped wooden beam across the floor, the scrape of it cutting through the silence.

"Walk it. Forward to the end, backward to the start."

The beam was perhaps six inches wide and fifteen feet long. Simple enough on steady legs. My legs were not steady.

The first student—a broad-shouldered boy—made it halfway before his heel slipped. Sister Harken's two fingers found him before he'd even regained his balance.

I stepped up next. The cold had stiffened the leather wrapping, making the beam's surface unforgiving beneath my boots. I fixed my eyes on the beam's far end and began.

▷

Forward. Heel, toe. Heel, toe. The truth dancing forms whispered through my memory. *Feel the surface. Let it tell you where to step.* I resented my boots—most truth dancing was done barefoot, and the leather sole deadened the beam's feedback to a murmur. But the frosty paths and stone halls here demanded them. I kept moving, kept breathing, kept listening to the wood beneath my feet.

My legs faltered twice, but I reached the end. Turned. Started back.

"Two steps forward, one step back," Sister Harken called, adding complexity mid-crossing.

My body knew this rhythm. Knew how to move through space while space moved around me. I completed the sequence and stepped off the beam, careful not to let the relief show on my face.

Three of us had passed. Jonathan and the others still held their squats at the wall, faces tight with effort.

Sister Harken called for a water break.

The drinking trough stood along the north wall—a long stone basin fed by a pipe that ran through the wall from some cistern or spring uphill. Water flowed in a steady stream, clear and cold, pooling before draining through holes at the basin's far end. Students lined up, cupping their hands to catch the flow.

I took my place in the queue, feeling the pleasant ache of muscles pushed to useful limits. Behind me, two boys spoke in low voices—close enough to overhear.

"You lost, fair and square. New kid made it to the end."

"No way. Fifty-fifty, the first one didn't make it past the third step."

"Fair is fair, Dec. The bet was they'd both be out."

I kept my eyes forward, pretending not to hear. The line shuffled ahead. My turn came. I bent toward the flowing water—

A boot caught the back of my knee. My leg buckled. Before I could catch myself, a hand shoved my head down, and my face plunged into the basin.

Water flooded my nose, my mouth. I came up sputtering, blinking, hands braced against the stone rim. Cold streamed down my face and soaked into my wrappings.

I spun to find a boy watching me with pale eyes and a satisfied smile. He wasn't tall—maybe a couple fingers on me—but he carried himself like he owned the room. Long straight hair, blonde-brown and slightly greasy, hung past his shoulders; he pushed it behind his ears as he studied my reaction. I recognized him now as one of the three who'd made it through Sister Harken's test alongside me.

"Ya done yet?" His smile didn't waver. "Got a line of thirsty people waiting for you to take your precious time." He stepped closer, close enough that the sour reek of slag-smoke and unwashed wool filled my nose. "Your grandstanding got me flock duty, love boy. In winter."

Love boy. I blinked. Took a half-step back before I could stop myself. Spirit School.

I looked past him, searching for Jonathan, but he was already across the room, warming his hands at one of the braziers, chatting with another student. Too far to have seen the exchange. No witnesses. No allies.

Sister Harken's voice cut across the hall, calling us back to formation.

I'd like to think I was prudent. I was a lord's son. I knew how to bow when diplomacy served better than blows.

"Sorry about the bet," I offered, keeping my voice level. "I didn't know."

The boy—Declan—rolled his eyes. "Of course you're sorry." He shoved past me toward the trough, driving his shoulder into mine hard enough that I had to catch myself with a quick step. "No backbone either. Pathetic." He reached to fill his hands with water, adding over his shoulder: "What else should I expect from someone who comes from the *love* school?"

Several nearby students looked away, suddenly fascinated by the ceiling, the walls, anything but the confrontation at the water trough.

I walked back to the formation still thirsty despite the water dripping from my chin, wiping my face with my sleeve as I went.

△

Sister Harken had us pair off for the next exercise. She selected the matches herself, pointing with a finger bent at the second knuckle, its nail yellowed and hard as horn.

Her finger landed on me, then Dec.

His smile hadn't changed.

"Double or nothing," I heard him mutter to his friend as he walked over. Then he was standing across from me, arms loose at his sides, eyes measuring.

"Measure drill," Sister Harken announced to the room. She beckoned forward one of the older students who'd been assisting—Brother Jeffrey, a lean second-year with patient eyes. From the wall she took a dowel, a thin length of ash roughly the span of an outstretched arm, and set one end against her sternum, the other against his. "One partner leads, the other mirrors. Maintain consistent distance—imagine this rod connecting your centers. The follower matches the leader's movement exactly. Forward, back, lateral. Stay in proper stance. Weight balanced, knees bent, feet never crossing."

She handed the dowel off and began to move. Brother Jeffrey matched her—flowing movements that maintained a perfect, unchanging gap between them regardless of direction or speed.

"This teaches you to read your opponent," she continued. "To move without telegraphing. To control space. To judge reach." Her eyes swept the room. "Leaders ready. Begin."

Dec's smile sharpened. "I lead."

I dropped into the stance Sister Harken demonstrated, knees bent, weight forward. Dec began to move—slow at first, testing. Forward. Back. Sliding left.

My body responded before my mind could catch up. I could read the intention in the shift of weight, the angle of the shoulder, the direction of the gaze. The skill transferred, letting me track Dec's movements and match them breath for breath.

△

His jaw tightened. He moved faster. Sharp lateral cuts, sudden reversals. He was trying to catch me off-balance, to make me stumble so Sister Harken would tap me out.

I matched him. Step for step. Change for change.

Truth dancing was submission, not contest—but the principles served both. I flowed where he flowed, withdrew where he advanced, maintained the invisible rod between us with a consistency that made his face go red with frustration.

Sister Harken walked past, observed us for three heartbeats, and moved on without comment. No taps.

"Switch," she called. "Followers now lead."

I became the one moving. I kept my movements clean, controlled—no tricks, no deceptions. Just the drill as it was meant to be performed.

Dec followed adequately. His footwork was solid enough. But I could see the resentment building in the set of his shoulders, the whiteness of his knuckles.

Before he could act on whatever he was planning, Sister Harken called us into a new formation.

"Push drill. Face your partner. Hands on shoulders. On my signal, try to unbalance them. Only footwork and weight shifts—no shoving." She paused, letting the prohibition land. "Whoever steps out of stance or stumbles loses."

Dec's hands found my shoulders, his grip tighter than necessary, fingers digging in like he was trying to leave marks through the cloth. Mine found his.

Sister Harken raised her hand. "Begin."

Dec took a bracing step backward, released my shoulders, and *shoved*.

With my hands still on his shoulders, the heels of his palms caught me square before I could react—raw strength pushing me backward. My feet scrambled for purchase. My stance broke. I hit the floor hard enough to knock the breath from my lungs.

When I looked up, Dec was already turning away, arm raised, grinning at his friends as if he'd won a prize bout.

Sister Harken's whistle cut through the room. "Next pairs! Winners stay. Losers work with Brother Jeffrey on fundamentals."

She hadn't seen. Or if she had, she hadn't cared.

I picked myself up from the floor. My elbow throbbed where it had struck the wood. My pride hurt worse.

At the wall, Jonathan caught my eye. His raised eyebrow asked a question: *You all right?*

I gave a small nod. *Fine.*

Then Jonathan was looking past me, his head tilted slightly as if working through a problem.

Sister Harken dismissed us with a curt nod as daylight faded. I made my way back to the trough and drank until the cold ached in my teeth, watching Dec accept congratulations from his friends as the declared victor of the push drill.

Jonathan fell into step beside me as we filed toward the door.

"El, that was great," he said.

I stared at him.

"The push drill," he clarified, grinning. "Full contact. No fainting, no folding. Just regular getting-shoved-onto-your-backside." His eyes were bright.

"I'll be sure to celebrate once my tailbone stops throbbing."

But truly, I hadn't even considered it. I'd been too focused on Dec's hostility to notice what *hadn't* occurred.

The winter air hit us as we stepped outside, sharp enough to make my eyes water. Snow had begun to fall in earnest, fat flakes that resisted melting against our still-warm robes.

We were halfway across the field when I heard raised voices.

Two figures blocked the path ahead, confronting Dec and his friends. Both were older—second years by the look of them. They looked familiar. A third figure stood a few paces back—Brother Jeffrey, arms folded, watching. When he saw us, he turned and walked back toward the training hall without a word.

"...was that?" one was demanding. "At the water trough and push drill."

Dec's hands came up, palms out, the picture of innocence. "New guy just needed some humility. Nothing wrong with that."

"Do it again," the other said, his voice carrying even through the falling snow, "and I'll bring it to Tristan."

Dec's expression flickered—too brief to read—before settling into exaggerated terror. His friends snickered on cue. He made a show of cowering, hands raised in mock surrender, before straightening with a smirk. "Just having some fun, brothers. No harm done."

The two older students held their ground for a moment longer, then turned and walked toward us.

I recognized them now. I'd seen them among the kindred at our first governance class—seated further up the rows, laughing at some joke I hadn't caught.

"Sorry about Dec," the taller one said. "You're in Sebastian's new hearth, right?" When I nodded: "I'm Andrew. This is Nort." He gestured toward his companion, a thin young man with a crooked nose who smiled. "Don't let Dec get under your skin. He'll tire of it once you stop being interesting."

"Who's Tristan?" Jonathan asked.

"Leads Dec's kindred. Third-level." Andrew's expression suggested this explained everything. "Good man."

"Thank you," I said. "For stepping in."

Andrew waved it off. "Dec's been warned before. He'll behave for a while." His eyes lingered on my wet wrappings, my damp hair. "Welcome to Ember, brothers. Training hall has a way of sorting things out eventually."

They walked on toward the main hall, leaving Jonathan and me in the falling snow.

"Well," Jonathan said after a moment. "Still excited to learn swords?"

I should have laughed, but all I could manage was a weak smile. My pride burned beneath my breastbone like a coal that wouldn't cool.

Love boy.

The hearth gathered for dinner as usual—wide bowls of something I didn't recognize, thick noodles swimming in a dark broth that smelled of salt and slow-cooked beef. Torn flatbread lay stacked on a clay plate between us along with a small saucer of pale-yellow spice paste. The four of us sat cross-legged on the floor. My muscles had limbered during the walk back from the training hall, but I lowered myself onto the stone with less grace than I would have liked.

"So," Sebastian said, tearing off a piece of bread. "How was your first day with Sister Harken?"

Jonathan launched into it before I could answer.

"El made it through every drill. The stance work, the beam walk, the measure drill—he was one of three left standing when she called the water break." Jonathan's eyes were bright as he recounted the afternoon. "You should have seen him on that balance beam. I could barely hold the opening stance."

I focused on my noodles. The warmth spread through my chest, and I realized I'd been hungrier than I thought.

"The push drill was something else," Jonathan continued. "El got shoved flat on his back—hard enough to knock the wind out of him."

Sebastian's eyebrows rose. "Shoving isn't typically permitted in a push drill."

"It wasn't."

"Who did the shoving?" Sebastian asked.

"Someone named Declan."

Sebastian slowed his chewing. "I know Dec. He has a reputation."

Me too, Adam signed.

"Jonathan didn't even tell you about what happened at the water break," I said.

The hearth went quiet. Jonathan set down his bread.

"What happened?" Sebastian's voice had lost its lightness.

▽

I told them about the bet, the boot catching my knee, the hand shoving my face into the trough. *Love boy.* I kept my voice level, but I felt the heat rising in my chest as I spoke.

When I finished, Adam's hands moved in sharp, emphatic gestures; I couldn't catch it all. Jonathan watched, then laughed—a bright, startled sound.

"He says: *Want me to rough him up?*"

The image of Silent Adam, tottering after Dec, fists raised. Sebastian snorted. Jonathan pressed his lips tight around a mouthful of noodles, lest they come tumbling out. My lips twitched.

"Seriously, though, El." Sebastian's smile faded. "I can bring this to Tristan. He leads Dec's kindred."

I shook my head. "He said I have no backbone. I'd rather prove him wrong."

Adam's hands moved. Sebastian watched, then translated: "*Leave a bent post standing, and the next man levels his work to it.*" He extended two fingers toward Adam, held them a moment, then turned to look me in the eyes. "Justice delayed curdles into revenge, El."

"I can handle it."

"I'm not saying you can't. Just don't mistake suffering for strength when you're choosing it."

"Who says I'll be the one suffering?"

The words came out darker than I intended. Jonathan gave me a strange look—his spoon paused halfway to his mouth, head tilted like he was hearing a note slightly off-key. Sebastian and Adam exchanged a glance and laughed it off, but I caught the pause before their laughter, the beat of silence where something else might have lived.

I bent to my noodles and said nothing more.

We cleared the bowls and stacked them near the door. The evening stretched ahead—my fingers already twitching toward the handspeak practice Adam and I had established. I reached for my sideflute to demonstrate a phrase, and Sebastian let out a theatrical groan.

"Every night," he said, collapsing onto his bunk. "A man can't even read in peace."

"You could join us," I offered.

"I'd rather sort coal." Sebastian pulled his book from beneath his pillow. "Maybe I'll ask Declan if he wants to play chess at *his* hearth. Probably quieter there."

Jonathan stirred. "Actually," he said slowly, "there might be a better solution." He turned to me. "They have a library here. History-focused, mostly—law cases, political theory, judgments from the old courts. It's largely unused." A smile crept across his face. "Books make excellent insulators."

Adam's hands moved: *Perfect.*

Jonathan led us through corridors I hadn't yet explored, back to the great hall and down a long passage that sloped gently into the mountain's heart. The air grew cooler, the torchlight sparser.

The library doors were heavy oak, iron-banded, set into an archway carved with geometric patterns. A small desk stood just inside, where a thin man with wispy hair was organizing a stack of parchment.

He looked up as we entered—and his face transformed.

"Jonathan?"

Jonathan's grin widened. "Brother Jacob."

The clerk—Brother Jacob—rose from his desk and clasped Jonathan's hand with both of his own. "Two years! More? I thought you'd abandoned us for somewhere with windows."

"Waterfall has a gorgeous library, but it's not nearly so dusty as I like." Jonathan gestured toward us. "My hearthmates. Elenden and Adam."

I offered my hand. Brother Jacob took it—his hand ink-stained but warm. "Welcome, welcome." His eyes moved to Adam and he dipped his head—a small bow, familiar rather than formal.

Adam raised two fingers to his brow. Brother Jacob returned the gesture.

"We were hoping to use one of the reading alcoves," Jonathan said.

"Use them?" Brother Jacob laughed. "You could host a banquet in the back rooms and I'd hardly notice. The library hasn't changed much since your last visit. Don't see much traffic outside of the law semester, and even then..." He waved a hand. "Half the students just want the light, not the books. Go on—you know the way."

The library was bathed in lamplight. The ceiling rose perhaps twice a man's height, and shelves stretched from floor to ceiling, filled with volumes that had clearly sat undisturbed for years.

"The lamps are specially designed," Jonathan said, noting my glance. "They extinguish if disturbed—knocked over, dropped, anything. After the burning of the Citarian archives, every serious library adopted something similar. The stone and cool air help too."

The space had been carved directly from the rock—I could see where different chambers connected through precise cuts in the stone walls, creating a maze of alcoves and reading rooms.

"It's the oldest library I know of," Jonathan said as we walked, keeping his voice reverently low despite our solitude. "Mostly histories of different eras. Lawsuits and judgments. Political theories from before the Empire's founding." He ran his hand along a row of spines. "Not much call for it these days, but the collection is remarkable."

We found a well-lit alcove near the back—a small table, two stools, a lamp that Brother Jacob must have kept burning out of habit or hope. The shelves here held treatises on mining rights and water disputes, their leather bindings cracked with age.

"I need to write Sorcha, then maybe I'll browse a bit," Jonathan said. His eyes had that gleam they always got around books. "See if there's anything I missed when I was here before." He winked at me. "Don't stay up too late; tomorrow is a working day."

He disappeared into the stacks.

Adam and I fell to our work. We began as we always did—handspeak first. He insisted on grammar and vocabulary beyond simple gestures: the difference between greeting a stranger and greeting a friend, the subtle shifts when addressing someone of renown versus a spouse, the quick forms for when you were rushed and the fuller ones for when you weren't. There were even signs meant to be hidden—small movements, close to the body, the handspeak equivalent of a whisper. My fingers had grown more fluid over the past days. Adam corrected me patiently, signing each phrase slowly until I could echo it back.

Then I excused myself—fumbling the sign, unsure whether Adam counted as elder, teacher, or brother/friend—and returned to Brother Jacob's desk to beg a sheet of parchment. He handed it over without question. Back at the alcove, I spread it on the table.

"I want to try something different tonight," I said, signing as I spoke. I pointed to the marks I'd drawn—five lines, the round notes positioned at different heights, the stems and flags that indicated duration. "This is how music is written."

Adam leaned forward, studying the notation.

I played a simple phrase on my sideflute, then pointed to the corresponding marks on the parchment. Played it again. Pointed again. Adam's eyes moved between the instrument and the page, and I could almost see him making connections—the way a note's position corresponded to its pitch, the way the shapes indicated how long to hold each sound.

He raised his pipe and attempted the phrase. Wrong key, but the rhythm was close—and his fingers climbed when the notes did.

I corrected his starting position. He tried again. Closer.

We worked through three more phrases before I noticed the other lamps in the library were going dark, one by one.

Brother Jacob appeared at the alcove's entrance with an odd brass key in his hand to extinguish the lamp's special wicks.

"Evening bells passed," he said apologetically. "I need to close up."

Adam and I exchanged a glance. His hands moved: *Next time, we hide from him.*

I laughed and tried to sign back: *Hard hide loud music.* My grammar was terrible—I could feel the wrongness of it even as my hands moved—but Adam raised a finger and pointed briefly at me anyway. Close enough.

We gathered our things and made our way back through the darkening stacks. Jonathan had already left.

The walk back to our quarters was quiet save for Adam's gait beside me—slide, step, slide, step—echoing off the stone.

Jonathan was already in his bunk when we entered. He waved without lifting his head from the pillow. Sebastian was asleep, a book fallen open across his chest.

I washed my face at the basin and returned to our room. Adam readied for bed behind me. His movements filled our stone room with sound—the scrape of his stool against stone, the shuffle of his feet as he changed, the rustling of his bunk as he lowered himself onto it. I climbed into my own bunk and lay staring at the ceiling.

Silent Adam.

He didn't seem stealthy. His gait was careful, measured, the walk of a man protecting aching joints. And yet...

I thought of how he'd appeared behind us that first day at Ember—seemingly from nowhere. I resolved to ask him properly when the time was right. There had to be a trick to it.

My eyes closed before I could decide whether my question ought to be signed with formal grammar or the easy shorthand between friends.

Chapter 69

Justice

Nearly two moons passed at Ember, and every four days turned like a wheel: governance, then generals and swords, then justice, then labor. The rhythm carved grooves into my bones until I woke knowing whether my hands would hold a stylus or a shovel, whether my legs would carry me to lecture halls or the cool darkness of the mines.

General days no longer frightened me. Through Brother Daren's patient teaching, mathematics had begun to yield its secrets. The ratios that had condemned me at Mountain now felt more like puzzles waiting to be solved. I still struggled with the harder proofs, still watched other students race ahead while I labored over basics they'd mastered. But the numbers had stopped being enemies. They had become, at least, reluctant acquaintances.

Rhetoric required no such reconciliation. Fletch's lessons had worked those patterns deep, and I moved through logical fallacies and argument structures the way my fingers found their homes on my pipes. Science and philosophy fell somewhere between—subjects I could follow without leading, more like my halting handspeak.

The generals' mornings passed quickly. It was the afternoons I dreaded.

Sister Harken had not softened. If anything, her standards grew sharper as winter deepened. But my body had begun to answer her demands. The stance work that once set my thighs trembling no longer did. She moved on to harder tests. The balance beam had become too easy, so Sister Harken took it away. What replaced it was always worse—tallow-slicked planks, boards set on rockers, a half-round log left to roll freely underfoot. Then came blindfolds. My ankles learned to read the surface when my eyes could not. When she called for the measure drill, I was among the last pairs standing. Truth dancing had taught me the language. Sister Harken was expanding my vocabulary.

She still didn't let us handle swords, but I might have found satisfaction in my progress. I might have, if not for Declan.

The first class after our encounter, I kept my distance. When Sister Harken paired us off, I positioned myself across the room, partnered with a quiet boy from my kindred named Greg who moved like he was apologizing for taking up space. We worked through the drills without incident. I told myself this was wisdom—avoiding unnecessary conflict, choosing battles worth fighting.

But I watched Declan from the corner of my eye. Watched him pair with a smaller student, a boy who couldn't have been more than twelve. Watched the way his 'weight shifts' became shoves when Sister Harken's attention turned elsewhere. Watched the smaller boy stumble, recover, stumble again. Watched the tight set of his jaw as he refused to complain.

The second class, the same. Declan found new partners—usually younger, always smaller—those least likely to protest. His cruelty had a cunning to it. He never broke rules openly enough to draw correction, never pushed when Brother Jeffrey's attention was anywhere nearby. His violations lived in the spaces between instructions, in moments that could be mistaken for clumsiness or enthusiasm.

By the third class, I made my decision.

When Sister Harken called for pairs, I crossed the floor and planted myself in front of Declan before he could select his usual prey. His pale eyes narrowed.

"Need another lesson, love boy?"

I said nothing. Simply waited.

His smile crept wider, savoring the moment. "Fine by me."

I told myself I was protecting the others. Told myself this was justice—placing myself between the wolf and the flock. If Declan wanted someone to push around, let it be someone who could push back. Let it be someone whose pride could carry the bruises his cruelty left.

What I did not tell myself, what I could not yet see, was how that pride had already begun its work.

The measure drill was simple enough. Declan led; I followed. He tested me with sharp cuts and sudden reversals, trying to catch me off-balance. I matched him step for step. When we switched, I kept my movements clean—no tricks, no retaliation.

He cheated anyway. A heel clip disguised as footwork. An elbow that strayed too wide. Small violations, deniable violations, and each one fed something I called resolve.

I said nothing. Did nothing. Absorbed it.

Better me than them, I thought. And beneath that thought: *Remember this. Remember what he is.*

Weeks passed. The pairing became routine. Whenever Sister Harken called for partners, I found Declan. Whenever Declan looked for easier targets, he found me instead. A kind of ritual, he and I—predator and willing prey.

He never stopped testing.

One afternoon during a grappling drill, his thumb found the soft place between tendon and bone on the inside of my wrist and pressed until my hand went white. I held his gaze. He held the pressure. Sister Harken passed behind him, and his grip released as if it had never been. My fingers tingled for the rest of the hour. The crescents scored into my hand lasted longer.

He had grown his nails long. I rarely saw the scratches until the hot water found them in the washroom each evening—thin lines across my forearms, shoulders, and sides.

Another day, a 'stumble' during footwork practice drove his knee into the meat of my thigh. I limped through the remaining drills. Jonathan mentioned it at dinner, and I told him I'd misjudged a lateral step. The lie came easily. Too easily.

Words, too. Always low enough that only I could hear. *Mama's boy. Coward. Beggar-brother.* He had a gift for finding the word that stuck longest. He never learned I was a lord's son, and I thanked the Spirit for that small mercy—what he could do with the ammunition he had was enough.

I absorbed them all. Told myself I was being noble. Told myself this was what standing between the weak and the strong looked like. The heat building in my chest was righteous indignation—the proper anger of a good man witnessing wrong. And because the wrongs were done to me rather than someone weaker, I mistook my silence for strength and my forbearance for forgiveness.

But forgiveness does not keep accounts.

It does not replay each slight in the dark hours before sleep. It does not calculate responses, imagine confrontations, rehearse the words that would cut deepest if ever spoken aloud. It does not lie awake flexing hands, shaping the strike—the angle that would land just below the sternum—and then set it aside as proof of restraint.

I did not name it hatred. Not then. I called it awareness. Called it preparation. Called it vigilance.

Each small cruelty became another entry in the ledger I kept somewhere behind my ribs. I balanced the books nightly, alone in my bunk, tallying what was owed with the patience of a miser.

Do your masters teach you how to fight, or only how to bend?

The cuts accumulated. They scabbed over. And beneath that hardened deadness, the ink dried permanent.

Governance class remained a refuge.

Brother Gentian's lectures carried us across oceans and centuries, into ways of thinking so foreign they made for strange discussions and stranger dreams.

The kindred discussions that followed each lecture became hours I anticipated. Twelve minds wrestling with ideas too large for any one of us to hold. Tam, the northern boy, argued for systems that trusted people to govern themselves. Kane pushed back with questions about human nature and the evidence of history. Jonathan traced connections between philosophies that seemed opposed, threading them together with precedents he'd unearthed from some dusty tomes or forgotten texts.

I spoke less than the others. Listened more. When I did venture an opinion, I found the kindred willing to hear it—willing to challenge it, too, which somehow felt like the greater gift.

Not everyone shared my enthusiasm.

"What's the point?" Tam complained one afternoon, gathering his things as the bells released us. "We're never going to form a government. None of us are going to be emperor. It's all just... theory."

Adam's shoulders shook with silent laughter. Tam didn't notice.

"You could join the Watch," someone offered.

Tam snorted. "Who wants to govern a small fire school? Waste of time."

Kane stirred—unusual for him, preferring to guide rather than argue. "Perhaps," he said quietly, "you've never suffered under a system that got it wrong."

But when Brother Gentian announced the final project at the end of our eighth week, even Tam went quiet.

"Each kindred will propose a government for the Empire," Gentian said, pacing across the front as though the ideas were too exciting to present sitting down. "You will draw upon everything we have studied. Every system. Every society. Every success. You will present your proposal before selected faculty and members of the Watch."

What Gentian was asking us to do, to set the Empire's own structure on the scale and find it wanting, would earn a flogging in most provinces and a noose in a few. I tried to imagine a professor at the Imperial Academy standing before his students and saying, *Design a better version of the thing that pays my salary.* The image wouldn't form.

"Their assessment of your government will be your grade for this class."

The room stirred. I caught Jonathan's eye across the kindred circle. His grin had sharpened into something hungry. Even Tam was leaning forward now, his earlier dismissal forgotten.

A government for the Empire, graded by the masters. Every piece of our scattered discussions, every strange philosophy from distant lands, every argument we'd had about human nature and the purpose of power—all of it suddenly had a destination.

I should have been excited. Part of me was. But the ledger behind my ribs had opened to a new page, and the questions forming there had less to do with protecting hearths than with ensuring people like Declan could never warm themselves beside one.

My handspeak was getting worse. Or rather, I was becoming fluent in nonsense.

Adam and I had moved our nightly lessons permanently to the library. Most nights, Jonathan came along, dragging another stool to our alcove. Brother Jacob was visibly delighted to have more regular company among his shelves.

The arrangement suited everyone. Sebastian got his silence. Adam got his music lessons on the rowan pipe. His breath control had steadied—he'd learned to work with the hum instead of against it. We could manage simple duets now, nothing elaborate, but the phrases wove together without stumbling. He was reading music now, too, and the sound of our pipes threading melody through the library's stone alcoves had a warmth to it that often drew Brother Jacob to linger nearby.

I was pleased with Adam's progress. He was less pleased with mine.

The trouble wasn't comprehension. After weeks of nightly practice, I could follow most conversations in standard handspeak, could track the quick exchanges between Adam and the kitchen master, could catch the shifts in tone when brothers signed across the dining hall. Adam had been thorough—teaching me not just the common dialect but miners' shorthand, the formal grammars used in Watch proceedings, the older signs that bridged cultures. My eyes had learned to listen.

My hands had learned to assume.

I couldn't stop it. That was the worst of it. My memory for the signs was good. I would sign a phrase and feel the shapes land correctly—fingers confident, wrists loose, transitions smooth. Adam would watch, his face a portrait of patience under strain. Then he would sign the phrase back to me the way I'd done it, and I would see nothing wrong.

"You just told him the coal tastes like sunrise," Jonathan said, returning his eyes to his book rather than meeting mine.

I stared at my hands. "I said the coal *quality* was excellent *this morning*."

"You signed three of those words. The rest was... creative." Jonathan's crooked smile surfaced. "You're mixing dialects, El. Shorthand for the verb, formal for the subject, and something I don't recognize at all for the modifier."

Adam's shoulders were shaking.

Jonathan had watched me fumble languages before—we'd set aside our *Azurath* work at Ember, but apparently the impatience I'd demonstrated as his student had followed me. He theorized that I had absorbed too many vocabularies at once without mastering the grammar beneath any of them—collecting words the way a magpie collects bright objects. I could *read* each dialect clearly—context filled the gaps, the way you could understand a man speaking with a thick accent even if you couldn't imitate it. But when I *signed*, my hands grabbed whichever word-shape felt most natural, pulling from three or four different systems in a single sentence. The result was barely intelligible to Adam, who knew every dialect, and baffling to everyone else.

"You're like a parrot raised by four different masters," Jonathan said. "Each word is correct. None of them belong together."

Adam signed something slow and deliberate, making sure I caught every shape.

Your confidence is outrunning your competence.

"He says your confidence is outrunning your competence," Jonathan translated.

"I know what he said!"

The words came out harder than I intended. Jonathan raised both hands in surrender. Adam watched me, perfectly still. Then he pointed at me and signed, intentionally: *That. That is the problem.*

My hands started to form a reply—then stopped, because I wasn't sure which grammar to use, and for the first time I could feel the gap I'd been standing over without looking down.

Adam waited. Then he signed, formal, master to student: *Good.*

Still, our lessons were paying off. Adam's duets grew more assured, my reading of handspeak sharpened, and if my signing remained a patchwork of borrowed dialects, at least I was learning where the holes were. Knowing what you don't know, Brother Daren had once said in mathematics, is one of the more useful kinds of proofs.

Every seventh day, one of the other kindreds prepared the kindred meal as their labor. What I thought of as duty was something closer to a tournament. Kindreds planned their menus days in advance, debating recipes with intensity typically reserved for sword forms. A southern kindred served peppered lamb over saffron rice that silenced the hall mid-bite. A week later, a group heavy with Qiran boys answered with dumplings folded tight as letters, swimming in a dark broth with spices I couldn't name but my tongue remembered long after. Even the failures had ambition—one kindred attempted a layered pastry that collapsed into dry flaky rubble, though they served it proudly like generals who'd lost the battle but refused to leave the field. The cooking was never the point.

All thirteen members of each kindred gathered at a long table, along with monastery regulars and guests who rotated through with the weeks. Kane sat at the head, not because he demanded it but because no one else did, and he was always last to sit. Last to speak, too. When he did speak, it was to ask how something had turned out, some struggle you'd mentioned three weeks ago and already forgotten. Andrew and Nort usually flanked him, their laughter setting the table's pitch. Tam stationed himself opposite whoever disagreed with him most recently, hungry for a debate. He would have been right at home at Redcloud.

Over the weeks, I came to know them. Greg, who apologized for existing but argued like a barrister when the subject touched history. Two brothers from the southern provinces—Marcus and Marius—whose names I muddled for the first month. One quiet, one relentless, both with the same dark eyes. A boy called Fin who couldn't hold a tune but sang anyway, usually to Adam's visible delight.

But there remained a distance I couldn't close. Jonathan felt it too—I could tell by the way he laughed a beat behind the others.

We had come late. We might leave in another month. And even among the hearth, there were things we did not say, could not say, that stood like closed doors between us and the rest. The others had mined together, eaten together, argued and frozen and sweated together through months we'd missed. Sebastian and Adam bridged the gap—Sebastian with his easy nature, Adam with a warmth that needed no speech—but the jokes that made Marcus spit his drink, the stories that sent Nort into fits, the single word that could invoke some memory of disaster in the tunnels: these belonged to a history we hadn't earned.

Sometimes the guests at our table seemed to belong more naturally than we did. The blue-wrapped air tester joined us once, folding his long frame into the space beside Kane. He signed with Adam in the miners' shorthand I could now follow, and the kindred greeted him like family. He'd earned his welcome at any table.

I envied him. It was like hearing laughter through a doorway. The sound is warm and real and you can bask in it, but no retelling will land the same.

And yet. Every seventh day, the larger table filled. Every seventh day, Kane asked what we'd studied, what we'd struggled with, what we'd built or broken. Every seventh day, someone told a story that made the rest groan or laugh, and gradually—so gradually I almost missed it—the stories began to include us. Jonathan's dry observations. My fumbled handspeak. The time Sebastian swore Adam had used some trick to pass us all in the dark of the tunnels.

It wasn't acceptance. Not yet. It was something slower and more honest—the kindred doing what kindreds did. Wearing us into the grain of itself, the way water shapes stone. Not by force. By the seventh day, again and again. By the arguments that spilled out of governance and into the corridors. By the justice cases we couldn't stop debating over meals. Until the table began to feel less like a place we visited and more like a place we returned to.

Justice days began the same as Governance—in the amphitheater, with Brother Gentian pacing the speaking floor, his pockets rattling with roasted nuts. But where governance asked *how should we arrange power?*, justice pressed closer to the bone.

The first class opened with Gentian pointing to the stone above the amphitheater's entrance. Words I had walked past a dozen times without reading:

Justice is not something we invent. It is something we submit to.

Gentian stood beneath them and let the silence hold.

"Emperor Theron's quote," he said. "Eighth Emperor of the second founding; the same man who quelled a provincial rebellion and had his own brother executed for treason." He looked up at the carved letters. "Was Theron just?"

No one answered.

"Today we begin where justice must always begin: not with law, not with punishment, not with courts—but with the object and subject of justice: lying, thieving, conniving *people.*" He cracked a nut between his fingers and chewed. "One of the sages has said 'The just person precedes the just society.' Very well then. What is a person? And what makes them just? A river doesn't argue with its banks. A salmon doesn't petition for redress when the bear's jaw closes. An oak doesn't envy the pine." He turned back to us. "Every created thing fulfills its nature without quarrel." His voice dropped. "Yet here we sit—the one creature with the audacity and impulse to look at itself and say: *Something is amiss. It must be set aright.*"

The curriculum was dialectical. Each kindred received a single copy of a text—passed between hearths, sharing one day each before class—and the discussions drew on those readings. Gentian assigned collected judgments from the founding era, cases where laws had been applied and the outcomes picked apart by generations of scholars. We argued over sentences. Tam insisted intent mattered most—a thief stealing bread for hunger deserved different treatment; Andrew countered that a victim's wounds healed no faster for their attacker's good intentions; Jonathan produced precedents that complicated both positions until no one was sure where they'd started.

As the weeks advanced, Gentian led us into terrain where the footing grew even less certain. One morning he arrived with a single question instead of his regular satchel of scrolls.

"There is a man," he said, pacing slowly. "A man from a small village. He has children—three, let us say—and they go hungry most nights. Not because there is no work, but because he is afraid to ask for it. Afraid of refusal. Afraid of the mill foreman's temper. So he sits at home and frets."

He cracked a nut.

"One evening, this same man watches the mill foreman beat his neighbor in the street. The neighbor is older. The blows are not ambiguous. Our man watches from a curtained window. He does nothing. He says nothing. Because intervening might cost him something."

Silence.

"The man is a coward," Tam blurted out.

Gentian pointed at him. "Is cowardice immoral?"

Most of us nodded.

"I'm pleased to note that most of you agree with our brown-wrapped brothers. Should it be illegal?"

The nods came slower. A few heads shook.

"When a man abandons his post in battle, we punish him. But not for cowardice—for desertion. For his broken oath. The law reaches the *act*, not the *vice*." He held up a finger. "Now. Our man who is merely a coward at home." He looked at Tam. "Should we arrest him?"

Tam opened his mouth. Closed it.

"A just society requires both law and virtue. Neither alone suffices." He paced back toward the center. "One of your readings this week included a line from a Val'dren chieftain, two centuries dead: 'The more laws, the less justice.' " He cracked a nut. "Let us consider his words."

"Law without virtue? The law becomes the weapon of the very men it was meant to restrain—selectively enforced, conveniently blind. The strong will bend it; the connected purchase exemptions from it; and the weak, whom it was written to protect, end up ground between its teeth."

Tam's hand went up before Gentian had finished. "But that's what governance is for. A self-governing society wouldn't allow the strong to prey on the weak. The people themselves would stop him."

"Would they?" Gentian resumed pacing. "What's to stop an unvirtuous people from becoming every bit as cruel as the tyrant? Fifty-one men with votes can write any law they please concerning the other forty-nine." He paused. "Men are no kinder in crowds than alone. Often less."

He turned.

"And virtue without law? That is the gentler lie. It pretends men are better than they are. That the fence is unnecessary because surely no one would trespass." He gestured broadly. "The first armed man who disagrees will simply take what he wants like a wolf takes from the sheep.

And the virtuous, having done nothing to stop him, will have nothing to offer but pity."

"Consider two men." He cracked a nut. "The first comes over the wall with a torch and burns the city. We all agree what he is. We write songs about the men who stopped him, or songs about the men who did not." He turned. "The second lives inside the wall. He takes from the common store and gives nothing back. He walks roads he did not pave, drinks from wells he did not dig, sleeps safe behind watches he will not stand. He destroys the same city." His voice dropped. "Only slower. Breaking no law."

The kindred discussions grew longer as the weeks passed. Justice made us argumentative in ways governance hadn't yet. Governance was abstract—we debated systems none of us would build. But Justice touched ground. Justice named things we recognized.

I said less in these discussions than I did in governance. But I listened with both hands flat on the bench, leaning forward, because Gentian was finally putting words to the thing burning in my chest—and I was certain I understood what he meant.

Chapter 70

Secrets

Over dinner one evening, Sebastian turned to Adam.

"I'm desperate for a game of chess." He gestured toward me. "Adam, do you think you could spare me Elenden for one evening?"

This wasn't the first time he'd asked. Each time before, I'd deferred to Adam's lessons. Sebastian never pressed, but I'd caught him more than once with his board open on his bunk, playing both sides against himself.

"Of course," Jonathan said, before Adam or I could answer. "I'll go with Adam to the library if he wants to practice. He doesn't always need you hovering."

"He does, actually. His breath—"

"His breath is fine. His rhythm is fine. You just like being needed." Jonathan's crooked smile took the edge off. "Besides, weren't you the one who told him he needs to learn to think through the music himself?"

I hesitated. Adam caught my eye across the table and smiled.

"I'll copy out some passages for him to work through," I said, grabbing paper from my pipe case. "The one in northern time. And the scale exercise—he keeps skipping the bridge between phrases."

After we'd cleared our bowls, Jonathan accepted the sheets of parchment I scratched out. He held them at arm's length as if the musical notation might bite him. "If he has questions about what any of this means, we're both in trouble."

I turned to Adam and signed what I hoped was casual common grammar: *Make sure not to rush the rests. Don't treat silence like something to be skipped over.*

"Have fun with him, Sebastian. He could use some humbling." Jonathan winked and left with Adam before I could respond.

Sebastian already had the board out.

It was a hinged case of pale ash that opened to reveal squares of alternating grain—light wood against dark walnut stain, sharp enough to read by lamplight. The pieces nested in felt-lined compartments, each one hand-carved.

I lifted the nearest tall piece and turned it in my fingers. Not a king—an emperor, seated on a miniature throne with carvings of tiny triangles worked into the headrest. The resemblance to the chess I knew ended there. Rooks had become hammer-wielding monks in brown-painted wrappings, their stances low and rooted. The Air sister bishops carried longbows. Careful brushstrokes outlined their grey sashes and fierce expressions. The knights—Fire brothers, red-wrapped, each brandishing a sword in a different guard position. And where the queen should have stood, a woman in blue gripped a longstaff, her painted wrappings flowing as though caught mid-stride.

"The master carver was a Water School adept," Sebastian said. "In case you couldn't tell."

I set the piece back on the board. "He gave Temperance the queen's position."

"A little biased, but the brother had a point. The piece that flows in any direction—forward, lateral, diagonal. No restrictions." Sebastian arranged the dark pieces on his side, and I moved to mirror him with the light pieces. He surveyed the assembled ranks. "Earth holds the corners, Air controls the long diagonals, Fire guards the flanks." He paused. "But no Spirit brothers, to speak of."

I looked at the board. The answer was obvious once you saw it.

"The pawns."

Sebastian's hands stilled over a knight. He looked at the row of small undyed figures—simply carved, bearing no weapons, wearing no color. Standing in front of everything else.

"No weapons. No color. And if they make it to the other side—"

"Huh." He picked one up and examined it as if seeing it for the first time. "I never thought of that." He returned the pawn with new respect.

We set the board and began. Sebastian played the way he lived—cheerful aggression, advancing pieces before he'd fully secured his position, trusting instinct over calculation. I played the way Corrin had taught me, during the winter when he'd broken his wrist and couldn't train. Slowly, looking three moves ahead, trading space for time. Rushing meant the game would end faster and I would be dismissed from his presence.

We were past the opening, the board grown thorny with threats and counters, when Adam appeared in the doorway.

I almost didn't recognize the expression. Adam's face—usually so composed it could have been carved from the same wood as the chess pieces—had gone white. His eyes were wide. His hands were already moving before his feet had crossed the threshold.

Come.

The grammar was not a request. It was absolute-requirement—the form reserved for a king commanding a servant. He had demonstrated it once when teaching me the registers. He had never used it.

Sebastian and I rose together. Jonathan appeared over Adam's shoulder, his face caught between confusion and alarm.

"What's going on?" Sebastian looked between them.

"I don't know." Jonathan's words came fast, tumbling over each other. "He was playing—working through something you wrote out, El—and he just stopped. Stood up wide-eyed. Looked at me and signed *Can you see it?* I said *See what?* and he—" Jonathan gestured helplessly. "He took off running. I've never seen him move that fast."

Sebastian turned to Adam. "What is it? What did you see?"

Adam didn't look at Sebastian. His eyes found mine and held—open wide and bright with something I couldn't name. His hands rose again, but the grammar had changed. Gone was the king's command. What replaced it was the lowest form in the language—beggar to master, the sign of one who had no right to ask and nothing to offer but need.

Please come.

I saw the library before we reached it.

Light spilled from the doorway and down the corridor like something that had been waiting to escape, warm and gold as late afternoon on open ground. I stopped mid-stride. Jonathan nearly walked into me. Sebastian caught his arm.

Adam was watching my face.

His eyes were wide and searching, and when I looked at him something in his expression broke into a grin so fierce it shook his whole frame.

His hands moved fast. *Yes! You see it. You see it!*

Shiranath.

I stepped through the doorway to the confused looks of my friends.

The library blazed. The walls and arched passages connecting the alcoves radiated a golden warmth that made the lamp-wicks look pale and thin by comparison. The light emanated from the ceiling: held in the rock the way warmth lives in a hearthstone after the fire goes out. The stone itself was luminous.

Brother Jacob stood behind his desk, blinking at us. He held a half-eaten apple in one hand and a cataloging stylus in the other.

"What in the name of—" He looked from Adam to me, to Sebastian and Jonathan crowding the doorway behind us. "You tore out of here like the mountain was coming down. Is everything all right?"

Adam turned a slow circle in the middle of the library, face upturned. His mouth was open.

"El. I can be patient, but I'd prefer not to be." Sebastian was watching Adam. "What is going on?"

A creeping suspicion gathered around my wonder. I held a placating hand up to Sebastian and addressed Adam. "Show me. Show me what you were playing when this happened."

Adam was already moving—that tottering gait suddenly purposeful—toward the alcove where we practiced each evening. The others followed. On the small table where our parchments lay scattered, one sheet stood out from the rest. Yellow. Unmistakable.

My stomach dropped. The Kindling Song. The Val'dren music I kept in my pipe case—I must have included it alongside the other pages without thinking.

"He complained about your handwriting," Jonathan explained, picking up one of my hastily scratched exercises and holding it up as evidence. "Shifted through the stack until he found something legible."

I stared at the yellow parchment, then at Adam. "You played this? On the pipe?"

Adam nodded.

It wasn't possible. *The Shiranath respond only to voice*, Master Septain had said. But then—Adam hummed when he played.

"You played this perfectly," I said.

Adam's shoulders shook.

I took a breath. Weighed the words.

There are moments when secrecy stops being prudence and becomes cowardice. Brother Jacob had hosted our hearth every evening for weeks without asking a single question. Adam could see the stones. Jonathan already knew most of it. Sebastian deserved the rest.

I told them.

Not everything—not the dragons and deep things that lived beneath those stories. But about the *Shiranath*: listening stones, set into rock by an ancient people whose arts we'd lost, woken by specific melodies. How I'd first encountered them in catacombs beneath Haven. How certain eyes could see their light while others couldn't.

I looked at Adam as I spoke. When I mentioned the sight—how some could see and some could not—Adam caught my eye and held it. His hand rose slowly, one finger extended, and pointed at me.

The words fell over the room like dust after a cave-in. Brother Jacob lowered his forgotten apple to the desk. Sebastian's mouth opened, then closed.

Jonathan filled in what he remembered from our talks—the Singers, the temple notation, the theory that *Azurath* script predated every known language. Jacob, for his part, had gone very still. The look on his face was reverent—the expression of a man discovering that the ground he'd stood on for years had been sacred the whole time.

Brother Jacob spoke first. His voice had found its footing again. "If what you're telling me is true—if these stones are what you say—this needs to go before the Watch. Or at least to Master Roman."

He was right. I knew he was right. But my eyes had drifted past him, down one of the narrow aisles between the shelves, and what I saw there stopped the words in my throat.

Blue letters. Faint as foxfire, half-hidden behind a shelf of unsorted scrolls—but unmistakable. *Azurath*. Here, in Ember's library, tucked behind a shelf that hadn't been moved in what looked like decades.

"Jonathan." My voice came out strange. "*Azurath*. Adam must've woken them as well."

Adam was already beside me. He was staring too. His hands moved in quick permission-grammar, turning to Brother Jacob: *May we move these?*

Jacob peered at the shelf—saw nothing, of course, but stone and dust and the spines of old scrolls. His hand went to the brass key at his belt, a librarian's reflex. "Some of those scrolls haven't been cataloged in my tenure. If anything is damaged—"

Adam touched Jacob's arm. Jacob exhaled through his nose. "Carefully," he said. "Some of those scrolls are very old."

We cleared the shelf together, all five of us. Sebastian and Jacob lifted the scrolls. Jonathan stacked them on the reading table. Adam and I watched the wall emerge.

The lettering followed a curve—an arch, carved into the stone where the shelf had stood. The indentations were barely there. Centuries of dust and disuse had filled them nearly level with the surrounding rock. But the blue behind them blazed to my eyes, and when I looked at Adam, he was smiling and nodding.

"Jonathan, think you can translate?"

Brother Jacob fetched parchment and a lantern. Jonathan and Sebastian made a trip back to the hearth for Jonathan's journal and reference notes. Adam and I waited in the alcove. The golden light held steady around us, patient as the stone it lived in. At Haven the stones had burned thinner—silver, almost cold, closer to starlight than to sun. Here the glow came warmer, amber, as though the mountain had soaked it in forge-heat before offering it back. I wondered how long they would stay lit. Adam sat on one of the stools, his gaze moving between the ceiling and the wall the way a man might gaze at stars after years indoors.

I sat across from him. His face held something I didn't want to interrupt. I kept my hands still.

Don't treat silence like something to be skipped over.

They returned, arms full, out of breath. Jonathan set down his materials and frowned.

"Jacob, could you bring that lantern closer?"

Adam and I were sitting in a wash of gold that made the lamplight look thin as candle-glow by comparison—and they couldn't see it.

I knelt before the arch and began copying each character, working slowly, confirming each stroke with Adam before committing it to paper. The shapes were familiar from my lessons with Jonathan on the road—the phonetic system, each symbol a sound rather than a meaning. My hand was steadier than my pulse.

Brother Jacob leaned over my shoulder as the characters took shape on parchment.

"Old temple notation," he murmured. "But… I don't recognize the language from the intonation."

"Singer," Jonathan said. He was already on his knees beside me, eyes bright with hunger.

"Singer?" Jacob looked between us.

"A name we came up with. The people who carved the *Azurath*—the blue script El and Adam can see." Jonathan took the parchment from me and studied the transcription. "I need to check some things. Give me a moment."

Jonathan spread his notes across the reading table, working through the transcription with a focus that shut out everything else. He muttered. Crossed things out. Wrote new possibilities in the margins. Consulted a battered page of phonetic charts and a book he carried from Waterfall. Adam watched his hands as if they were signing.

At last, Jonathan leaned back. "I have it. Mostly. The first word is either—" He tapped his stylus against his teeth. "The root could mean 'unspoken truths' or just 'secrets.' The Singer form doesn't distinguish between the two the way Thamarian does. A truth you don't speak and a truth you hide—same word."

"Does it matter?" I asked.

I don't think he heard me.

"Jonathan."

He looked up.

"Just pick one."

He glared at me—but the impatience of four other faces staring back must have registered, because his crooked smile won out. He gave a dramatic sigh and swept his hand toward the wall as though presenting a dignitary.

"The *Azurath* reads: *Unspoken truths are locked doors.*"

No one spoke. Brother Jacob mouthed them silently.

"Inspirational," Sebastian said, after a long moment. "In a way."

"Feels like something that belongs in a library," Jacob added.

Adam's hands cut the air—impatient, excited.

Sebastian translated: "*And the other part?*"

I looked at Adam. "What other part? That's the whole inscription."

No. Adam rose from his stool and crossed to the wall. He pointed—not at the blue arc of letters I'd just spent half an hour transcribing, but at a space below the arch. The center of the curve.

The white words, he signed. *Here. In the middle.*

I stared at where he was pointing. Saw nothing. Not even indentations. Just stone, blank and grey.

"Adam. I don't see anything." I kept my voice gentle. "Master Limerick called them *Argentil*—words that burn white, not blue."

His face changed. *Half-sight?* he signed. His expression was something closer to grief than confusion.

He saw more than I did. True sight. A lifetime seeing what others could not. A country of one. And tonight, he had allowed himself to believe he'd found a countryman.

"Can you write it down for us?" I asked.

Adam accepted the parchment and stylus. His hands, so sure in handspeak, trembled over the smaller work of letter-forms. The characters emerged slowly—some confident, others redrawn where his shaking grip had blurred a stroke. Jonathan and I leaned close, asking careful questions. *Is that curve open or closed? Does the second mark connect to the third?* Adam answered each one with an emphatic nod or apologetic correction.

Jonathan worked the translation faster this time. He knew the system now, knew where to look.

He leaned back.

"*Speak and enter.*"

Brother Jacob and Adam stared at each other. Sebastian, Jonathan, and I traded looks.

"It sounds like a riddle," Jonathan offered.

"It sounds like something I should bring to Master Roman." Sebastian's voice had lost its lightness.

I said nothing. I was thinking about all the unspoken truths I had laid up in my heart. The inscription burned in my conscience more than my eyes.

Unspoken truths are locked doors. Speak and enter.

Adam stood at the wall, his hands tracing the invisible letters in the middle.

Brother Jacob cleared his throat. "I'm inclined to agree with Sebastian. We would do well to heed the inscription ourselves and bring this before Master Roman." He paused, looking around the group for confirmation. "What say you—" His mouth opened, closed. I watched him swallow whatever honorific he normally offered. "Adam?"

Adam broke his gaze from the wall and pointed at Jacob.

"Settled, then." Sebastian straightened. "We go tomorrow, first thing. Brother Jacob, would you come with us?"

"I wouldn't miss it." Jacob was already reaching for the brass key at his belt. The hour was very late. The *Shiranath* burned on, but he couldn't see them, and the lamps needed extinguishing.

Sebastian would notify Master Roman and clear our absence with Kane from tomorrow's Justice class. Our scattered pages of music and translations were gathered into a single stack that Jonathan tucked inside his journal.

We returned to the hearth. Sebastian knelt beside the chess game where it still lay on the floor, mid-battle. He slid both hands beneath the board and lifted it whole, pieces and all, carrying it level to his bunk and setting it where no one would step on it.

"Don't think any of this gets you out of finishing our game, El." He straightened. "I had you in six moves."

"Maybe," I admitted.

He grinned. "Tomorrow, then. After we've changed the course of history, or whatever it is we're doing."

Jonathan was already in his bunk. "Wake me up if you discover any more ancient secrets before morning."

Adam signed something in the dark—too dim for me to read. Sebastian laughed softly, and that was enough.

I lay staring at the ceiling. Somewhere below us, through fathoms of stone, the *Shiranath* still burned.

Unspoken truths are locked doors. Speak and enter.

"We're excused from Justice today," Sebastian said, distributing bowls of porridge. He'd already been to Master Roman's office. "Roman will see us after morning bells. I told him it was important." He glanced at Adam. "I may have implied you were the one requesting the audience."

Adam raised an eyebrow but didn't object.

"Brother Jacob?" I asked.

"Meeting us there."

We ate quickly. Jonathan tucked his journal under his arm without being asked.

Master Roman received us in his office—the same cluttered chamber of black stones and ink-stained wood, the same brazier breathing warmth into the rock. Brother Jacob stood near the door, clutching a leather folio to his chest like a shield.

I told it plainly. The *Shiranath*. The Kindling Song. Adam's playing. The golden light that had bloomed in the library ceiling. The blue inscription hidden behind the shelf.

Roman listened without interruption. His fingers steepled beneath his chin, his copper eyes moving between Adam and me as I spoke. When I finished, he was quiet for a long time.

"You don't believe us," Sebastian said.

"I do believe you," Roman corrected. "But I'm not particularly surprised." He leaned back. "The mines predate the monastery by centuries. Perhaps longer. When the first brothers settled here, the library and several of the deeper chambers were already carved. The stonework is older than anything we built—older than the Empire, by some estimates."

"Singers," Jonathan said.

Roman's gaze sharpened. "That is one theory. There are others." He turned to Adam. "You can see this script?"

Adam nodded. Roman studied him the way a man studies a map he thought he'd memorized and finds redrawn.

"Show me the wall," he said.

We led him to the library. Brother Jacob hovered at a distance while Roman examined the cleared shelf, the arch of faded indentations, the stone beneath. He ran his fingers along the curve, tracing what he couldn't see.

"*Unspoken truths are locked doors,*" he repeated. "*Speak and enter.*" His hand dropped. "I want this added to the monastery records. Brother Jacob, I'll need your catalog entry—full description, location, date of discovery, names of those present." He paused. "And I'll send word to the Watch."

The Watch came. Over the following days, members arrived in ones and twos—weathered men and women who descended into the library, studied the wall, listened to our account, and departed with expressions ranging from guarded interest to polite doubt. Two masters came as well: Brother Gentian, who cracked a nut and pronounced the inscription "philosophically sound, if cryptic," and Sister Harken, who examined the stonework with a swordsman's eye for hidden mechanisms and found none.

Jonathan gave the same explanation each time, and each time, the visitor would squint at the bare stone. Adam would point. The visitor would look harder. And see nothing.

The visits tapered off within the week.

Without other eyes to confirm what Adam and I saw, the discovery sank into the monastery's memory the way most strange things do—not denied, exactly, but gently reclassified. The inscription became part of the lore surrounding Silent Adam, another chapter in the quiet legend of the man. Remarkable, yes. But remarkable the way old stories are—worth preserving, not worth rearranging your life around.

The one discovery that did hold wider attention was simpler. The *Shiranath* extinguished at sunrise. Every morning, without exception. Adam and I tested it across several days—arriving before dawn, watching the golden light hold steady in the ceiling, then fade as the first true daylight crept down the bronze-lined channels outside. By the time the light shafts carried full sun, the stones had gone dark.

Master Roman noted this for the records. Brother Jacob added it to his catalog.

Beyond that, nothing changed—except that Adam had insisted we move our practice to the alcove nearest the inscription, and I now hummed the Kindling Song each evening before our lessons. The golden light made everything easier to see, the alcove felt warmer, the hours less like study and more like something I didn't have a word for. Brother Jacob stopped checking the lamps in our alcove. The first evening they went out, he stood at the entrance with his taper and squinted into the space where Adam and I sat reading by light he couldn't see. He held there a moment—then nodded once, to himself, and moved on to the next alcove without a word.

I lost three more chess games to Sebastian. He offered to let me play white every time as consolation. I told him I was learning his weaknesses. He said at this rate I'd have a comprehensive catalog by the time I was old enough to grow a beard.

On those evenings, Adam would always excuse himself to the library. Jonathan accompanied him, but Adam would have gone alone. He never said as much—never signed a reason beyond *practice*—but I saw the way he reached for the rowan pipe the moment dinner was cleared. Not impatience. Need.

Once, late in an evening when Jonathan had already returned to the hearth and Brother Jacob was making his rounds with the brass key, I looked up from my notation and found Adam standing at the wall again. His hand hovered over the center of the arch. His back was to me. His shoulders were still. He traced shapes in the air—not the blue letters I could see, but the *Argentil* in the center. The words only he saw burning in the stone.

Speak and enter.

I watched him trace them the way you might trace a name on a grave marker—remembering. Or being remembered.

I thought I saw him wipe his eyes before he turned. But I couldn't be certain, and he was smiling when he faced me, and some things you don't ask about.

He picked up the rowan pipe and we played until Brother Jacob's key found the last wick.

Chapter 71

Provision

A knock at the tower door. The evening meal.

Merauve rose from his chair, gathering his coat. Elenden's account of the inscription still turned in his mind like a coin he couldn't stop fingering. He set it aside.

"If you'll excuse me," he said, already moving. "I have matters that will require my attention over the next two days."

Elenden's gaze followed him—those sea-blue eyes. Then the young man's head tilted, not toward Merauve but toward something else. Listening. His expression went briefly distant.

When his eyes cleared, they found Merauve at the door.

"I will be ready when you return."

Merauve held his gaze a moment longer than necessary, then stepped into the corridor and drew the door shut behind him.

The meal cart waited in the passage, attended by an orderly whose posture suggested he'd been standing at attention for some time. Merauve lifted the covers in turn. A braised shoulder of lamb, its surface lacquered dark with reduced wine. Root vegetables roasted to the edge of caramel. A dense bread studded with seeds.

"The lamb," he said, replacing the other covers. "One setting. Serve him directly. If he speaks, do not reply."

The orderly nodded and began arranging the tray.

Merauve turned to the senior guard. "Standard protocols. No visitors for the next two days. No exceptions."

"Sir."

"Should anyone inquire after my movements, I am occupied with Inquisition matters and unavailable."

"Understood, sir."

These guards had served well—weeks of vigil over their charge, and not once had discipline slipped. Reliable men. Discreet men. The sort who followed orders without the dangerous curiosity that afflicted so many.

If Sirius made good on his offer, Merauve would need such men around him. He descended the tower stairs.

The kitchens occupied the ground level of the eastern wing; their noise reached him before their smell did. Steam and woodsmoke thickened the air in the corridor, undercut by the sharper notes of garlic and rendered fat. Evening service was in full swing—the clatter of pans, the percussion of knives against cutting boards, voices calling orders across the line.

Merauve paused in the doorway. The head chef—Brendan—stood at the center, his bulk turning with surprising grace between a stockpot and a pair of roasting trays. Despite the chaos orbiting him, he spotted the Inquisitor before Merauve announced himself.

"Inquisitor." Brendan wiped his hands on his apron—a gesture of greeting rather than necessity, since the cloth was already beyond saving. "We're mid-service for the officers' hall, but there's a seat at the pass if you'd care to sit."

Merauve took the offered stool at the end of the long preparation counter where the finished plates staged before the servers carried them out. From here he could watch the kitchen's mechanism without interrupting its rhythm. A bowl of broth appeared at his elbow without his asking—rich, beefy, still rolling from the heat. Beside it, a linen napkin folded around polished cutlery.

"I won't keep you long," Merauve said. "I wanted to thank you for accommodating my irregular requests these past weeks. The tower meals have been well received."

Brendan's knife never paused over the shallots. "Not at all. Keeps the work interesting." He swept the mince into a waiting pan, where it hit the oil with a sharp hiss. “Cooking three options for a choosy man is better sport than feeding forty officers who’d be equally happy with gruel.”

A server rushed past, collecting two plates. Brendan tracked the departure with a glance, ensuring presentation survived transit, then turned to face Merauve fully. The kitchen noise covered their conversation as thoroughly as any closed door.

“Inquisitor.” His voice dropped. The big hands stilled. “My sister. I never properly—” He stopped, started again. “The physicians had given us a date. You understand? They’d measured it out in weeks. And then your man arrived with the transfer papers, and the sanatorium in the south accepted her within the ten.” He met Merauve’s eyes. “She’s walking again.”

Merauve waved the gratitude aside. “A simple administrative matter. The southern facility had capacity; your sister’s case warranted it.”

Brendan held his gaze a beat longer—he understood exactly how much paperwork and political capital *simple administrative matters* required—but he nodded once and returned his attention to his work.

Merauve sipped the broth. Set the bowl down.

“I have a separate request. Discreet.” He reset the utensil settings as he spoke. “Traveling provisions sufficient for two. Up to a ten’s duration. The food may need to be dry-stored for some time before use—a week or two.”

Brendan shook the sauté pan once, scattering the shallots across the heat, and reached for the salt without looking. No surprise registered.

“Will they have access to water?”

“Assume limited.”

“Weight or sustenance—which matters more?”

“Sustenance. But it must travel light enough for two packs.”

“Cook-fires?”

“None.”

Brendan’s fingers drummed once against the cutting board. “Dried meat. Hard cheese in wax. Ship’s biscuit—I can bake a batch tonight without drawing attention. Honey for energy, keeps indefinitely. Dried fruit." He paused. "Salt tablets, if they're sweating. I've also got rendered tallow I can portion into tins."

"Do it." Merauve dabbed his mouth with a napkin, slipped it into his coat pocket, and stood. "I'll collect the bundles in the morning. Before first bell, if that suits?"

"I'll have them ready, sir."

Merauve crossed to the doorway, then paused. "Your discretion in this is appreciated, Brendan."

The chef was already turning back to his line, hands finding the next task. "Discretion in what, Inquisitor?"

The stables were nearly empty at this hour—the day's work done, horses shifting in their stalls, the soft sounds of slow-pulled hay. A groom looked up from his sweeping, registered Merauve's uniform, and returned to his work without comment.

Merauve found the stablemaster's log on its hook beside the tack room door. He turned back three pages—requisition entries for the past ten—and studied the format. Column widths. Ink weight. The stablemaster's cramped notation, each entry initialed in the same abbreviated hand.

Merauve uncapped his pen and drew a short curving stroke in the margin of a page near the front of the log—an older entry, months past review. Too dark. The crisp black line sat among the faded notation like a snake in the grass. He studied the surrounding pages. The stablemaster's ink had a watery, diluted quality, each stroke bleeding slightly at its edges.

He found the source on the shelf beside the duty roster: an inkwell with its cork seated loose from habitual neglect. Merauve dipped his pen. The ink came up thin—a brownish wash that matched the log's entries precisely. He added a requisition dated two days prior: one horse, Inquisition courier duty, to be held available starting tomorrow morning. He matched the stablemaster's hand—the looping *horse*, the truncated *courier*—and initialed it with the man's abbreviated mark. Then he blotted the entry twice with his napkin, pressing until the fresh ink sat no brighter than the lines around it. If questioned, the stablemaster would trust his log over his memory.

That settled, he walked the stalls.

What he needed was reliability over speed—a mount for scouting supply-cache locations. Two days of riding over uncertain ground.

He passed over the officers' chargers—too conspicuous, too likely to be missed. The courier mounts were lean and fast but bred for relay sprints, not sustained work. In the fourth stall from the back, a familiar bay gelding stood hip-cocked and drowsing.

Copper.

The horse lifted his head at Merauve's approach, ears forward, curious. Broader through the chest than Merauve remembered from the parley with the Kervani band, well-fed on fortress grain these past weeks. Merauve let himself into the stall, and Copper swung his muzzle toward the Inquisitor's coat pocket.

"Hello again." Merauve ran a hand down each foreleg. No heat. No swelling. Shoes firm—the farrier had seen him recently. He lifted a hoof, checked the frog, set it down. The gelding bore the inspection easily.

Merauve returned to the log and noted Copper's stall number seventeen beside his forged entry, then checked the rotation schedule. Not assigned to patrol or courier duty for the next five days.

He hung the log back on its hook and left without speaking to anyone.

Upon returning to his quarters, Merauve shed his coat, hung it on its hook, and moved to his desk.

The hidden drawer yielded to its magnetic catch. Inside, beneath a false bottom he'd installed himself, lay forged identity papers—official forms, official signatures, flexible contents, prepared months ago for contingencies that seemed important at the time. He spread them across the desk beside a lamp turned low.

The first set identified an Imperial auditor and his clerk, traveling on routine inspection business. Serviceable, but the seals were old. Current protocols had changed the cipher sequence in the lower left corner. Merauve dipped his pen and made the correction—three strokes, precise as surgery.

The second set required more attention. A merchant, bound for the southern provinces with documentation from the Haven trade office. The physical descriptions needed adjustment. He scratched out the original measurements and entered new ones, matching the ink weight to the existing hand. Elenden's height. His build—nearly back to full-weight now, but a clerk's measurements allowed some latitude.

He held the finished documents to the lamplight, examining them from the angle a border guard would use. Passable. Not perfect—perfection invited scrutiny.

He returned the papers to the hidden drawer, closed it, locked it, and returned both keys.

The fire needed another log. He fed it, watched the bark catch and curl. He retrieved the napkin from his coat pocket and laid it across the fresh flame. The linen darkened, crisped, caught. He watched it burn to nothing.

Tachet went to its mount. Boots aligned beneath the chair. He extinguished the lamp and lay in darkness.

Cassius left midday yesterday. If the Lightbringer pushed himself—and he would—he might reach Ember Monastery before dawn. The return journey would take at least as long. He still had two days. Perhaps three, if verification proved difficult.

He would be back in time.

He rose before first bell.

Physick Grendle's office burned lamplight at any hour—the man slept in snatches between cases, or not at all. The vinegar smell thickened to a sting as Merauve pushed through the door. Grendle looked up from a mortar and pestle, unsurprised. Merauve was inside for less than a quarter hour. When he emerged, the Physick followed him three steps into the corridor, speaking low and fast. Merauve answered without turning. Grendle's mouth pressed into a line, but he nodded and went back inside.

Jerome next.

The junior interrogator's quarters were on the second floor of the barracks—a room Merauve had never entered and did not intend to enter now. He knocked twice. Jerome answered in a half-buttoned shirt, face creased from sleep, one hand already reaching for the lantern. He listened in the doorway, knuckling one eye like a child. By the time Merauve finished, the sleep had left his face entirely.

"Understood, sir."

"See that you do." Merauve held his gaze. Then left.

The kitchens were dark save for a single lamp near the cold ovens. Brendan had left two canvas bundles on the flour shelf, tied with butcher's twine and tagged with a number—the Inquisitor's requisition code, nothing more. Merauve hefted each in turn. Compact. Dense. He'd need to repack them. Something that would seal them from the elements. He tucked one under each arm and slipped out through the service door.

Back in his quarters, he locked the door and stood still.

The room needed to tell a story. Not the truth—a different story. One that confirmed what everyone already believed about him: that he was vain, ambitious, and hiding a few indiscretions. Boring enough to dismiss. Interesting enough not to look deeper.

He began with the desk. He carried the lodestone across, knelt, and fitted it into the depression beneath the support beam.

Snick.

Next, the key from the ceiling beam. The drawer open, and with it the hidden panel. He retrieved the forged papers and slid them into an oilskin wallet alongside his small journal. The contingency notes from his late planning sessions went next—not into the wallet but into the fire, page by page, watching each sheet curl and blacken before adding the next.

He gathered Chen's rice paper and the ring. The compartment held nothing now but shadow and the smell of old wood. He closed the drawer, turned the key, and knelt again to shift the lodestone from its seat.

Now the traps.

He laid a strand of hair across the seam where desk met drawer—dark enough to vanish against the wood grain—and wet the ends with his tongue, pressing them flat.

He returned the key to its hiding place among the beam's carved flourishes—but not before drawing a single thread from his coat's inner lining and winding it twice around the key's blade. Dark thread against dark iron, invisible unless you knew to look. Anyone who found the key and used it would tear or break the thread without noticing.

Let them find the key. Let them open the drawer and discover the honeypot—correspondence damning enough to satisfy the curious.

The wardrobe door he left ajar by the width of a coin. But between door and frame, at knee height, he wedged a splinter of wood. It would drop if the door swung wider. It would snap if the door was pushed shut.

The letter took longer.

He composed it in his best administrative hand—a request for leave to investigate diplomatic leads surfaced by the recent Val'dren movements, addressed to no one in particular. Vague enough to explain his absence. Specific enough to sound genuine. He signed it, blotted it, and left it centered on the desk beneath the brass paperweight.

His trail pack lay open on the bed. He laid the oilskin wallet in first, then the map and compass in the outer pocket. Flint and steel nested in the wool blanket's folds. The waterskins went to the outside strap where he could reach them mounted. One of Brendan's packs, wrapped in leather, filled the remaining space. He cinched the straps, tested the weight across his shoulders, and adjusted the blanket so the load centered at the bottom.

Tachet went to his boot.

He surveyed the room one final time. An officer's quarters, tidied before an absence. The letter on the desk invited exactly the right questions. The papers in his locked drawer answered exactly the wrong ones.

He shouldered the pack, lifted the second bundle of provisions under his arm, and left.

The stables were quiet. Horses dozed in their stalls, weight shifting in slow rhythm. A barn cat threaded between posts. The sweet dust of hay wasn't yet stirred by boots or brooms. A single groom sat on an upturned bucket near the entrance, mending a bridle by lamplight.

Merauve passed him without speaking and went to the tack room. He selected a saddle from the common rack—one of the heavier trail saddles—and gathered a bridle, a breast collar, and two sets of saddlebags. He carried them down the aisle in one trip—the leather and iron heavy across his arms.

Copper heard him coming. The gelding's head appeared over the stall door, ears pricked forward, nostrils working. When Merauve let himself in, the bay swung his muzzle toward the Inquisitor's belt and pockets.

Merauve set the saddle across the partition and began brushing the gelding's back with quick, sure strokes. Copper's coat was thickening against the autumn cold, and the brush raised fine dust.

The saddle went on next. Merauve settled it, adjusted the gullet, tightened the girth in three stages the way Corbin had shown him on the ride to the Kervani camp—snug, wait, snug again, wait, final cinch. The breast collar buckled at the chest. He loaded the saddlebags: provisions distributed evenly, weight balanced, nothing shifting. The second bundle he bagged and lashed behind the cantle with a diamond hitch.

Copper stood through it all, turning once to lip at the saddlebag buckles until Merauve pushed his nose away.

He bridled the horse, gathered the reins, and led him into the aisle.

The groom looked up from his mending. His eyes moved from Merauve's face to the loaded horse to the pack on Merauve's back.

"Checking out number seventeen."

The groom set aside his work and reached for the stablemaster's log. He found the entry—Merauve watched him scan the page, find the forged requisition, compare the stall number—and initialed it out. His pen scratched once in the margin column.

"Should have him back in a couple of days."

The groom nodded and returned to his bridle.

Merauve led Copper through the stable doors into the grey half-light before dawn. The fortress slept around them—a guard's silhouette on the eastern wall, a thread of smoke from the kitchens where Brendan's ovens were already firing for the morning's bread. He mounted, settled his weight, and turned Copper toward the south gate.

The sentry waved him through without challenge.

The road opened ahead of him, pale and empty in the early dark. Behind him, the fortress diminished with each stride—stone becoming shadow, shadow becoming distance, distance becoming memory.

He had two days to prepare, and he meant to use them.

The southern road woke early.

Tradesmen's carts already busied the first mile beyond the gate—timber haulers bound for the mills, a farrier's wagon trailing the smell of coal and hot iron, couriers overtaking everything on lean horses. Merauve kept Copper to an easy walk, nodding at those who acknowledged the uniform, letting himself be seen. South. Official business. Nothing remarkable.

A quarter mile past the crossroads, where the road bent toward the river, he left it.

The turn was unhurried. A horse picking its way down a bank toward water—nothing a passing eye would question. But once the road noise faded behind the screen of willows along the drainage, Merauve swung west and held the line. He followed the creek bed until it bent south, then crossed it and struck across open country, keeping the willows between himself and the road until distance rendered him invisible.

The morning opened around him.

The weather had turned generous—one of those late autumn days that arrives like an apology for what's coming. The sky was clear and bright, making distant ridgelines look close enough to touch, and the sun, still low, warmed his shoulders through his riding leathers. Frost lingered in the shadows but melted wherever the light fell, and the grass released a sweetness as it thawed—rare green beneath the gold, alive despite the season's instructions.

Copper moved well beneath him, ears forward, pleased to be covering ground. The gelding's stride lengthened on the open terrain, finding a rhythm that ate distance without demanding effort. Merauve let the reins fall to his neck and rode with his weight.

It had been over a ten since he'd left the fortress walls to meet the Kervani. He'd forgotten how the body settled on horseback, the way tension bled from the spine with each stride. The land beyond the fortress' perimeter had nothing to catalog, no vulnerabilities to file, no weakness to exploit. Just ground unfolding in front of him.

He caught himself watching a raptor, the fortress' namesake if he wasn't mistaken, hunt the stubble fields—hovering on the wind, tail fanned, still against the moving sky. A hundred feet of empty air between it and the vole it was studying.

Merauve circled north.

The country roughened as it rose. Cultivated fields gave way to scrub pasture, then to the rocky uplands where the Thornwall's foothills began to climb. Merauve consulted his map against visible landmarks: a dead oak on a ridge, lightning-stripped to grey bone years past; a dry stone wall running east to west with no farm attached; the fork where two sheep tracks diverged toward different valleys.

By mid-morning the fortress was well behind him and the road traffic with it. He'd seen no one for the better part of an hour—only a shepherd's distant silhouette, too far off to identify a rider's face.

He dismounted where a stream crossed the sheep track and let Copper drink. The gelding dropped his head and pulled long draughts while Merauve loosened the girth a notch and stretched his legs.

The first bundle of Brendan's provisions he opened standing beside the stream. He untied the butcher's twine and peeled back the canvas.

Everything nested tight: strips of dried venison dark as old leather, hard cheese sealed in wax, ship's biscuit wrapped in parchment and stacked like tiles. Honey in a stoppered flask. Dried apricots and figs pressed into dense cakes. Salt tablets in a waxed-paper envelope. And at the bundle's core, three small tins of rendered tallow.

Merauve broke off a piece of the cheese and cut a strip of venison with Tachet's edge. He ate standing, watching Copper drink. The cheese had a sharp bite that cut through the dried meat. The venison was dense and clean-tasting, salted well enough to keep without overpowering the meat.

He retied the bundle and remounted.

The cache site he chose lay another hour north, where the terrain broke into a tumble of granite boulders at the mouth of a narrow valley—the beginning of the route toward Raven's Gap. A traveler heading for the Thornwall would pass through here, but the landscape gave no reason to stop.

The boulders offered what he needed. Where three large stones leaned together, their bases had eroded to leave a gap barely wide enough for a man's arm—deep, dry, sheltered from rain by the overhang above. Merauve crouched and reached in. His fingers found dry sand and old leaves. No animal sign. No droppings. The gap was too narrow for anything larger than a fox, and too shallow for denning.

He wrapped the first provision bundle in the oilcloth from his pack, then wedged it deep into the crevice, packing the surrounding space with stones until the bundle was invisible from the opening. Over this he arranged loose rock and dead bracken—not a concealment that would survive determined searching, but enough to defeat casual notice. He dragged a flat stone across the approach to scuff his boot prints, then stood back.

▽

From ten paces, the boulder pile looked natural. From five, it looked untouched. He knelt and checked from ground level—a tracker's angle. Nothing.

On a smooth face of the easternmost boulder, he scratched a small mark with Tachet's point: a single vertical line crossed near the top. Meaningless to anyone who didn't know to look. He noted the landmark bearings—the grey oak on the ridge behind him, the stone wall's terminus below, the angle of the valley mouth—and committed a rough sketch to his journal. In scenarios where Elenden was secreted out, he would need to find this stash alone.

The light was already tilting west when he finished. He'd spent longer than intended. The planning had absorbed him the way Elenden's testimony sometimes did—the hours collapsing into themselves, time gone without feeling spent.

He made camp in the lee of the same boulder field, spreading his bedroll where the rock still held the day's warmth. Copper he staked on a long line where a patch of grass survived between the stones, and the gelding set to grazing contentedly.

The sky deepened overhead. No clouds. The stars awakened in the east while light still held in the west—that brief hour when both shared the sky, the constellations emerging like writing on a page held to the light.

Merauve lay on his back, hands behind his head, and watched them come.

The True Star sat where it always sat, low on the northern horizon. He found it without searching—everyone could, these days. Even those who refused to call it by name. It burned with a particularly steady light that distinguished it from the flickering of its neighbors, as if it drew from a source the others lacked.

He thought of those tracing constellations by firelight, like Patricia's people uprooting their lives to follow the sky. Lying here beneath it—the whole vault turning while that single point held still—he could see how a man might begin to believe it meant something.

He thought of Cassius. Of the Lightbringer's return and inevitable demands. Of how the various ploys might answer them—most designed to show Cassius exactly what he wanted to see: a body. Meanwhile, his prize would be beyond reach. The thought of tricking Cassius warmed him more than the blanket.

He had his reasons for saving Elenden. Good reasons—strategic, defensible, each one bearing weight on its own merits. The boy was an intelligence asset of extraordinary value. His testimony had already yielded the Fire Monastery's location; what else might it yield, given time? A living source outperformed a dead one by any measure. And a man who held what Cassius wanted held power. It was that simple.

He thought of Elenden in his tower room, watching this same sky through a window barely wider than his shoulders.

Sleep came without announcement, and he did not dream.

Merauve woke all at once, the bedroll's warmth long since surrendered to the frost. He lay still for a moment, breathing the cold air—then shed the blanket and let the morning steal what warmth remained. Not unlike the plunge, though considerably less voluntary.

He rolled out, stamped circulation into his feet, and began breaking camp.

Copper stood with his head low, breath steaming, one hind hoof cocked. Frost whitened his mane. Merauve fed him a piece of hard biscuit and saddled up.

He struck west.

The country changed within the hour. The foothills' green and granite gave way to something older—a landscape losing its grip on water. Grass thinned, broke into patches, surrendered to dust and scrub. The soil paled to the color of rust and old bones.

The Cindrel Vale.

He had studied it on maps—the wedge of dry country that pressed against the Thornwall's western shoulder, running south until it merged with the true deserts beyond the Empire's practical reach. Patrol routes

▷

avoided it. Traders avoided it. Even the Val'dren, who made all lands their home, skirted its edges. A man entering without water would die in it.

But a man fleeing west under pursuit might enter it.

He rode until the landmarks became their own kind: a bleached tree standing alone, a wash of pale gravel, a ridge of rust-colored stone. He noted each one, measuring distances by Copper's stride count, building a route he could describe to someone who had never seen this ground. The second cache he placed beneath a deep stone overhang high above the dry wash—no attempt at concealment. Either it would be needed within the ten, or the desert could have it.

A last resort. He did not pretend otherwise.

Copper's ears swiveled constantly—reading the silence, finding it disagreeable. Twice he shied at nothing Merauve could see, and once he stopped dead until a shape in the scrub resolved itself into a juniper stump.

"Fair enough." Merauve turned him east.

The sun stood at its peak. If he pushed, he could circle back to the south road before the light failed and make Fortress Kestrel by sunset.

He gave Copper a quarter hour's rest where the scrub turned back to grass, loosened the girth, let him graze. Then he tightened it and asked for speed.

The gelding answered. Whatever complaints he harbored about the Cindrel's silence vanished when pointed toward home. His stride opened into a canter that covered ground like a hand sweeping a table—steady, purposeful, relentless. Merauve posted in rhythm, weight forward, letting the horse choose his footing.

The foothills rose and fell beneath them. The sheep tracks reappeared, then the stone wall, then the drainage where he'd left the road. He followed the creek bed south until the willows parted and the road emerged—empty now, the day's traffic long since delivered to its destinations.

He turned Copper onto the packed earth and held the canter north.

The fortress' profile appeared above the road's final rise as the sun touched the western ridgeline. The stone tower caught the last amber light—warm for a moment, almost welcoming, as shadow climbed its base.

Something was wrong.

Chapter 72

Val'dren

The south gate stood open, but the evening torches burned in their brackets earlier than protocol warranted. On the eastern wall, figures moved where the watch usually stood single—doubled now, a third climbing the stairs to join them. A runner crossed the courtyard at speed and disappeared into the keep.

Merauve eased Copper to a trot. His gaze swept the walls. More movement on the north side—soldiers called from their evening meal, still pulling on coats.

He walked Copper through the south gate. The sentries noted his approach but did not challenge—an Inquisitor returning at dusk on a lathered horse warranted attention, not questions. The fortress closed around him: stone and shadow and the smell of supper fires cut with something sharper. Tension.

He was calculating the route to the stables—unsaddle, cool Copper, check his quarters, check his traps—when Thorne's voice reached him from the torchlit colonnade.

"Inquisitor Merauve." The Major's stride was brisk, his jaw set. "Your timing defies coincidence."

"Major." Merauve dismounted, keeping the reins in hand. Copper's neck was dark with sweat, his breathing deep and steady. "I see we have visitors."

"Six horsemen at the north gate. Arrived less than an hour ago under a parley banner." Thorne fell into step beside him, dropping his voice. "Val'dren. Armed, but making no hostile moves. They brought their own translator and asked to speak with—" He paused, as though the phrasing still irritated him. " 'The one who keeps faith with the traveling folk.' "

Merauve detached his travel satchel from the saddle and slung it across his shoulder. The wallet inside pressed against his ribs.

"Your assessment?"

The Major grunted. "I'll not have six armed riders inside this fortress, surveying its defenses." Thorne's voice dropped further. "The scouts report Val'dren companies have been moving north through the western approaches for the better part of a ten. Conservative estimates put their numbers at three hundred. Possibly more." He let that settle. "If this goes badly, Inquisitor, we are outnumbered."

"Then we should ensure it goes well." Merauve stroked Copper's neck. "We see what they want—two of them, no weapons. We confirm their rationale for moving north. We give them no cause for hostilities."

"I intend to be present."

"I would expect nothing less. This is your fortress, Major."

Thorne studied each of Merauve's eyes in turn. "Any decisions touching base security, logistics, or the disposition of my men remain my authority. Clear?"

"Perfectly."

"Good." Thorne glanced toward the keep, already organizing. "Then I'll present the terms and give you fifteen minutes. I assume you'll want to clean up—"

"I'll present them."

Thorne's eyebrows rose.

"The Val'dren are horse people," Merauve said. "They'll measure a man by how he treats his animal. Let me go to them as I am."

A groom appeared at Merauve's elbow, reaching for the reins. Merauve shook his head.

Thorne considered it. His eyes moved from Merauve to Copper—the lathered horse, the satchel over the shoulder, the riding leathers still dark with the day's work. Then he nodded once.

"Let's go."

They crossed the courtyard together, Merauve leading Copper by the reins. The gelding's hooves rang on cobblestone—heavy with the day's miles. Merauve glanced toward his quarters as they passed. Then the tower that rose above the keep's roofline, its narrow window catching the last of the light.

He did not look up.

The north gate was barred but not bolted—a distinction that spoke to Thorne's judgment. Beyond it, visible through the iron lattice, six riders waited in the gathering dusk.

Their horses stood beautifully. Even at a distance, Merauve could see their deep chests, the clean legs, the way each animal stood collected and calm. The riders sat at ease, voices low, unhurried.

The gate guards drew back the bar at Thorne's signal. The iron lattice swung inward.

Merauve stepped through with Copper at his shoulder. He raised both hands, palms open. The reins hung loose in the crook of his arm.

"Greetings in the name of His Imperial Majesty. I understand one of you speaks Thamarian."

A young woman near the group's center edged her horse forward. She guided the animal with her legs alone, both hands raised to mirror his gesture—empty, open. She was between fifteen and twenty, sharp-featured, with long dark hair pulled into a tail that fell straight and heavy past her shoulders. Her eyes swept Merauve, then Thorne, then dropped to Copper.

She studied the horse longer than she studied either man.

"You're the fourth stone-foot I've told." Her Thamarian was clipped but fluent, each word bitten off. "Yes, I speak your sloppy language. Are you going to invite us in, or not?"

"Nora, I presume."

The name struck like a crop across a flank. Her chin jerked back. For a beat she only stared. Then her eyes narrowed.

"Once." Her voice was quiet. "No more. I am named Niska."

"Here are the terms," Merauve announced. "Yourself and one representative. Unarmed. You'll parley with Major Thorne"—a nod toward the man beside him—"and myself inside the fortress. We guarantee safe passage in and out."

Niska held his gaze a beat longer, then she turned in her saddle and spoke to the group, directing her words to a broad-shouldered man at the formation's center. Even in the failing light, Merauve recognized him from Elenden's description—the dark skin, the heavy brows, hair braided with beads and feathers, the beard gone grey at its edges. The elder Pakonaskow, Papa, sat his horse—settled, certain, part of the thing itself.

Niska spoke. The elder listened. Then his head tipped back and he laughed—a sound that carried across the open ground and startled Copper into flicking his ears. White teeth flashed against his dark beard.

He said something brief. Niska turned back.

"He says you flatter us with your fears." A pause. "We accept—if you can receive us now. We wish to be away tonight."

"Give me fifteen minutes to see to my horse."

Niska's gaze dropped again to Copper. She gave no smile, but her chin inclined a fraction.

"Of course."

Merauve did not thank her.

"Fifteen, then."

He turned with Copper and walked back through the gate. Thorne fell in beside him, matching his pace to the horse's.

"You know her?"

"A guess. My prisoner spoke of a Val'dren child bearing her description." Merauve kept his voice low. "Translated for her father—the large man in the center." He ran his hand along Copper's shoulder as they walked, feeling the heat still trapped beneath the coat. "She was seven at the time."

Thorne absorbed this without comment. They crossed the courtyard toward the stables, Merauve's hand already working the girth buckle loose.

"So this is about your prisoner?"

"I don't know."

"The Kervani? The stars they follow?"

"I don't know that either."

"You understand the stakes." Thorne said it flat.

"Three hundred riders could overwhelm this garrison before a relief column reached the first hill." Merauve lifted the saddle clear and set it on the rail. The pad beneath was dark with sweat. He folded it over the bar to dry, then found a cloth and began rubbing Copper down in long strokes, working from neck to barrel. "Yes, Major. I understand."

Copper leaned into the pressure, his head dropping. Steam rose from his coat into the cold air.

Thorne watched the work. Whatever he thought of an Inquisitor tending his own horse while a diplomatic crisis waited, he kept his counsel.

"I'll yield the discussion to you, Inquisitor," Thorne said at last. "But I reserve the right to intervene on any matter touching the safety of this garrison. Understood?"

"Perfectly." Merauve moved to Copper's offside, working the same long strokes. The horse shifted his weight and sighed. "Have a translator standing by," Merauve said. "Not at the table. Among the door guards." He glanced at Thorne. "The Val'dren will bring Niska, but I want someone who speaks Valdris close enough to confirm what she's telling us—and subtle enough that she won't know they're listening."

Thorne's expression sharpened. "Signals?"

"Simple. If the translation holds true, nothing. If she departs from what's being said—" Merauve tapped his collar twice. "Your man adjusts his belt, shifts his weight. Something a guard might do. We'll know."

Thorne nodded slowly. "I'll send for my best Valdris speaker." He straightened, already turning. "The Val'dren will be escorted in—meet you at the reception chamber."

The sound of Thorne's boots faded before Merauve had finished with Copper's offside.

Merauve finished the rubdown. He found a measure of oats in the stable's feed bin and poured it into Copper's bucket, holding it steady while the gelding buried his nose and ate. The sound of grinding filled the stall. Merauve stood with one hand on the horse's neck, feeling the pulse slow beneath his palm.

He set the bucket down and latched the stall gate behind him. The tower windows were lit above the keep's roofline.

He looked away and walked toward the reception chamber.

The formal reception chamber carried the pervasive smell of lamp oil and a faint odor of seal wax from whatever business had last transpired. The polished table caught torchlight along its grain. Glass windows overlooked the courtyard on the eastern wall—dark now, reflecting the room back at itself.

Thorne had kept the staging spare: four chairs, a water pitcher, two guards flanking the door. The room could impress when the Empire needed impressing. A theater of sorts. Tonight it needed to work.

Niska entered first. Her eyes swept the chamber, cataloging, dismissing. She took the chair across from Merauve without waiting to be offered it.

Her father followed. Up close, the man's presence filled more space than his frame warranted. His boots met the stone floor heel-first, each stride wide-set and deliberate. His dark eyes found Merauve, held there, then moved to Thorne. He lowered himself into the chair beside Niska the way he'd sat his horse outside, then rested his hands flat on his thighs.

They had surrendered the weapons without argument at the gate.

"Water?" Merauve gestured toward the pitcher.

Niska translated. The elder shook his head once.

Thorne crossed to the table's far end and claimed the remaining chair, arms folded across his chest. The door guards held their posts. Merauve noted the one on the left—auburn braid tucked beneath a standard-issue uniform collar, grey eyes forward, hands clasped at the small of her back. Alena. The translator.

"Where is the one you call Elenden?"

Niska's Thamarian sounded loud in the quiet room. No preamble. No diplomatic overture. She hadn't even translated the question for her father—this one was hers.

"The Kervani say you hold him captive here."

Merauve folded his hands on the table. "The man you speak of is indeed a prisoner of this fortress. He faces charges under Imperial law, and an investigation is ongoing. If the inquiry clears him, he goes free."

He left the alternative unspoken.

"What charges?"

Still Niska alone. The elder's gaze had drifted to the eastern windows, studying the dark glass as though the reflection held something more interesting than the conversation.

"I'm afraid the specifics of an active investigation cannot be shared outside approved channels." Merauve kept his voice even. "I'm sure you appreciate the distinction."

Niska's jaw tightened. She turned to her father and spoke in rapid Valdris—not translating so much as reporting. Her hands moved as she spoke, sharp gestures that punctuated her words. Every shade of feeling crossed her face: frustration, protectiveness, the hot edge of contempt.

The elder listened without expression. When she finished, he asked a single question. Niska answered with a clipped phrase that sounded like disagreement.

The elder spoke again. A single statement, pitched low—the resonance of a man accustomed to being heard. Niska's face changed—disbelief first, then something harder. She fired back a volley of Valdris, her voice climbing. The elder did not respond. His eyes returned to the window.

Merauve's eyes found Alena at the door. Her chin dipped a fraction—barely perceptible, there and gone. Her focus remained on the Val'dren pair, her posture unchanged.

The argument burned itself out in Niska's silence. She stared at her father a moment longer, then turned back to Merauve. Her cheeks were flushed, her mouth a thin line.

"My father—Pakonaskow, Breaks-the-Clouds—offers himself as blood-stead."

Beside him, Merauve heard Thorne shift his weight in the leather chair.

A substitute, a body exchanged for a body. In the Virtue Duels it meant one man standing in another's place for trial by combat. Outside them, it carried the same weight: a hostage freely given, bound by honor rather than chains. Both meanings converged on the same principle. A life for a life.

Merauve kept his hands still on the table. "A significant offer. Why would he make it?"

Niska's eyes rolled toward the ceiling—a gesture so unguarded it nearly made him smile. "Because men are fools. They can only repay." She gestured at her father without looking at him. "Pakonaskow owes Two-Horse a debt. He rescued me." She turned to her father as she said it. The elder's expression did not change. "My father has carried that debt for years, and apparently this stone cage is where he's decided to settle it."

Two-Horse. Breaks-the-Clouds. Val'dren names. Merauve filed a question about what *Niska* translated to.

"That answers one question," he said. "But why would we accept? You're asking me to release a prisoner under active Imperial investigation in exchange for a man who has committed no crime. Where is the equivalence?"

Niska's chin came up. She answered without translating. "He is Chief-Elder of the Val'dren. A willing blood-stead is recognized by every tribe as a covenant of trust. For as long as you hold him—alive and in good condition—you hold brotherhood with every rider who answers to him." She paused. Her voice dropped, stripped of its usual bite. "And you spare the bloodshed when we come to free Two-Horse ourselves."

The threat sat in the open between them, unadorned.

Thorne cleared his throat.

"May we take a moment to counsel?" Merauve rose without waiting for an answer, gesturing Thorne toward the far wall, near Alena.

The three of them stood close, voices pitched low.

"The translation?" Merauve asked.

"Clean." Alena's eyes remained on the Val'dren pair. "She didn't soften a word. Though she fought him hard on the offer—told him he was throwing his life into a pit for a stone-foot. Told him he owed no debt as she was still *kail* when Two-Horse rescued her."

Merauve turned to Thorne.

The Major spoke low, his jaw working. "Do I understand correctly? They're offering this fortress a guarantee against attack. We give them your prisoner, and in return we hold their leader as surety?"

"That's the shape of it."

"Then I'd be a fool not to consider it." Thorne's eyes cut toward the table. "Three hundred riders, Inquisitor."

"Which only deepens the complexity of our situation." Merauve kept his voice barely above breath. "Despite her claim, we cannot verify that Niska speaks for all the Val'dren. And a blood-stead in our keeping could serve as pretext as easily as prevention—a leader held captive is also a leader who needs rescuing."

"If they wanted him by force, they could try for him within the week."

"True."

Thorne waited. Merauve looked at the table where Niska sat rigid and Pakonaskow sat still, and something turned in his mind.

An option was opening that he had not prepared. Sirius would have received his communication by now. Any reply—by seal or by saddle—was likely still days away. Cassius would return sooner. But a prisoner transferred under diplomatic protocol—exchanged for a blood-stead, escorted by the Val'dren under the formal assurances of Imperial law—was a prisoner whose release bore a paper trail. Defensible. Documented. The act of a cautious officer managing a volatile border situation, not spiriting away a prisoner in the night. If Sirius sanctioned it, Cassius could not prevent it.

He had prepared other ways. But this was cleaner. If it had a chance.

"I have a counterproposal," Merauve said. "For you."

He spoke for less than a minute. Thorne listened, eyes narrowing. "Agreed."

They returned to the table.

Merauve settled into his chair and met Niska's gaze. "Pakonaskow's offer is generous, and we recognize the weight it carries. But I cannot release a prisoner under active investigation on my own authority. To do so would violate the law I'm sworn to uphold, and it would not serve your father well to have rescued his friend only to see him recaptured as a fugitive."

Niska's nostrils flared. "Then you've chosen war. Why did you bother with counsel if you cannot decide for him?"

Merauve opened his hand, palm up. "What I propose is this. One or both of you remain as our guests. See for yourselves that the prisoner is alive and well. Allow me two days to send word to my superiors regarding your offer."

Niska translated. Her voice was flat, stripped of advocacy—she clearly expected refusal.

Pakonaskow listened. His shadowed eyes still on the window.

Then he met her eyes, raised one hand, and pointed at Niska.

The reaction was immediate. Niska's fist struck the table—not hard enough to move the pitcher, but hard enough to make the water shiver in its vessel. She turned on her father with a torrent of Valdris, her voice low and fierce, words tumbling over one another. Papa said nothing. He sat with his hands on his thighs and watched his daughter spend her fury the way a man watches a summer storm from beneath good shelter.

Merauve risked a glance at the door. Alena's eyebrows had risen a fraction. Her lips pressed together—suppressing something.

Niska's voice broke off. She sat breathing hard, staring at her father as if he had betrayed her. Papa held her gaze. Still said nothing.

She turned to Merauve.

"He accepts your terms." Each word arrived bitten off, cold as iron. "I do not. Open this stone cage and let me back to my people."

She was on her feet before anyone moved. Alena stepped aside as Niska reached the door—the scout's hand finding the latch, pulling it wide without being asked. Merauve rose and hurried to follow her into the corridor.

"We intend no ill will," he said to her back. "This was your parley, his offer, not ours. We are simply asking for the time to honor it properly."

Niska stopped. She turned, and her eyes held something older than anger.

"You don't understand what he's done." Her eyes held unshed tears. "The Val'dren will not touch this fortress while Pakonaskow is your guest. Not a rider, not a scout, not an arrow. He is our Papa. All of us." She stepped closer. "He may make himself your guest. But if he becomes your captive—if you harm him—if you so much as let him grow sick under your care without giving us Two-Horse in return for his blood-stead—"

She did not finish.

Merauve held her gaze. "He will be treated as an honored guest. I ask only two days. You have my word."

"Your word." Niska shook her head as she walked toward the gate.

The north gate's bar drew back at Merauve's wave. The iron lattice swung open, and Niska passed through without looking back. A young soldier hurried out from the guardhouse behind her, a canvas sling over his shoulder—the surrendered weapons bundled like firewood. The remaining riders had dismounted, their horses standing loose-reined in the darkness. At Niska's appearance they straightened—questions in their postures, hands near weapons. The soldier reached them as Niska did, and the weapons were passed back.

She spoke to them in Valdris. Quick, clipped, final. One of the riders looked past her toward the gate, searching. When Papa did not appear, the man's hand closed on his sword hilt.

Niska caught his wrist. The hand released. The rider turned and gathered his horse's reins.

They mounted. Niska swung up last. Before she turned her horse north, she leaned from the saddle and caught the reins of her father's mare—a handsome dun who tossed her head. Niska held firm, wrapping the leather once around her pommel.

She looked back once at the fortress, its stone walls lit amber by the torches.

The Val'dren party moved north into the gathering dark. Papa's mare trailing at the column's end, riderless.

"Close the gate." Thorne spoke from behind him—the Major had followed them out, though Merauve hadn't marked when.

The bar dropped home. Iron rested against iron.

Merauve stood in the torchlight, watching the darkness where the riders had vanished. Beside him, Thorne waited.

"Two days," Merauve said. "That's what I promised her."

"Two days," Thorne confirmed. "And then?"

"Then we weigh our options."

Thorne grunted.

"I've sent inquiries up the chain about the traveling peoples. Val'dren movements. Requested guidance, reinforcement, anything." He folded his arms. "Every response I've received has been a polite variation of 'you're on your own.' "

Merauve turned from the gate and looked toward the keep. The tower's lit window caught the edge of his vision.

This time, he looked up.

"Then I'd suggest we guard that diplomat with our lives, Major." He met Thorne's gaze.

Thorne studied him. Then nodded once.

"I'll post a detail on his quarters tonight."

Their boots rang together across the courtyard, heading in different directions.

Back in his quarters, his traps were untouched. The letter beneath the paperweight sat precisely where he'd left it—the Val'dren parley had closed that loop neatly. Pity no one had read it.

He slept deeply and without complication—a blessedly unbroken night back in his own quarters. He woke to grey light. Three hundred riders in the valley to the north. Their chief behind these walls. And for what seemed like the first time, leverage he hadn't needed to forge.

He moved through abbreviated forms, welcomed the cold plunge, dressed in the deep purple vest with silver threading. From the shelf inside his desk he took the leather satchel—checked its contents by touch through the flap: wallet, ring, rice paper—and slung the strap across his shoulder. The face in the window glass looked rested. He could work with that.

Thorne had quartered Pakonaskow in the diplomatic suite on the keep's second level—a room that offered comfort without concealment, its windows overlooking the courtyard where activity would remind the elder he was surrounded, and where his presence could remind the garrison he was honored. Two guards flanked the door: veterans, selected for temperament as much as competence. Merauve approved of the choices.

The visit was brief. With Thorne's permission, Merauve recruited Alena as translator and the three of them—Merauve, Alena, and Pakonaskow—climbed the tower stairs in silence. The elder moved well for a man his age, though his wide-set stride was slow on the narrow steps. He studied the stonework as they ascended.

At the top, Merauve slid back the viewport.

Elenden sat at his table by the window, morning light falling across the remains of breakfast. His color was good. Alive. His eyes lifted toward the viewport's opening, though he could not have seen who stood beyond it.

"As you can see," Merauve said, pitching his voice for Alena to translate, "the prisoner is well cared for while under investigation. He receives regular meals, medical attention as needed, and quarters with natural light."

Alena rendered this into Valdris. Pakonaskow listened. His eyes barely moved across the narrow frame of the viewport. His expression gave nothing.

His chin dipped. Then he turned and gestured toward the stairs.

They descended in the same silence they had climbed. At the diplomatic suite's door, Pakonaskow entered without farewell. The guards resumed their posts. Alena glanced at Merauve, awaiting dismissal.

"Thank you, Alena. We may need you again before the day is out."

"Sir."

Merauve stood in the corridor a moment longer. The visit had taken less than a quarter hour. The elder had not spoken a single word since entering the keep—not to Merauve, not through Alena, not even to himself, according to the guards. He had looked. He had seen. And the looking, Merauve suspected, had been courtesy rather than condition—Pakonaskow had settled this matter the moment he pointed at Niska and stayed. Men who were 'Papa' to hundreds did not make such decisions lightly. Nor unmake them.

Merauve climbed the tower stairs again. The guards drew back the bolt at his approach.

Elenden was finishing the last of his breakfast—bread torn into pieces, a cup of something still steaming. He looked up as the door swung inward, and the faintest smile crossed his features.

Merauve crossed to his chair. Withdrew his tobacco pouch. Selected a leaf.

"You'll never guess who I met."

Chapter 73

Holes

"You'll never guess who I met."

Elenden set down the last of his bread and rested his hands on the table.

"I could not guess. No."

That brief distance crossed his features—the listening expression Merauve had cataloged a dozen times but never decoded. It passed in a breath. When his eyes cleared, he shook his head slightly.

"Someone has come a very long way," Elenden said quietly. "A father stands where his daughter stood. Someone who carries a debt from pride they need not carry."

Merauve's tobacco leaf stilled between his fingers.

"It is not you. The Spirit has shown me this much." Elenden's gaze dropped to his own scarred hands on the table. "But the rest is hidden from me. It is your truth to share or to keep." His eyes lifted. "I do not know why."

Merauve finished rolling the leaf. He rose, crossed to the hearth, and knelt to light a sliver of kindling from a glowing ember. He carried the flame to the rolled leaf and drew until it caught and held. He returned to his chair trailing smoke.

"A woman by the name of Niska." He watched the smoke rise. "Spoke for a delegation of six riders to our north gate last night."

Elenden's stillness broke. His eyes widened, and for a moment the gravity gave way to something much lighter.

"*Niska.*" He smiled like opening a gift. "It means goose. She would hate that I told you. But the name fits. It's a good name." The laugh that followed was bright, unguarded—and then it faltered. His eyes found Merauve's. "But then. A father where his daughter stood." The color shifted in his face. "Pakonaskow?"

"The elder is here." Merauve let the words land. "Pakonaskow is quartered on the keep's second level. Somewhere beneath us."

"Papa," Elenden said softly, "what have you done?"

"He arrived with his daughter last night and offered himself as your blood-stead."

Elenden was quiet for a long time. His fingers traced something against the table.

"His offer stands, pending approval from my superiors." Merauve drew on his tobacco. "Niska was not pleased. She called her father a fool—among other things my translator was too discreet to render. She said you rescued her."

Elenden closed his eyes. His lips moved. When he opened them again, the warmth had not gone, but something deeper ran beneath it.

"We are not to that part of the story yet, Inquisitor."

Before Merauve could respond:

"There is something you must know first." His voice was always earnest, but now it sounded almost urgent. "Our time in this tower room draws to its close—like a river changing pitch when it nears a fall. You feel it. I feel it. The thread we have been following since the morning you first sat in that chair nears its end."

Merauve said nothing. His tobacco burned between his fingers.

"You have been patient with beginnings, Inquisitor. You have followed the thread through knots and tangles and stretches where it seemed to lead nowhere." He met Merauve's eyes. "It was allotted me three weeks and three days in this room. I have spent them as faithfully as I know how. But the skein runs thin, and what remains must be told before it is cut."

Morning light fell through the narrow window in bright stripes across the floor between them. Below, courtyard sounds rose faintly: boots on cobblestone, a shouted order, the ring of iron on iron.

"My road does not end in this room, Inquisitor." Elenden held his gaze. "Nor does your own."

▷

Merauve studied him. *Three weeks and three days.* He did not ask how he was so certain. He knew how Elenden would respond.

But a different answer had begun to make far more sense.

What if the whole arc of this testimony—the trust, the slow unveiling, the gratitude that tasted so much like honesty—had been shaped from the start? A patient hand guiding the interrogator toward the very conclusions his prisoner needed him to reach. Was the Val'dren migration a ruse? A scheduled intervention by a blood-stead? If he knew, down to the day...

Merauve's fingers tightened on the arm of his chair.

You are being played.

The certainty of it blazed through him—white, absolute, sharp as Tachet's edge. He knew this feeling. He had built his career on it: the moment an interrogation's true architecture revealed itself, when the subject's mask slipped and the game beneath became visible. His gaze cut to the satchel at his feet—the cache locations sketched in his own hand—and the impulse seized him: *burn it. All of it.* He had missed it; the man across the table had been three moves ahead—

Elenden's hand moved.

Not toward Merauve. A small motion—his scarred fingers closing to a fist against the table as though holding something down. His gaze sharpened, but not at Merauve. Past him. Through him.

"I came here to tell you the truth." Elenden's voice was quiet and unhurried. "All of it."

Those same words. No micro-correction in the jaw. No asymmetry in the brow. The hands had closed, yes, but toward the table, not away from the body—conviction or containment, not concealment. The pupils held steady. His breathing hadn't changed.

Not once had the young man produced the constellation of signs that betray a lie. Either Elenden deArthis possessed a singular gift for deception that surpassed anything Merauve had encountered—or the simplest explanation held.

Merauve's suspicion did not vanish. But it loosened like a hand unclenching, finger by finger. Merauve breathed. The tightness in his chest eased by degrees he could not account for.

Truth or lies. He would be the judge of that. Pakonaskow sat below—insurance. Tachet rode in his boot. The satchel held options.

"Well then, by all means." Merauve raised the tobacco to his lips, drew once, and exhaled toward the ceiling. He settled deeper into the leather. "Continue."

One of the mining foremen—a barrel-chested man named Hollis—presented his proposal to Master Roman the evening before one of our kindred dinners. I wasn't present, but Jonathan was, and he recounted the exchange with a dry relish.

Hollis had mapped the library's adjacent voids using survey techniques borrowed from the deeper shafts. His analysis was thorough: structural drawings, load calculations, proposed approach angles that would bypass the inscribed wall and enter whatever chamber lay beyond from the corridor side. He'd even sourced the timbers for shoring.

Master Roman listened to the full presentation. Then said no.

The wall and whatever lay behind it would remain undisturbed until the archives were given a chance to yield an answer. Brother Jacob had already taken a charcoal rubbing of the stone—pressing thin parchment against the arch and working the charcoal flat across its surface until the faintest indentations emerged as pale ghosts against the dark. The *Azurath* inscription was visible only to Adam and me, its carved channels too shallow for anyone else to confirm by touch alone, but the rubbing had caught something. Faint lines. Suggestions of curves. Not proof—but enough to enter into the monastery's records, and enough to begin a search. Ember would not defile sacred stones to satisfy curiosity just yet.

Hollis, to his credit, accepted the ruling without argument. But I caught him studying the library's eastern wall on three separate occasions that week, his surveyor's eye tracing the corners just so.

The archive search grew. Brother Jacob had recruited two of the older scholars to assist, their progress marked by the growing stack of rejected volumes on the reading table. Most references to ancient inscriptions led to dead ends—they'd since moved on to references about the library. Jonathan helped where he could, but the deeper catalogs were written in a formal Thamarian so dense with ecclesiastical phrasing that even he had to read each line twice.

I checked in when I could, but the kindred's final project had consumed my imagination.

Brother Gentian had given us three weeks. We were halfway through the second, and the kindred had produced, by my count, two complete proposals, seven partial frameworks, and one evening that ended with Tam and Nort shouting across the slate so loudly that Kane had to stand between them. On those nights, Adam's rowan pipe lay cold in its case and Sebastian lost his chess partner—though neither complained. The arguments were better entertainment.

The large slate—a slab of smooth grey set on an easel in our meeting alcove—had become our battleground. Every session began with someone wiping the previous night's work and replacing it with their own, which the next speaker would critique, amend, or cheerfully demolish.

Tam's position hadn't shifted since the first governance lecture. "Every citizen votes," he said, chalking his model across the slate's upper half in letters that leaned forward as aggressively as he did. "On everything. No kings, no lords, no councils that claim to speak for people who never asked them to. You want to build a road? The people who'll use it decide. You want to raise an army? The people who'll fight in it vote."

"And when they vote to take their neighbor's land?" Andrew leaned against the wall, arms folded. He was one of the biggest in our hearth—stocky, patient. "What then? Your citizens vote to strip the rights of anyone who disagrees with them. Or anyone they grow jealous of. History's full of it."

"Then you educate them."

"You can't educate a mob, Tam. You can only hope it disperses before it finds a rope." Andrew pushed off the wall and took the chalk. Below Tam's model he drew a simple tree: a trunk dividing into branches, branches into smaller branches. "Families. Households choose a head. Heads choose a village elder. Elders choose a lord. Lords answer to a greater lord, and so on, up to the crown. Each level accountable to the one below and the one above."

"That's the Empire," Jonathan observed from his corner. "You've just described what we already have."

"No. In the Empire, lords inherit by blood. I'm saying they should be chosen—but chosen by those who know them. Not by strangers."

Nort, who rarely spoke without Andrew beside him, surprised us. "There's something to the inheritance, though." He squinted as he thought. "Not blood for its own sake. But a lord who knows his children will inherit—his *children*, not some stranger elected after he dies—that lord thinks in generations. He plants orchards he'll never eat from. He maintains the roads because his grandson will ride them."

"Or he hoards wealth for his heirs and bleeds his people dry," Tam shot back. "Nort, you've just described half the Central Provinces."

Sebastian mediated. Jonathan made notes. Adam watched with something like amusement, his hands occasionally forming a sign that Jonathan would translate—usually a joke that cut to the root of whatever argument had just been made, delivered with impeccable timing.

Kane sat at the edge, saying little, guiding less than usual. I'd noticed this over the past week—a deliberate withdrawal, as though he'd decided the kindred needed to find its own footing rather than follow his.

I listened to all of it. Drew lines in my own notes. Crossed them out. Drew new ones.

But I wasn't thinking about systems. I was thinking about Declan.

What kept forming in my mind—like a pattern emerging from tangled thread—was a system that didn't depend on the quality of the people running it. Tam's democracy assumed virtuous citizens. Andrew's feudalism assumed virtuous lords. Nort's inheritance assumed virtuous families. Every model placed its faith in the character of men, and every model collapsed the moment those men proved faithless.

What if the rules themselves could be made incorruptible? Not the people within them—I wasn't fool enough to believe that—but what if the system *compelled* punishment for every violation, regardless of who committed it? What if no official, no lord, no emperor could look at a Declan and decide it wasn't worth the trouble?

The idea grew from something Fletch told me at Redcloud. When you laid a foundation stone, everything above it must be true to it. If the foundation holds, the wall stands. If the foundation isn't true, everything above it falls—and it doesn't matter how well you laid the upper courses. If you lay the foundation stone level, every crooked course above it *shows*. The foundation doesn't prevent bad work. It exposes it.

I'd been working through the idea for days. Alone, mostly, in the margins of my notes during rhetoric exercises and in the quiet hour before sleep.

I wasn't designing a government. I was designing a noose.

My opening came on the ninth evening.

Tam and Andrew had exhausted each other. Their chalk lines covered the slate in overlapping systems that contradicted more than they resolved. Nort had gone quiet. Jonathan was rereading his notes.

Kane looked at me.

I don't know how he knew. Perhaps he'd noticed the growing stack of pages I carried to each session, or the way I'd stopped arguing other people's positions and started listening with a different kind of attention. Whatever he saw, he nodded.

"El. You've been quiet."

I stood up too quickly. My hands were unsteady. I picked up the chalk and wiped the slate clean.

"I want to propose something different. Rule without rulers." I wrote a single word across the top: *JUSTICE*. "Rule by Justice."

Tam squinted. "Rule by virtue?"

"Justice," I corrected. "We build a government that does nothing else."

The room was quiet, deciding whether to take me seriously.

"Every government we've studied puts its trust in *people*—voters, lords, kings, councils. And every one of them fails when those people prove untrue. What if we built a system that didn't require trustworthy rulers? What if the rules themselves were the authority, and every person in power—from the lowest magistrate to the Emperor himself—was bound by them absolutely?"

"Start with this." I returned to the slate. "Let's define some terms. Every person has at least three things that belong to them alone: their life, their freedom, and what they earn."

"Sounds like common sense," Nort said.

"Not to the Kaldren," Greg said mildly. "Their lords own everything—including the people."

I pointed at Greg. "Exactly. These things *should* be self-evident—but they aren't evident to everyone. That's why you write them down." I drew a vertical line down the slate's center and numbered the left side. "The rules work as a hierarchy—every lower rule yields to every higher one. If two rules conflict, the higher one wins. Always."

I wrote the first:

Justice is the protection of life, freedom, and property. Government exists solely for this end.

"That's the foundation." I let that settle. "One person can't always secure their own rights. When the threat is greater than any individual can face—a bully—" and here my face reddened, though I kept my voice level, "—an invading army, a lord with a hundred swords—justice requires collective action. That's what government is. That's *all* government should be. Nothing more."

Andrew crossed his arms. "Every tyrant claims he's just."

"Give him a moment." Kane's voice was quiet, but everyone obeyed it. "Let him lay it out."

I turned back to the slate for the second rule.

The government shall punish every violation of these rights—whether the violator is a citizen, a foreigner...

"Fine in theory," Andrew said. "But who's the worst violator of rights in history? Not bandits. Not bullies. Governments."

Greg's voice cut across the murmuring—quiet, but with an edge that stilled the alcove. "Let him finish writing at least."

"*...or the government itself.*" I underlined it. Greg flushed slightly—less at the attention than at being right.

"Rule number three:"

The government shall not violate any person's rights, except where a higher rule demands it—and no further than it demands.

I set the chalk down and faced them.

The silence lasted half a breath. Then the room broke open.

Three conversations started at once. Andrew and Greg had turned to each other; Tam was squinting at the slate; Jonathan's stylus was scribbling over his notes. I stood at the board with chalk dust on my fingers and no one looking at me, and for a bad half-minute I felt the whole thing slipping sideways like a cart losing a wheel.

Tam shoved back from the bench and crossed to the slate. The other voices dropped away. He traced the second and third rules with a chalk-stained finger. "The third rule sounds like the second."

"It's not." Nort had also been reading. "The second one says the government *hunts*. It punishes anyone who violates rights—including its own officials. The third says the government is *leashed*. It cannot act against anyone except where a higher rule demands it." He looked at me. "So the constable can restrain a murderer—"

"—because protecting the victim's life outranks the murderer's freedom," I finished. "But a constable can't search your home without cause, because your freedom outranks the government's convenience."

Jonathan spoke up. "You've built a system that has purpose—some agency, even—but does it have any accountability? How is the government going to punish its own violations? Who decides a violation has occurred? The same officials who committed the violation?"

"Citizen juries," Tam blurted, nodding for the first time all evening.

I turned back to the slate and added a fourth:

Any violation of these rules by a government official shall be reviewed by a jury of citizens—

The room broke into chaos once more.

"Randomly selected," Tam said, leaning forward. "Not appointed, not elected, not beholden to anyone in power."

"And they must have paid taxes," Nort added. "Skin in the system."

"And passed an examination on the rules," Greg said. "A juror who doesn't understand the law he's enforcing is just another mob."

"How many jurors? Twelve?"

"Five. One for every virtue—"

Adam's hands moved. Sebastian leaned forward to read them, then half-smiled. "Adam says we're laying cornerstones and arguing about the curtains."

The alcove went still.

Andrew broke it. "You've built a system with no head. Who commands the army? Who writes the laws? Who decides what these rules mean when two men read them differently?" He took the chalk from the ledge and drew a single vertical line beneath my hierarchy. "One authority. One seat. Otherwise you'll have three men pulling three directions and nothing gets done."

"That's the Empire," Tam said. "One seat. How's that working?"

"Better than no seat at all."

Nort leaned forward. "Andrew's right about this much—*someone* has to hold the sword. A jury can judge misconduct after the fact, but when the enemy are at the gates, you need a single voice that can act."

The quarter hour that followed was the hardest stretch of the evening. Andrew and Nort built their case with examples I couldn't dismiss—border wars where divided command had cost thousands, provinces where competing magistrates had paralyzed trade for a decade. Jonathan sat quiet through most of it, turning his stylus between his fingers.

It was Kane who cut through.

"You're all assuming rulers judge and fight and legislate because that's how it's always been done." He looked at me. "Elenden. You said rules without rulers. Can a rule settle this one? Who writes the laws? Who judges? Who commands the military?"

I stared at the slate. Andrew's single vertical line stared back.

A fence post on a hillside. Fletch standing with a pick on his shoulder, waiting for my words to direct his hands. The post had leaned from true, and I'd learned three things that morning: you needed a standard that didn't depend on local conditions—something that revealed the plumb line. You needed judgment to read the ground and know which direction to push. And you needed strength enough to move the post—but not an ounce beyond, or you'd err the other way.

Three tasks. I wiped the line away and in its place, I wrote the fifth rule:

Government power shall be divided into three branches—those who write the law, those who judge it, and those who enforce it.

Jonathan read the slate a second time, then a third. His stylus had gone still. "Those who write the law draft statutes that serve the higher rules. Those who judge it test every case and every statute against those rules—and strike down any that contradict them. Those who enforce it command the military and carry out the law—but remain subject to the rules first, the statutes second, and the judges and citizen juries third."

"What happens when those branches disagree?" Andrew pressed.

"The rules settle it. A statute that violates a higher rule is void the moment the judges say so. An enforcer who violates a citizen's rights faces the juries."

I stepped away from the board. My hand was white with dust.

Andrew stared at the slate for a long time. "What about roads?"

"What about them?"

"Roads. Bridges. Harbors. Public wells. Coinage. The things no single citizen builds but every citizen needs. Where do they come from in your system?"

I'd thought about this. I'd thought about it more than anything.

"They don't come from this government."

Tam's head came up. "What?"

"*This* government exists solely to prosecute, then to work to protect rights if it can. Building roads isn't protecting rights. Educating children isn't protecting rights. Feeding the poor isn't protecting rights." I paused. "Those things are *good*. They're *virtuous*. They may be *necessary*. But they are not the work of this government."

"Then who does them?" Nort asked.

"Communities. Guilds. Virtue schools. Families. The same people who've always built roads and fed the hungry—before kings claimed credit for it. Maybe a town government can levy their own taxes to do them." I met their eyes in turn. "The moment you give a government the power to provide, you give it the power to withhold. The moment it builds your roads, it decides who walks on them. The moment it feeds your children, it decides which farmer to take the food from."

"This government has one virtue," I said—and the word cradled the bruise I'd been building around. "Justice. And it does nothing else, because every additional power is a door through which tyranny enters."

Andrew spoke first. "It's idealistic."

Sebastian still leaned against the wall, arms folded. "All government is idealistic," he said. "The question is which ideals."

"It leaves holes," Andrew pressed.

Jonathan tapped his stylus against his notes. "It leaves room. There's a difference."

Kane hadn't moved from his seat. His dark eyes had tracked the chalk lines across the slate. When he spoke, everyone listened.

"It's not finished," he said. "But it's a start." He looked at me, then at the rest. "Let's use this as a base and build from here."

Tam exhaled—a long breath that might have been concession or relief. "I still want the citizens voting."

"The juries give them something better than voting," Jonathan said. "The final word on government misconduct. Accountability without popularity."

"It's not enough."

"Then draft a new rule." Jonathan tapped the slate. "If you want broader citizen involvement, draft it. Show how it serves Justice."

Tam's jaw worked. Then he nodded—his eyes promised arguments at kindred dinners to come.

Sebastian began copying the rules onto clean parchment. Adam signed something to Jonathan, who paused, then translated: "He says the mining charter at Ember already works like this. Rules above men. Even Master Roman can't override some protocols—they're written into the founding documents of the Watch."

I hadn't known that.

Andrew took the chalk from my hand and began sketching subsidiary structures—how the branches might be selected, how their powers might be limited, what checks would prevent any one branch from absorbing the others. Nort added notes on military constraints. Tam started drafting ideas for citizen voting, his handwriting as aggressive as his arguments.

The slate filled. Voices overlapped—not shouting now, but the hum of people building something together. Jonathan arbitrated disputes. Kane asked questions that sharpened every answer. Sebastian kept the record. Adam watched it all.

I stood at the edge of it, chalk dust on my fingers, and felt something I'd forgotten since my days at Redcloud—the joy of an idea.

We were still arguing well past midnight. Kane called a halt.

"Tomorrow," Kane said. "We pick it apart. Find every hole before Gentian does."

We filed out into the corridor, voices still trailing threads of the discussion. Jonathan fell into step beside me.

"It's good, El. It may be better than good." He paused. "But it needs a name."

"It has a name. Justice."

He tilted his head. "Men will die with their king's names on their lips. *Justice* is a virtue, not a banner. I'm not arguing the concept—I'm arguing the name." He smiled. "We'll find it. Something that sounds like what it means."

I rubbed the chalk from my hands and said nothing; he was probably right.

We walked a few more steps before he spoke again. "You know what Gentian will ask."

I knew. "What happens when the people inside it stop caring about justice."

"And?"

I thought about it. Thought about Declan. Thought about a whole society of Declans.

"Then the system falls," I said. "They all do. But maybe this one falls more slowly? At least they'll know when they're falling..."

"Get some sleep." He smiled. "Tomorrow after chores, we'll break it."

Chapter 74

Deafening

The morning of the great blizzard, breakfast was bowls of boiled wheat sweetened with milk and a red fruit I couldn't name. The nestled eggs were still steaming in the carved hollows of the tray. The grains had been cooked soft enough to cling to the spoon, and after the first bite I was scraping the bowl before I realized I was hungry.

"Eat up; it's labor day," Sebastian said, settling cross-legged beside us. "We're needed at the forges."

Jonathan's face fell. "I'm still hoping to take El shepherding. The views from the high pastures are worth the climb."

"When the weather is nice." Sebastian pointed a finger at Jonathan. "But the weather is *not*. Storm coming down from the north. Wind and snow both, and plenty of each." He gestured toward the light channel above our door, where the usual amber glow had gone the color of weak tea. "Better to trade a cold chore for a hot one on a day like today."

Adam's hands moved in quick shapes I missed behind my bowl's rim.

"Exactly." Sebastian pointed a finger at Adam while watching him sign. "The forges are essential to everything Ember does. Coal becomes heat becomes iron becomes tools becomes trade. Without the smiths, there's no monastery. Supporting them is an honor." He grinned. "Even if it doesn't feel particularly honoring."

We tied our face wrappings and made our way down.

The forges occupied a series of caverns carved among the mountain's roots, where natural ventilation met human ingenuity. We'd hauled slag before, but never been on forge duty. Heat struck us before we'd cleared the entrance—a wall of it, thick and shimmering, carrying the smell of hot metal and burned coal. The light here came from the fires themselves: orange and white and blue-white where the flames burned hottest, dancing in the bellows' rhythm like something alive.

The smithy master met us at the threshold. A smith twice his size stepped back to let him pass; another paused mid-swing to catch his nod before resuming. Darin was the sort of man you'd forget the moment you looked away—middle-aged, middle height, unremarkable in every visible way—but no one in this room seemed to lose track of him. When he raised his hands to greet us, he signed rather than shouted.

Welcome. You'll rotate through stations. Questions to me.

Darin handed each of us lumps of pale beeswax, soft and faintly sweet-smelling. Sebastian demonstrated: tear off a piece, roll it warm between your fingers, press it into each ear until the world goes muffled and distant. The hammering that had been piercing became merely loud. The roar of the forges dulled to a pulse I felt more than heard.

We would work the bellows, haul coal, and sweep. My hands blackened within the first hour. When I opened my fist to wipe sweat from my brow, pale lines showed where the coal dust hadn't reached the creases of my fingers or the map of my palm.

At least we didn't have to fetch water. Jonathan paused at a junction of bronze pipes running along the ceiling and traced their path with one finger.

"See how they've routed it?" He signed as he shouted. "Water from the cisterns passes through here before it heads up. The fire heats the water, the water heats the stone, the stone keeps us warm while we sleep." He smiled. "The whole mountain is one system."

I heard the words *work the bellows* and thought them an easier assignment. The bellows were enormous: leather lungs the size of a man, operated by handles that required your whole body to move.

When I was young, one of the masons expanding our east tower had been caught beneath a fallen stone. I watched from a window as they carried him to the courtyard, his mouth working like a landed fish, each breath a war his body was losing. The physick said his lungs were whole but couldn't expand—the weight had bent something in his ribs that wouldn't unbend.

Working the bellows felt like that. Like breathing through lungs that fought to stay empty.

The smith at each station needed a specific tempo—fast enough to keep the fire at temperature, steady enough that the heat wouldn't spike and ruin the metal he was working. Too slow and he'd wave you faster. Too fast and the metal would burn. The rhythm demanded arms, shoulders, core, and legs braced against the stone floor. Within minutes my muscles were screaming. After what felt like hours but was probably half of one, sweat had soaked through my wrappings and plastered my hair to my skull.

I started counting silently to keep the rhythm. Then counting gave way to a tune surfacing from memory, one of the nursery songs mother sang to me. Its beat matched what the smith needed. I let it play behind my eyes while my arms kept moving:

Feet that wander, feet that roam,
May every path fain lead you home,
Hill and hollow, field and fen,
Round the bend and back again.
Past the gate and past the wall,
Hear your mother's evening call,
Candle's lit and baking bread—
Almost home, and then to bed.

Childish words, but they kept my hands from faltering. I wondered if my mother had sung it to my brothers too, or only to me.

When Adam appeared at my elbow, I didn't notice at first. He stood watching for a moment, then caught the smith's eye and made a gesture I didn't catch. The smith nodded.

Adam's massive hand closed over the bellows handle beside mine. He took the weight smoothly, matching my rhythm, then waved me clear with his free hand. *Go*, he signed. *Rest.*

I stumbled toward the sweeping station and leaned against the wall, chest heaving.

Unlike the rest of Ember, which kept to two meals a day, the forges also fed their workers at noon. The fires couldn't stop, so the smiths ate in rotation, but we were called out together. Sebastian appeared at my shoulder with a cloth bundle of bread and cheese, and I could have wept with gratitude.

"Can we—" I gestured vaguely toward the corridor, toward anywhere that wasn't pulsing with heat and noise.

Sebastian nodded. "We'll need to eat on the way, but yeah. Let's head up."

We climbed toward the surface, the air cooling with each turn. I pulled the wax from my ears, and the world rushed back in. I could hear the wind sighing upward through the stone hallways. I unwound my face wrapping and let the cold fill my lungs, sharp and clean as water from a mountain spring. The ringing of hammers faded behind us like a fever breaking.

Snow had come to Ember.

Outside the central hearth, fat white flakes drifted down from a sky the color of iron. They fell without hurry, almost lazy in their descent, as if they had all the time in the world to bury everything beneath them. The cold bit at my sweat-damp skin, but I didn't care. After the forges, the chill felt like mercy.

We stood at the hall's entrance and watched the snow accumulate on the stone railings, the steps, the distant pastures where sheep looked like grey lumps against the white. The forges had filled my skull with noise until I'd forgotten what its absence felt like. But the snow swallowed sound—the world grown soft and muffled, wrapped in white.

I don't know how long I stood watching. Long enough that Sebastian finally tugged my sleeve and guided me back inside, past the great hearth where the fire crackled and spat.

"Time we head back."

The afternoon passed in rotations. Bellows again—twice more—until I thought my arms might simply detach from my shoulders and crawl away to find someone who would treat them better. Coal hauling between, which felt like rest by comparison. Sweeping, which was paradise. Adam found me struggling at the bellows each time and stayed until he could relieve me or signal the smith for a rotation. His stamina was inexhaustible.

By the time Darin signed *finished* and (formal) *gratitude*, the light channels in the corridors had gone to grey, and I had lost all sense of time. We trudged back to our quarters, trailing coal dust, speaking little.

I washed until the water ran clear, then washed again for good measure. The heat from the pipes in the walls felt different now that I knew where it came from—still marvelous, but less mysterious.

We settled onto the floor for dinner, and I let the meaty broth seep into my aching muscles. I was composing the words—*Adam, might we skip practice tonight?*—when a bell rang in the corridor.

Sebastian looked up and raised his hand. We all fell silent.

The bell chimed once. Twice. Three times.

"That's for hearth leaders." Sebastian was already rising. "I'll be back."

The door closed behind him. I looked at Adam and decided on a different stalling tactic. My fingers moved slowly, forming the signs with care in a friendly grammar:

Your name. Why Silent Adam?

Adam's eyebrow rose. He considered me for a moment, then pointed to his throat.

His mouth opened. His lips shaped a word. What emerged wasn't speech—but it wasn't nothing, either. A low sound, steady and resonant, rose from somewhere deep in his chest like the humming he did when he played. It held for a moment, then broke apart like wind through dead leaves. The tone was there, if quiet. The words were not.

My fingers formed the response carefully: *Mute. Not Silent.*

Adam extended a finger to me and held it there for a heartbeat. His throat was broken, but his name was something else. He was reaching for more signs when the door swung open.

Sebastian's expression was tight.

"Two sheep missing from the high pastures," he said.

Jonathan sat up straighter. "I *knew* we should have been on shepherding duty."

Sebastian's smile flickered but didn't hold. "The bell wasn't for the sheep. It's for the shepherd who went after them. Storm's turned to blizzard up top—visibility's down to nothing. Kindreds are forming search parties." He turned to Adam. "Can you fetch a lantern from the supply room? Jonathan, El—" He hesitated. "You can stay here, if you want."

Jonathan was already standing. "You're going. We're going. Hearths stick together, right?"

Sebastian extended two fingers toward him. "All right. Get bundled up. We leave as soon as Adam returns."

The corridor outside was alive with footsteps and clanking buckles, the rustle of heavy clothing, voices calling names. Someone laughed, too loud and too brief—the sound of nerves dressed as courage. Doors opened and closed. I pulled on my warmest layers, wrapped my face against the cold that waited outside, and tried not to think about how tired I felt.

A suspicion surfaced. Cold and sudden, like water through a crack in ice.

"Sebastian." I kept my voice level. "The lost shepherd. Do we know him?"

Sebastian's hands paused over his pack. He didn't turn around.

"It's Declan."

I knew.

Before Sebastian spoke the name, before his mouth had finished shaping the first syllable, I knew.

And what's more—something that tightened and twisted like a snake beneath my ribs—I knew that if anyone found him tonight, it would be me.

No.

The refusal rose hot and sudden. Let him freeze. *Your grandstanding got me flock duty, love boy*—well, here it was. The mountain was teaching him what I couldn't.

Serves him right.

The thought should have shamed me. It didn't.

Sebastian's warning echoed: *Justice delayed curdles into revenge.* Maybe it had. Maybe I didn't care. Maybe I grew a backbone after all.

"—for the horn signals. This anchor line is our lifeline." Sebastian's voice cut through my thoughts. I'd missed half of what he'd said. "It's tied off here with the others. We'll head north-northwest, but we can only go as far as the rope allows. When we reach the end, we turn back. No exceptions."

He demonstrated the harness—a short length of rope with a bronze clip that threaded through the main anchor line, allowing movement while maintaining connection. Jonathan was already fastening his. Adam waited patiently.

Sebastian moved down the row, checking each harness. Jonathan first, then me. His hands paused at my belt. Tugged the knot. Tested the clip. Then his eyes found mine.

I looked away.

His hand found my shoulder. "He would do this for *you*, El."

I thought of Declan's pale eyes, his satisfied smile.

"I'm not sure he would," I said.

Sebastian held my gaze a moment longer. "Then don't make it about him." He squeezed my shoulder once and moved on to Adam.

The anchor line ran from an iron ring beside the great hearth, disappearing into the howling white beyond the hall's entrance. A dozen other lines already hung from the iron circle—other search parties, other directions. Jonathan clipped in after Sebastian. Then me. Then Adam.

I chose the middle deliberately. Not first to find anything. Not last to be blamed for dragging behind.

The storm swallowed us whole.

Wind pried at every gap in my wrappings, drove ice into the corners of my eyes, turned my breath to frost before it left my lips. The forge's heat had been oppressive; this cold was its dark twin—absolute, intimate, interested in nothing but leeching every memory of warmth from my body. Within twenty paces, the great hearth's glow vanished. Within thirty, Jonathan became a suggestion ahead of me, then nothing at all.

The rope became my world. My gloved hands caught it, gripped it, followed its tension forward through blindness. I might have been walking across the moors of my childhood or off the edge of a cliff—the white void offered no distinction. Each step required faith: lift the foot high, commit to the descent, trust that ground existed somewhere below.

Time dissolved. The wind's howl swallowed all other sound—Sebastian's calls, Jonathan's whistles, even my own breathing seemed to happen somewhere outside myself. My thighs burned with the effort of high-stepping through drifts that varied from ankle-deep to thigh-deep with no warning. The rope vibrated with the movements of those ahead, a thin pulse of connection in a world gone formless.

We aren't going to find him. The thought was a relief. The storm was too thick, the mountain too vast, the chances too slim. We would reach the end of our line, turn back, report our failure, and Declan would become a story told in hushed voices. *Remember that shepherd who went after his sheep in the blizzard?* I would nod along with everyone else.

Look

The word came without sound—quick and unapologetic like I should have been expecting it. I knew that voice.

I didn't want to look where it pointed.

My feet kept moving. One step. Another. Follow the rope. Follow the others. The voice was wrong—had to be wrong—because if it was right, then I would have to choose. And I had already chosen.

SEE

Gentler now. Patient. The way Master Colm spoke to Kyle.

My eyes rose.

The wind paused—the mountain's breath between gusts. But through that momentary gap, I saw a shadow huddled against a low stone wall, dark against the grey-white nothing, knees drawn to chest.

Then the wind returned, and the shape vanished behind curtains of snow. That could've been anything. A shadow. A trick of the mind.

If it *were* Dec, he would have heard Sebastian calling. Surely he would have answered. Surely I could keep walking, keep following the rope, keep—

"El! End of the line!"

Sebastian's voice, closer than I'd expected. The rope ahead was slack in my hands—they were gathering, turning back. Adam's lantern emerged from the white behind me, amber and wavering. Then Jonathan's outline ahead. Finally Sebastian, holding up the end of the anchor line.

"He's not here!" Sebastian shouted over the wind. "We've run out of rope. Adam: lead us back—we follow the line and update the search parties."

Adam nodded and turned. Began working his way back along the anchor line, the rope between us slowly uncoiling at my feet. Jonathan clapped my shoulder in greeting, already grinning at the thought of warmth.

Then he saw my face.

His grin died. "El? What is it?"

I couldn't answer. The words caught somewhere between my chest and my throat, tangled with all the reasons I shouldn't speak them. *No backbone.* Maybe Declan was right, because here I stood with the truth pressing against my ribs and I couldn't make myself say it.

The rope kept uncoiling. In a moment I would have to move or be dragged.

My arm rose. My hand pointed toward the wall I could no longer see.

Jonathan squinted into the white nothing. Turned back to me. "What? I don't see anything."

"Maybe—" My voice came out a croak. I tried again, louder. "Maybe we should check over there."

Jonathan's whistle cut through the storm—two fingers in his mouth, sharp as a blade. Sebastian materialized from the white only feet away, stamping his feet and slapping his arms against his sides. His face was wrapped so thick only his eyes showed.

"El thinks we should try that direction!"

Sebastian looked where I pointed. Looked at me. Shouted. "El? What's this?"

I couldn't make myself argue for the life of someone who'd made mine miserable. Couldn't raise my voice in his defense. I'd held my tongue about him for two moons. Now it held itself. The rope at my feet kept uncoiling, Adam's steady progress pulling it away.

"We can't stay out here forever," Sebastian said, more to Jonathan than me. No judgment in his voice—just fact. "They'll start to worry about us if we don't return." He waited. "El?"

I stared at the snow between my boots.

Sebastian reached past me, caught the rope leading to Adam, and gave it two sharp tugs. The line went still. A moment later, the lantern's glow reappeared, Adam's form taking shape behind it.

Sebastian spoke—words I couldn't catch, mouths close to ears. Then Adam set the lantern down in the snow. His hands emerged from their wrappings, fingers spread so the signs could be read.

He reached out. Cupped my chin. Lifted until I had no choice but to meet his eyes.

Adam's eyes held no accusation. No impatience. He studied my face for a moment as if he knew exactly what war was being fought behind my closed lips.

His free hand moved: *Speak.*

I shook my head. Gave a cut across the air with my arm.

The disgust I felt wasn't for Declan—it was for myself: for the shameful hope that we would simply turn back, for the part of me that wanted Declan to pay for every petty cruelty with his life. I was making my friends waste precious time. Their fingers were going numb, their faces raw with cold, and I stood here fighting a battle I should have already won.

But every time I tried to let it go—to walk away, to pretend I'd heard nothing—my gut tightened like a cord about to snap. If I ignored truth now, the next time would come easier. And the time after that. Until ignoring became habit, and I became the kind of man whose pride stopped his ears as surely as beeswax.

I couldn't say it aloud. Couldn't raise my voice in support of him. But I could move my hands. I pulled off my own gloves. The cold bit immediately, but I needed my fingers free.

We should check there.

Adam tilted his head as if listening to something beyond the wind. His eyes moved to Sebastian, held there for a long moment.

Sebastian nodded once. Grabbed the slack rope and pushed forward into the white, line trailing behind him. Jonathan fell in beside him. Adam stayed with me, waiting.

Not twenty feet from where we'd stood—tucked in the lee of the stone wall, exactly where the shadow had been—they found him.

"Adam! El!" Sebastian's voice rang through the storm. "We got him!" A pause. "He's alive. Can't walk."

Sebastian sounded three horn blasts—*found, need aid*—but the wind scattered them like startled birds before they'd crossed the distance to my ears. If I could barely hear them, the searchers at the hall had no chance.

I didn't move. My head hung. The wind howled around us, but I barely felt it.

Adam touched my arm. When I looked up, his hands were waiting.

Did you see? True sight?

I shook my head.

How? His signs were gentle, curious. *How did you know?*

How could I explain what I couldn't explain to myself? That a voice had spoken where voices couldn't reach? That I had tried to ignore it—had *wanted* to ignore it—because that boy freezing against that wall had felt like justice?

My right hand rose slowly. Formed a fist. Pressed it hard against that place beneath my sternum—the center Feng had taught me to guard.

Adam's eyes widened slightly.

Jonathan's outline took shape from the white—stumbling along the rope toward us, one hand shielding his face.

"Sebastian says to follow the anchor line back!" His voice came in gusts, the wind tearing pieces from each word. "Tell them we've found him but he can't walk—they need to bring a sled!" He held out his hand to Adam. "Leave me the lantern. Go with El."

Adam pressed the lantern into Jonathan's waiting hands. Then he gestured toward the rope, clipped in behind me, and waited.

The way back felt longer than the way out. I followed the anchor line hand over hand, the rope my only truth in a world of white. Without Adam's presence behind me, I might have believed myself lost in an endless nothing, paying the price for my hesitation.

Then light. Warmth. The great hearth's fire blazing through the snow, figures emerging from the white to meet us.

"—Sebastian's line. Sebastian? That you?" Kane, the kindred leader, stepping forward.

Adam moved past me. His hands shaped quick signs. Kane's eyes went wide—then he was shouting orders. A padded sled. Heated stones. Blankets. Two brothers took off at a run, clipping in to our line and running out into the storm.

Kane turned back to us, gripping Adam by the shoulder. "Well done, both of you. Rest by the fire. We have it from here."

We walked to the hearth. The heat pressed against my frozen face, my numb hands, but I couldn't feel it. Not really. I stood as close as I dared and let the warmth try to thaw me.

Adam stood beside me. Patient as ever. But even his patience had its limits.

His hands moved: *El. How?*

I didn't answer.

How did you know?

I was on the edge of tears. I didn't deserve Adam's gentle curiosity or his respect or the warmth of this fire while Declan lay freezing twenty feet from where I'd almost walked away.

Adam's hands began to form another question.

I thought I had disgusted myself enough for one night. I was wrong.

Because slowly, deliberately, I closed my eyes to Adam. A single tear broke free as the lids came down—pushed from its place by the closing.

Chapter 75

Speak

I must have fallen asleep.

One moment I was sitting with my back against the warm stone, eyes closed, shutting out Adam. The next, voices were threading through my consciousness: Sebastian's low murmur, Jonathan's questions tumbling over each other.

I kept my eyes closed. Tight as the fist that curled around my throat and refused to let go.

Sebastian and Jonathan were looking at me. I could feel it the way you feel the sun through shut lids—a warmth that presses without touching. I turned my face toward the wall.

"He's been like this since we left?" Jonathan asked, quiet enough to be kind, loud enough to be heard. I opened my eyes and turned toward them. Adam's back was to me, his signs invisible. But I saw the way Sebastian's expression shifted as he read them—concern folding into resolve.

"We've all had a long day," Sebastian said at last. "Let's get some rest. We'll talk in the morning."

But we didn't.

Or rather, I didn't.

Morning came through the light channel in pale amber, and I watched it crawl across the floor from my bunk without moving. Jonathan stirred below me. Sebastian brought food. Adam sat on his stool near the door and waited.

They tried.

Jonathan sat beside my bunk and talked about nothing—the latest archive ideas for the inscription, names for the government proposal, whether we'd ever draw shepherding duty. He steered wide of anything that might brush against Declan. His voice was a hand extended across a gap, patient and open. I heard every word. My mouth stayed shut.

Sebastian tried differently. He brought problems: a question about kindred rotations he claimed to need my opinion on, a passage from his reading he said he couldn't parse. The questions were generous lies, and I loved him for them. But my jaw might as well have been wired closed.

The strange thing was that I *wanted* to speak. My body rebelled against the silence—every instinct screamed to surface, to gulp air, to answer. But between the wanting and the doing, something had broken. Some bridge I'd crossed a thousand times without thinking had collapsed last night, and now I stood on the wrong side of the gap, watching my voice retreat to where I couldn't reach it.

I'd hurt them. I knew that. I was still hurting them. Could see it in the way Jonathan's cheerful patter grew thinner as the hours passed, in the careful way Sebastian avoided meeting my eyes. I was repaying their kindnesses with a turned shoulder.

Adam I couldn't face at all.

The memory sat behind my ribs like a stone: his wide eyes in the dark. And I had answered by shutting mine.

Every time his stool creaked, every time I felt his steady gaze settle on the back of my head, guilt twisted a notch tighter. I turned toward the wall and pulled the blanket higher.

Sebastian's frustration broke the second day.

He'd been pacing—short laps between the bunks, his boots marking the same four strides. Jonathan had stepped out to fetch water. Adam sat motionless on his stool.

"I don't get it, El." Sebastian stopped at the foot of my bunk. "What are you so afraid of?" His voice cracked on the question. "Did *you* lead him out there? Did you put the snow on the mountain? Did you make Dec go after those sheep?"

I flinched but didn't turn.

"Because from where I'm standing, the only person you're punishing is yourself. And us." A pause. His breathing was hard, like he'd been running. "Mostly us."

The silence stretched. I heard him rub his face with both hands.

"I'm sorry." The anger had drained, leaving something hollow. "That wasn't fair. I just—" He sat heavily on the lower bunk. "I don't know how to help you if you won't let us."

I wanted to tell him it wasn't a choice. That my silence wasn't a door I'd locked but a mountain that had grown overnight, bouldered with guilt and shame and something I couldn't name. But the wanting only made the gap wider.

Sebastian left. When he returned, Jonathan came with him. They spoke to Adam in low voices near the door—low enough that I was clearly meant to overhear without being addressed.

"I think we bring this to Kane," Sebastian said.

Adam's hand rose: flat palm, tilted slowly side to side. *Maybe.*

He looked at me. I dropped my eyes to his hands.

His hands moved again—longer this time.

When the heart is broken, sometimes the body must lead the way. Let me show him fire katas.

Sebastian and Jonathan exchanged a glance. I felt the air shift—relief, or the beginning of it. A plan where there had been none.

"I'll speak to Brother Gentian and Kane," Sebastian said. "Get El excused for the next few days."

I closed my eyes and let the blanket settle over me like a burial shroud.

Jonathan sat on the edge of my bunk. His hand found my shoulder through the blanket, and he let it rest there.

"I'm here," he said. "When you're ready."

Sebastian appeared beside him. "El. I'm sorry for what I said earlier. I didn't mean—" He stopped. Tried again. "We care about you."

Then they were gone, and the room held only Adam and me.

Adam hadn't moved.

I stared at the stone above my bunk and felt the tears come again—hot and useless, sliding into my hair, itching at the edges of my ear. It felt like drowning in shallow water: knowing the air was right there, inches away, and being unable to lift my face to reach it.

I heard Adam rise from his stool. His tottering steps crossed the room. A weathered hand appeared at the edge of my bunk, palm down, resting on the wool blanket near my shoulder. Not reaching for me. Just there.

I don't know how long we stayed like that. Long enough for the light channel to shift from amber to the flat grey of a passing cloud and back again.

When I finally rolled to face him, his eyes were steady. He didn't sign. Didn't gesture. Just watched me: without demand, without hurry, as though whatever I contained was worth the waiting.

My hands rose on their own—clumsy, trembling. I shaped the signs in the formal register, student to master, the careful grammar he'd drilled into me night after night.

I'm sorry.

Adam's expression didn't change. His hands answered in a different register entirely: brother to brother, friend to friend, the grammar of equals who share a table and a fire.

I know.

Then the register shifted again, and the command grammar returned—the one I'd only seen him use once before in the library, the night his eyes had gone wide. King commanding a servant. Absolute requirement. A single word:

Come.

Adam took a coat from the hook behind the door and shrugged it over his shoulders. He pointed at mine. I put it on, my fingers fumbling the clasps. The simple obedience of dressing felt like the first solid ground I'd stood on in days.

He led me up through corridors I knew, past the great hall where the central fire burned, toward the iron doors set into the mountain's face. The guards opened it for him without question; one of them bowed.

Snow lay across everything—deep and brilliant, unbroken save for the paths the brothers had already cleared. The sun hung low and fierce in a sky scrubbed clean, throwing light so sharp it made my eyes water. After two days in the amber womb of the mountain, the brightness felt aggressive. Or penitent. As though the sun were trying too hard to make amends for whatever it allowed during the blizzard.

Adam turned from the main path toward a set of stairs I hadn't noticed before—shallow steps carved into the rock face above the monastery entrance, rising at an angle steep enough that I had to use my hands where shadow had let ice form. The stone beneath was rough-cut but sure. Old stairs.

At the top, the mountain leveled into a broad shelf of rock, perhaps thirty paces across. A natural platform, partially sheltered by a cliff face rising behind it, open to the valley on three sides. On a clear day, you could see for miles—the snow-covered hills rolling away, the grey thread of the Drahan far below, the distant northern Thornwall catching light like a row of teeth.

I squinted against the glare and followed Adam's tottering gait along a partly shoveled walk. Brothers had already been at work out here—I could see where they'd knocked the accumulated snow from around the tall sticks that marked the light channels, freeing the bronze mouths to drink the sun and swallow it down into the deep. Without that maintenance, the rooms below would darken. The monastery saw through these openings.

I stood breathing hard from the climb while Adam walked to the center of a large drift and did a strange thing.

He began moving in slow, deliberate circles. Round and round, his boots pressing the fresh snow flat, each pass widening the circle by a boot's width. Then he reversed direction, walking back and forth in parallel lines that crossed the circle's interior. The pattern was methodical—building a floor where there was none.

When I understood, I stepped forward to help.

Adam held up one hand. *Wait.*

So I waited, hugging my coat, watching a grown man walk circles in the snow. The work had a kind of holiness to it—the patience of each pass, the way each step built on the last. He wasn't clearing the snow. He was claiming it. Compressing it into ground that could bear weight, the way a potter stamps clay before shaping it on the wheel.

When he'd finished—the circle perhaps ten paces across, the snow packed firm beneath a thin crust—he didn't use it. Instead, he led me back down the stairs and across the long cleared path to the training hall.

Wait here, he signed.

I stood outside the hall, stamping my feet to knock any wet snow off, sourly wondering when Declan would be sufficiently whole to return to Sister Harken's class. The thought was a dark fish surfacing in still water, and I let it slip away.

Adam returned carrying two practice swords. Wooden, wrapped in leather at the grip.

I stared at them. I recognized them.

I don't think Sister Harken would want me to have one of those, I signed.

Adam's face creased. *Too bad.*

He handed me a sword and led me back up the carved stairs, back to the platform he'd spent half the morning building. The sun had climbed higher during our walk to the training hall. The air was cold but the light fell warm where it reached us, reflecting off the packed snow like thousands of tiny glass candles.

Adam planted his practice sword tip-down in the snow beside him and signed, each shape slow and deliberate.

This ground will hold for walking. But it's new. Packed once, not frozen over many passes. It won't hold yet for pivots, lunges, or weight shifts. He glanced at the surface, then back at me. *Today we work on grip. Only grip.*

He led me through a series of stretches first—shoulders, wrists, forearms. Basic movements that loosened the cold from my joints. When I raised an eyebrow at a particularly gentle rotation, he signed: *These are not proper fire-school kata. These wake the small muscles. Every muscle must pull its weight, or their burden will fall to others to compensate. Use the wrong muscle for the job, and even if you escape injury, you will still be limited.*

Fire-school katas are always done with blades. They are forbidden to teach before level 2.

Adam gave me a serious look.

Please don't tell Sister Harken. She'd break my other hip.

The joke caught me off-guard. Something fluttered to life in my chest—not quite a laugh, but the memory of where laughter lived.

Then Adam picked up his practice sword and showed me how to hold it.

Like a bird, he signed with one hand, curving the other around the grip. *Tight enough it can't fly away. Loose enough you don't crush it.*

He adjusted his grip, settling the pommel against the heel of his palm. *Hold it like a hammer. The bottom sits here.* He pressed the pommel into the fleshy base below his little finger. *Your thumb and forefinger do the fine work—steering, adjusting, feeling. The three lower fingers provide the power.*

He turned the sword so I could see the alignment. *The V between thumb and finger sits on top of the handle, lined up with the blade's edge.* He ran his other thumb along the imaginary line. *The web of the hand tells the blade where to cut.*

I copied him, wrapping my fingers around my own practice sword. The leather grip was cold, the wood beneath it dense and heavy. Heavier than my staff, and balanced differently—the weight sat further from my hand, wanting to tip forward.

Adam watched. Corrected the angle of my wrist with a gentle touch. Adjusted my thumb's position by pointing until I shifted it myself.

I tried an experimental flourish—a simple rotation.

Adam caught the movement. He raised an eyebrow. I had to sheath my sword in the snow to explain with both hands.

Something I saw the soldiers do in the training yards when I was a boy. My fingers hesitated. *I thought it was real swordwork. No one would teach me.*

He smiled and shook his head. Then his hands demonstrated a series of proper wrist exercises—small, controlled rotations and figure-eight patterns that kept the blade moving without engaging the arm.

Power comes from here. He pressed a fist to his own stomach, then touched his shoulder. *The arm carries the blade. The wrist tells it where to bite. A strong arm with a slow wrist is a hammer, not a sword.*

I worked through his exercises while the sun tracked across the packed snow. The cold kept my grip honest—numb fingers couldn't cheat as well, couldn't rely on dexterity when strength failed. Adam corrected me twice more, then sat with his sword resting across his knees.

He was still for long enough that I stopped.

His eyes had gone distant—not like Master Limerick visiting some foreign place in thought, but more like someone standing at the edge of a deep place, deciding whether to step forward. When he noticed me watching, his hands rose slowly.

I wasn't always Silent Adam.

I waited.

I wasn't always silent.

"My voice used to sound like this."

I nearly dropped the practice sword. Adam's mouth had moved, but the voice came from behind me—a warm tenor, slightly rough, a voice that would carry across a crowded hall. I spun. No one. Just the empty platform, the snow, the wind.

When I turned back, Adam wore a tight smile.

*One of the tricks I picked up in **my** youth.* His smile deepened. *I had more teachers than I wanted.*

◁

The surprise of it cracked something loose in my chest. I felt words rush toward my teeth, felt my jaw begin to open—and then the chasm yawned wide again, and the words fell back into the dark.

My hands rose instead—I wasn't choosy about the grammar: *You can talk?!*

No longer. Adam's smile was layered—grief and mischief and years. *I can seem to talk. Just as I can seem silent.*

He demonstrated. Tapping his practice sword against the toe of his boot, he produced a dull rhythmic thunk, steady as a heartbeat. Thunk. Thunk. Thunk. Then—between one tap and the next—the sound vanished. His sword still struck his boot, the motion unchanged. But the air swallowed the impact as if it had never been.

My eyes went wide.

You can make yourself silent?

Adam pointed at me in reply.

So can you.

The words landed closer than I was ready for. I looked down at the practice sword in my hands.

Adam let the moment breathe. Then: *The snow needs time to harden. We'll come back tomorrow morning.* He gathered both swords and tucked them under one arm. *Besides—all these late nights are robbing me of my music lessons.*

He was using it. The music, the sword work, the morning air—all of it an excuse to keep me moving. I knew it. He knew I knew it.

I picked up my coat from where I'd laid it on the snow and followed him toward the stairs.

I let him. I missed my pipes too.

Despite my silence, life moved on.

Most evenings, the kindred continued to gather to work through the proposal. Kane had been briefed—Sebastian's doing, I assumed—and no one pressed me to explain my silence. But I caught the curious looks, the glances traded when they thought I wasn't watching. The boy who'd argued for justice with such heat now sat silent among them, hands usually folded, eyes on the floor.

I couldn't speak. But I could listen. And when the discussions turned to the structure of punishment—whether their government could guarantee restitution, whether the state owed victims what the guilty could not repay—I made my first contribution since introducing the idea.

No. Restitution cannot be guaranteed. I signed. Jonathan translated without being asked. *You cannot bring back the dead. You cannot ensure the thief can repay what he stole. But punishment can be guaranteed. The state can ensure that the cost of a crime is not borne by the innocent.*

Nort leaned forward. "So you're saying this justice-government isn't about making things right. It's about making sure they don't stay wrong?"

I hadn't said that. But he was closer than I was.

Tam opened his mouth to argue, then closed it. Opened it again. "That's bleak."

It's honest, I signed. *Justice cannot promise the world will be fair. Only that it won't look the other way.*

They still hadn't found a better name. Jonathan kept a running list of alternatives in his journal, each one crossed out within a day.

Mornings belonged to Adam.

Before dawn, while the monastery still slept, we climbed those carved stairs to our platform above the world. The snow circle hardened day by day—each night's freeze setting the previous day's work, each morning's first steps testing what the cold had built. Adam packed new snow over the old when needed, filling the gaps and soft spots, widening the circle by a pace each time. The floor grew beneath us slowly, in layers, one pressed firmly atop the last.

As the ground firmed, Adam risked more.

▽

The grip work expanded into guard positions—high, middle, low. He showed me how to transition between them without dropping my edge alignment, how to let the blade find its resting place at each station rather than muscling it into position. *Let it settle,* he signed. *It knows where it belongs.*

The stancework built too, though limited by what our patch could hold. Wide steps were disastrous—the ice beneath the packed snow punished any sudden weight shift with a treacherous slide. So Adam taught me narrow stances for close quarters, feet close, weight centered, the kind of balanced stillness that Sister Harken had been drilling without swords for months. Only now the blade in my hands gave the balance a purpose, and the ice under my feet gave me motivation.

Adam was good. I could see it in the economy of his movements, the way his practice sword arrived at each guard as though it had always been there. But he could only demonstrate with one hand. The other was always signing—explaining, correcting, refining. And when the instruction required both hands on the grip, his words vanished. He would set down the sword and sign, then pick it up and show, then set it down again. The lesson fractured into halves that never quite joined.

My shorthand was improving rapidly. Necessity is its own grammar—when you need a word, you build it from whatever pieces lie nearest. Adam was showing me the compressed vocabulary of blade-terms that resembled miners' shorthand. *High-guard* became a single gesture. *Edge-true* another. But shorthand couldn't carry nuance. It couldn't explain *why* the wrist turned at the top of a cut, only that it did.

I begged him to use his voice.

Adam raised his hand and held his finger toward me, steady.

I looked away.

Fair enough, I signed.

He smiled. But the frustration showed in other ways. Some mornings, when a particular movement eluded his explanation, he would demonstrate it three or four times in succession, each repetition slower, more exaggerated, willing me to see what his hands couldn't say. And

▷

I watched—watched the way he drove from his legs, the way his hips preceded his shoulders, the way every cut began somewhere below the sword.

I watched, too, the way his right leg caught on certain pivots. A hitch—a moment where the muscle asked for range the joint couldn't give. He compensated so smoothly that I might have missed it, except that I was an expert in reading bodies. The weakness lived in his hip. Old damage, structural—the kind of injury you get from impact, from a fall onto hard ground that drives force up through the leg and into the pelvis. A drop from height, perhaps. The hip had healed, but the healing had set limits that no amount of skill could erase.

When I asked him about it, he pointed at me again.

I stopped asking.

The government presentation arrived on a morning when the light channels carried only the thin grey wash of an overcast sky—no gold, just pale lights that looked like a ghost crown on the amphitheater ceiling.

Brother Gentian sat at the center of the panel, flanked by three members of the Watch—two men and a woman whose faces I didn't recognize. Kane had assigned the presentation to Andrew and Tam, a decision that seemed reckless when he'd announced it and now revealed itself as quietly brilliant. Andrew spoke with the steady conviction of someone who believed in the system he was describing. Tam attacked its weaknesses before the panel could, turning potential objections into evidence of rigor. They disagreed with each other three times during the presentation—genuinely, not for show—and each disagreement demonstrated that the proposal could hold two opposing minds without breaking.

I sat in the back row and watched the kindred's work take shape. Jonathan had rewritten most of the framework. Sebastian had organized the presentation. The model was mine, though Andrew presented it better than I could have. The whole was greater than any of us.

Brother Gentian cracked a nut when they finished. He chewed. He consulted the Watch members in low voices. Then he looked up.

"Its greatest weakness is the absence of successful precedent. You've built a government no one has tried."

Andrew started to respond, but Gentian held up a hand.

"That said—you've built it honestly. The tradeoffs are acknowledged, the mechanisms are clear, and you've resisted the temptation to promise more than the system can deliver." He glanced at the Watch. "Full marks for the kindred."

The kindred dinner that evening was loud with congratulations, most of it directed at Andrew and Tam. I ate quietly, letting the warmth of it wash over me. Jonathan caught my eye across the table and raised his cup.

With the government project no longer consuming our evenings, Adam and I returned to the library alcove.

Under the warm light of the *Shiranath*, my fingers found the minor scales without deciding to. My phrases came mournful, circling, the Aeolian mode pulling each melody down toward resolution and then denying it. Adam followed. His rowan pipe carried a different quality in the Aeolian—where mine grieved, his bled. The hum in his breath turned the notes into something that ached. Some evenings I slipped into the Phrygian, its flattened second lending the music an edge that cut where the Aeolian only bruised. On better nights, I rose to the Dorian—still minor, still shadowed, but with a breath of hope beneath it. Grieving without surrendering.

We never discussed it. Adam heard where I was and met me there.

Beside us, the inscription burned blue in the arch of ancient stone. *Unspoken truths are locked doors.* Below it, where I could not see, Adam's white words: *Speak and enter.*

One evening, Adam set down his pipe and pointed at the wall.

Maybe we should ask Brother Jacob to move the bookshelf back in front of it, he signed.

I stared at him. The joke was so dry I almost missed it—suggesting they re-bury the ancient inscription because its advice was uncomfortable.

My lips pressed together and spread wide. Not a laugh. But close.

I returned to regular classes as well.

Each generals' afternoon, climbing the training hall steps, my chest would tighten. I'd scan the room before entering—counting heads, searching for a set of pale eyes and greasy hair. Each time: nothing. Declan's usual place on the far wall remained empty, his circle of friends reduced by one.

I told myself the knot in my stomach was relief. Weeks passed. The absence calcified into fact. I stopped scanning the room.

Then one evening, Adam and I returned from the library to find Jonathan and Sebastian in low conversation. They broke off as we entered—too quickly.

I paused in the doorway. Adam raised an eyebrow.

Jonathan looked at Sebastian. Sebastian looked at the floor.

Go on, I signed. *I heard his name.*

Sebastian straightened. It was a small thing, a squaring of the shoulders, but I recognized it—the posture he assumed when he spoke as hearth-guide rather than friend.

"Declan is in good health," he said.

My stomach dropped. I'd been bracing for this—the day Dec walked back into the training hall, rosy-cheeked, grinning, as though nothing had happened.

"But he's been dismissed from Ember."

I couldn't make the words fit.

"He was already under review," Sebastian continued. "Prior incidents. When the blizzard hit, a group of sheep broke from the flock and he went after them alone. Against standing orders. Against counsel." He paused. "Thanks to—" He caught himself. "—us, he was found. But he stood before the Watch, and they judged that he'd put lives at risk—his own and those who searched for him. Combined with his existing record..." Sebastian's hands opened, palms up. "They escorted him across the Drahan yesterday."

The room was quiet. Jonathan watched me. Adam sat on his stool and waited.

I should have felt resolution. The ledger balanced, the account closed. Justice, delivered not by my hand but by the institution built to deliver it.

Instead I felt cold. Empty. The way a room feels after a fire goes out.

Declan was still out there. Walking back to whatever village had sent him. And I could picture it clearly: Dec finding the smallest boy in whatever place he landed, the smile spreading slow as oil on water. Ember hadn't changed him. It had merely removed him from my sight.

The bully expelled, the tormentor gone. I searched my chest for satisfaction and found nothing but ash.

Because what I wanted—what I hadn't let myself name until this moment—wasn't justice at all.

I'd wanted him to suffer.

I'd wanted him afraid, and cold, and alone, the way he'd made others feel. I'd wanted him to understand what it was like. And when the blizzard took him, some part of me—an *honest* part of me—had been glad. I hated him. He was gone, but that wasn't enough. I wanted him dead, not merely gone, and I resented the voice that wanted to save him.

Unspoken truths are locked doors.

Yes.

I looked at Adam. He was watching me. His eyes held a question he would never sign.

I looked at Sebastian and Jonathan. My hearth. The people who had sat outside my silence for days without complaint. They deserved better than locked doors.

Come, I signed in the brother-to-brother grammar. *There's something you need to hear.*

I was already moving toward the door. Adam rose from his stool. Jonathan and Sebastian exchanged a glance, then Sebastian grabbed a lantern and followed.

I led them back through the corridors, down the sloping passage to the library. Brother Jacob was at the door with his brass key, working the lamp nearest the entrance. He paused when he saw the four of us.

"We need the alcove," Sebastian said.

Jacob's eyes found Adam. Whatever he read there made him step aside. He held the door wide and pressed the key into Sebastian's hand. "Lock it when you're done."

The *Shiranath* were still lit, but the alcove felt cold. Sebastian unshuttered the lantern completely to light the way for himself and Jonathan as I pressed ahead. If I slowed down, I'd stop. If I stopped, I'd bury this thing again, and next time I might not find where I'd put it.

I stood beneath the inscription and faced the three of them.

Adam looked horrified. Jonathan leaned against the shelves. Sebastian stood ready.

I raised my hands and found them shaking. I opened my mouth.

No! Adam shot out a closed fist. *Me first.*

He stepped past me. Past Sebastian and Jonathan. He stood beneath the arch of ancient letters and placed his palm flat against the stone—against the center, against the white words only he could see.

His mouth moved. The familiar hum rose from his chest—that low, barely audible drone I knew from a hundred evenings beneath the rowan pipe. But this time it was joined by the voice I'd heard once before, pressed close inside my ear like a whisper—warm, private, meant only for the hearer. A tenor roughened by years of proclamations.

"My name is Vaylen. Son of Dorian. True Emperor of Thamaria."

Chapter 76

The Setup

Elenden opened his eyes slowly.

He had closed them somewhere during the telling—Merauve could not say when. The title had come. *True Emperor of Thamaria.* Then silence and the faint business of the courtyard below.

Merauve's tobacco went forgotten in his fingers.

The sea-blue gaze found him and held. Then Elenden spoke in a voice stripped of everything Merauve had come to expect: no parable, no pastoral unfolding. Facts.

"Emperor Vaylen's son—Vaylen the Second—was only thirteen. His mother died bringing him into the world, and his father had turned his attention to the old ways." Elenden's voice held no softness for what came next. "The Lightbringers saw a thirteen-year-old boy with no mother and a father who had begun to seek the Spirit of Truth."

"His cup-bearer was a Water-brother."

Elenden's hands rested open on the table, palms down. "The Lightbringers came to him with threats and a plan. Poison. Something caustic—it burned tissue on contact."

"The cup-bearer tried to warn people. The men he went to were already part of it."

"On the appointed day, the cup-bearer carried the cup to the table as instructed. But just before, he fed the Emperor black bread with ash from the cooking fires kneaded into the dough. Enough to force the body to reject what it swallowed." A pause. "It saved his life. It did not save his throat."

"The assassins heard the screams and went to ground."

Merauve did not move.

"The cup-bearer dulled Vaylen's pain with what he had and lowered him from the balcony on knotted sheets." Elenden paused. "The draught clouded his senses. He fell. The fall broke his hip."

"He was secreted to River Monastery. Triaged. Then moved again." Elenden's eyes held Merauve's without wavering. "Moved by an underground network: experts at hiding those the Empire wished to find. Eventually he reached Ember."

Merauve saw the network's shape—not as abstraction but as architecture. The underground passages at River Monastery. The routes Master Chen mapped in careful brushwork. The channels that threaded between Imperial patrols like water through cracked stone.

Routes Merauve had helped tend. At eighteen, he had guided frightened families through those channels under Chen's direction—never asking names, never looking too closely beneath lowered hoods or at the wounded carried between stronger shoulders. Had one of those nameless figures been an emperor with a ruined throat and broken hip?

His hand twitched toward the satchel at his feet. The folded square of rice paper, yellowed with age.

He stilled his hand and forced it flat on the arm of the chair.

"When the Water-brother failed to produce the body," Elenden continued, "he was turned over to the Inquisition. By their arts, they learned only one name: 'Master Chen'."

Merauve remembered the smell of wet clay and late summer—overripe fruit from the orchard wall, the gurgle of the river. Soldiers in formation.

"The Emperor's death was declared a sudden affliction—a hereditary weakness. The nation mourned." Elenden's voice was flat. "They dressed the Water-brother in Imperial vestments, buried him in the Emperor's casket, and set up their regency."

The fire popped. A log shifted, sending sparks across the hearthstone.

"But Lightbringers don't leave loose ends. They have been looking for Emperor Vaylen ever since."

Merauve drew breath to speak—what, he did not yet know—when the sound reached them.

Hooves on cobblestone, too many and too fast.

Merauve was at the window in three steps.

Below, the south gate stood open. Riders poured through—an escort of six, dust-caked, their mounts lathered. At their center, white robes caught the afternoon light.

Cassius.

Beside him rode a figure Merauve recognized by silhouette before the face resolved: narrow shoulders, dark grey robes, a purple hood drawn back from a severe face. High Inquisitor Sirius.

Cassius dismounted first. He planted himself at the courtyard's center and pitched his voice to carry through stone and glass—theatrical, commanding, meant for every ear in the fortress:

"By authority of His Imperial Majesty's Inquisition, and upon evidence presented to High Inquisitor Sirius, I bring formal accusation against a traitor in our midst."

Merauve held still—the silence between notes, taut with what follows.

He had rehearsed this moment in a dozen variations: Ember's coordinates confirmed, a raid to be organized, Elenden's usefulness at its end. Elenden's sense of betrayal countered with the satchel's contents. He had prepared for every version of this proclamation.

Except this one.

"Inquisitor Merauve—stationed at this garrison under pretense of loyal service—stands accused of treachery against the Empire. Of bartering Imperial intelligence. Of consorting with enemies of the Emperor. Of corruption by the heresy known as the Truth."

The courtyard went silent. Soldiers paused mid-stride. Something dropped against cobblestone and rang.

Merauve's knuckles whitened on the sill.

Cassius had not ridden south to verify the location of Ember Monastery.

He had ridden to intercept the courier. And what he brought back was not confirmation—it was Sirius himself, primed with accusations sown deep enough to make the truth irrelevant.

Below, Thorne emerged from the keep. The Major walked stiffly toward Sirius, who leaned from the saddle to hear him. Thorne's jaw was tight.

And there—emerging from the keep's entrance, a guard at his elbow—Pakonaskow. The elder stood motionless, his dark eyes lifting from the courtyard up to the tower window. He seemed to hold Merauve's gaze for one breath. Then looked north.

Elenden had risen from his chair. The young man's head was tilted. "Inquisitor?"

Merauve faced the window. When he spoke, the words came quick and flat—aimed at the bars, at the courtyard, at no one. There would have been a note of shame in his voice if he had known where to find it, how to pitch it on humility's register. He had neglected that particular instrument so long it no longer made a sound.

"You have told me your truth. Here is mine."

He drew one breath. Held it. Let it go.

"High Inquisitor Sirius charged me with recovering the location of the Fire Monastery within the moon. After what you have just told me, I begin to suspect why." His fingers found Tachet's hilt at his belt. "Cassius—the Lightbringer below—arrived shortly thereafter, offering power if I gave the location to him first." He met Elenden's eyes. "And killed you."

Elenden's expression did not change. If he was surprised that Merauve had used him or had weighed his life and spared it—he gave no sign.

"I did neither. I sent the location of Ember Monastery to Sirius four days ago under Imperial seal. Proper channels. Proper protocol." He paused.

Merauve's gaze dropped to the courtyard. "I expect that courier never arrived, for I told Cassius the same later that morning, to placate him."

Below, Thorne nodded at something Sirius said and lifted a hand, pointing toward the tower. Every face in the courtyard followed it.

Merauve stepped back from the window.

His gaze fell on the satchel beside the chair.

Three flights. Maybe a minute before they reached the landing.

Merauve lifted the satchel and slid it beneath Elenden's chair, pressing it into the shadow of the back legs. The leather settled against the dark wood without a sound.

He straightened.

"I am guilty of a great many things. I have killed to extract confessions—truths." He gathered his tobacco pouch. "How fitting I should die for a lie."

He drew his coat from the back of the chair. "Sirius has already judged, or he would not be here." Merauve looked at his hands. Long-fingered. Steady.

"Appeal to Virtue," Elenden said.

Merauve laughed at this. He drew the last measure of smoke from his leaf, held it, and tossed the stub into the fire.

Elenden ran his hands through his hair—a gesture so ordinary it struck Merauve as wrong, somehow. As though a painting had scratched its nose.

"You are innocent in this," Elenden said.

Merauve's hands stilled on the fabric of his coat. "I am not innocent in much else."

"I will stand for you."

Merauve stared at him.

"You can barely stand at all."

A fist struck the door. Three blows. "Inquisitor Merauve. By order of Major Thorne and High Inquisitor Sirius, you are requested and required to present yourself immediately."

Merauve held Elenden's gaze as he called to the guards. "Open the door."

The bolt drew back. Two soldiers filled the threshold—men Merauve had seen, whose names he knew. They did not meet his eyes.

Merauve straightened his coat. Adjusted the silver threading at his cuffs. Stepped toward the door.

He did not resist.

The bolt drove home behind him—the scrape sounded different this time.

"Your weapon, sir."

A senior sergeant by his rank tabs—one of Thorne's veterans—extended his hand. Merauve reached to his belt and drew Tachet. The blade caught the tower's lamplight as he flipped it: a thin edge of brightness, there and gone. He placed it across the sergeant's palm, hilt first.

The man's fingers closed around it. Merauve watched his blade disappear into another man's keeping. "Cursed be any other hand that wields you," he breathed.

Then, addressing the remaining door guard: "The prisoner remains under standard protocols. No one enters that chamber without Major Thorne's direct authority."

"Sir." The guard held his gaze a beat longer than protocol required.

Merauve descended.

Thorne met him at the base of the tower stairs. The Major's face looked tired—the skin beneath his eyes the grey of long-dead pine.

"I have been presented with a formal charge bearing the High Inquisitor's seal." Thorne's voice carried no further than the space between them. "I am obligated to act on it. You understand."

"I understand, Major."

"Your quarters are being searched." Thorne paused. Something worked behind his eyes. "Before we step into that courtyard, I am asking you once. Is there any truth to these charges?"

Merauve returned the Major's look. His question was genuine.

"Your concern for my fate is misplaced, Major." Merauve rubbed a boot against the back of his leg to polish it. "I fear they are not interested in the truth."

"I am concerned about the fate of my fortress, Inquisitor," Thorne corrected. His gaze tracked past Merauve to Pakonaskow, who stood watching the courtyard from beneath the colonnade.

Thorne straightened. "This way."

The courtyard was full.

The garrison smelled blood, or at least a show. Soldiers stood in clusters along the walls, arms folded or hands resting on belts. Officers had emerged from the keep. Faces Merauve recognized—men he dined across from, corrected, terrified into competence—watched from the shade of the colonnade. None looked away. None looked friendly.

At the center, Cassius paced beside Sirius like a hunting dog straining against its lead. The Lightbringer's white robes were bright in the afternoon sun; his hand rested on the pearl-hilted sword, thumb stroking the pommel in small circles. Beside him, Sirius had dismounted—sleeves pushed back past his elbows. A runner was speeding off at his direction.

To the right, soldiers had been at work. Merauve's personal effects lay scattered across the cobblestones like the aftermath of a shipwreck: clothing dragged from the wardrobe, books thrown open and face-down, correspondence spread in loose sheets that stirred in the breeze. His desk had been hauled from his quarters whole and now stood at an angle near the well, its drawers pulled and upended. As he watched, a sergeant drove an axe through the locked drawer. Wood splintered. Papers spilled.

The honeypot.

Merauve nearly smiled.

"Your Justice." He pitched his voice to carry—not to Sirius alone but to the walls, the men along them, the windows above. "To what do I owe the honor? I trust you received my letter."

Sirius' voice was the same flat delivery Merauve remembered from their first meeting over Anders' corpse. "A High Inquisitor's post. And you repay opportunity with treachery?"

Merauve waited.

"Imagine my surprise," Sirius continued, "when Sir Cassius arrives at my camp not two days past, breathless, bearing a story I would scarcely have believed from a lesser source." He clasped his hands behind his back. "An Inquisitor, he tells me, approached him during his travels through Fort Kestrel on Imperial business. Supplied confidential intelligence of an ongoing interrogation."

A horse stamped on the cobblestone.

"Moreover," Sirius added, "this same Inquisitor offered the Lightbringer first purchase—ahead of the Inquisition. Ahead of the Empire."

Merauve turned to Cassius for the first time.

The Lightbringer had stopped pacing. He stood with his weight forward, both hands on the sword's hilt now, the pearl pommel catching light between his thumbs. His smile was drawn tight as a snare.

"He lies," Merauve said.

A crow screamed from the battlements—a single ragged note that rang off the courtyard stone and died.

"I sent my findings to Your Justice under Imperial seal four days ago—Tensday, second bell, by mounted courier under priority routing. The objective I was charged to uncover, obtained through lawful interrogation and dispatched through proper channels." He held Sirius' gaze. "If that courier never arrived, I invite Your Justice to ask Sir Cassius why."

Cassius' sword cleared the scabbard in a breath. "Are you accusing—"

"*His* name is not on the charge." Sirius' voice cut like a blade. "Yours is." He looked at Cassius. "Sheathe that weapon."

The sword slid home. Cassius' jaw worked, but he stepped back.

Sirius returned the full weight of his attention to Merauve. "Do you deny speaking to him before this? Where is your letter? If you claim it was intercepted, do you also claim our ciphers broken? How does he come to know the object and subject of our investigation—something only two people outside this circle could know?"

"People like Garoth?"

Sirius' chin drew back a fraction—not much, but enough. The Inquisitor who had held Elenden for six months before Merauve, and failed—excluded from Sirius' count. At least one oversight.

The recovery came quickly. "A drowning man grasps at flotsam." Sirius made a small wave with his hand. "You are charged with conspiracy against the Empire, with trafficking confidential Imperial intelligence, and with corruption by heresy. By my authority and my witness, you are found guilty. Your commission is revoked." The words came as a recitation—formal, final. "Your days as Inquisitor are over. Arrest this man."

Two soldiers stepped forward.

"I appeal to Virtue. To Justice."

Merauve's voice filled the courtyard—not loud, but it reached every wall, every window, every ear pressed to the stone.

Sirius' face went rigid, then red.

"I **am** Justice—"

The last word rang off the courtyard walls—raw, unguarded. The silence that followed was worse.

"Major Thorne." The voice came from Merauve's left—pitched precisely: loud enough to command attention, quiet enough to seem deferential. An officer's instrument, honed across decades. "A word, Your Justice."

Sirius turned. Thorne stood at the edge of the proceedings, hands clasped behind his back. He inclined his head.

Thorne spoke quietly. Merauve could not hear the words, but he could read the shapes: *foreign dignitary... negotiations... formal witness... diplomatic catastrophe.* High Inquisitor Sirius' gaze sought Pakonaskow multiple times during the exchange.

The runner returned—a young orderly, carrying a tray with a bottle and cup. He hesitated at the edge of the confrontation, unsure whether to interrupt. Sirius took the cup without looking at him, swirled, sipped.

His expression soured. He held the cup away from his body as though it had insulted him.

When Thorne finished, the High Inquisitor stood motionless for several seconds.

"You have appealed to Justice. To Justice I commend you. You shall have your duel." He gave a dismissive wave. "With my blood-stead."

The Lightbringer's smile split wide. He stepped forward, the white robes luminous in the courtyard's fading light, and swept a bow so deep it bordered on mockery.

"I am honored to serve," Cassius said.

"Tomorrow." Sirius had already turned away. "First bell. Justice will not be delayed." He gestured to the orderly. "Bring me something drinkable."

Merauve's cell was on the keep's ground floor, facing the courtyard. A stone room with a proper door, a cot with wool blankets, and a window too narrow for a man's shoulders but wide enough to admit a bar of late-afternoon light. An officer's courtesy.

The Major had given him this much.

The guards were unfamiliar—two faces Merauve had seen at distance on the walls but never addressed by name. They stood at the correct interval, eyes forward, saying nothing. No deference, no flinch of old fear. Thorne had chosen them for distance and neutrality.

Merauve stood in the center of the room and listened to their boots shuffling on the other side.

He sat on the edge of the cot. Closed his eyes. Let the mind do what the body could not—pace, calculate, disassemble the board and rebuild it.

The bar of light crawled across the floor. Climbed the far wall. Thinned to a wire. Went out.

When the bolt drew back again, the cell held only the faint amber of a corridor lamp.

▷

Thorne entered alone, carrying nothing. The door stayed open behind him, the guards visible in the hall.

The Major's grey hair was combed flat, his collar buttoned to the throat. His hands were clasped behind his back, his shoulders loose. Only the cords of his neck and the white of his knuckles betrayed the day's crisis.

"I have moved your personal effects to storage. Your quarters are sealed." He unclasped his hands. "I managed to talk them down from burning the place."

"How considerate."

Thorne's gaze hardened and he crossed his arms. "I am not here for you, Inquisitor."

The title still. Interesting.

"I have three hundred Val'dren riders beyond my northern wall. A High Inquisitor and a Lightbringer inside it. One prisoner under active investigation, and a diplomat whose continued good health is the only thing standing between this garrison and a siege I cannot win." He drew a slow breath. "I need to know what this duel costs me—whichever way it falls."

Merauve leaned forward, elbows on his knees.

"Then let me lay it plain." His voice carried no performance. Simply the architecture of the problem. "If I duel Cassius and lose, custody of my prisoner passes to Sirius by protocol. The Lightbringer has already tried to kill him once under this roof." He let that sit. "If Elenden dies, Pakonaskow has ample cause to consider his offer of blood-stead betrayed. You may guess what follows."

Thorne's jaw shifted. "Surely Sirius would not simply execute the prisoner. I explained the situation with the Val'dren elder—he allowed your appeal."

"Sirius allowed it because Pakonaskow knows the old traditions, Major. Better than Sirius. Better than Cassius. He *believes* them." Merauve paused. "If Pakonaskow had witnessed a violation of the right to trial by Virtue—a summary verdict with no recourse—he would have walked out of this fortress that same hour. One does not offer blood-

▷

stead to truthless oathbreakers. Every rider in that valley would know us faithless."

Thorne said nothing.

"Even if I am victorious in the duel," Merauve continued, "there is no winning, for me. Sirius will strip me of rank regardless—he has already pronounced his verdict. Even if he lets me walk free for the sake of appearances, the prisoner becomes his charge." Merauve held the Major's gaze. "I will not pretend to know what Sirius intends in that regard. But I can assure you that a prisoner who knows what that young man knows does not survive an Inquisition—whether Cassius lives or dies."

He let Thorne sit with it. The corridor lamp threw their shadows long across the stone.

"I have... an alternate proposal." Merauve leaned forward. "Elenden has offered to stand for me."

Thorne said nothing for a long moment.

"Your prisoner."

"Yes."

"The man Pakonaskow came to retrieve."

Merauve held his gaze. "The same."

"Why in the name of stone and storm would he—" Thorne cut himself short, one hand raised. "You are proposing to put the one piece holding my northern situation together onto a dueling field against the Lightbringer?!"

"Hear me out." Merauve kept his voice steady. "I am no fool. If Elenden stands as *voluntary* blood-stead and falls, there is no longer an Elenden to rescue. The debt Pakonaskow came to honor is cleared. The elder is freed from his obligation. Your northern problem rides home."

Thorne's thick fingers drummed against his bicep.

"By that logic, what difference does it make whether your prisoner dies in a duel or dies by Sirius' decree?"

"To someone like Pakonaskow?" Merauve let the question breathe. "Everything."

He watched Thorne work through it—the Major's eyes moving across the floor as though reading terms in the stone.

"Think about it. Sirius gets what he wants: a guilty verdict and a dead prisoner. Pakonaskow sees what he needs to see to free him from his obligation. And you get a disaster averted."

"And what do you get?"

Merauve felt Tachet's absence keenly—an absence with edges, the missing balance at his hip.

"I am a reasonable man, Major." He turned his palms up on his knees. "I do not expect reinstatement. I hope to walk out of this fortress alive. Escorted or secreted, it makes little difference to me."

Thorne studied him. Merauve could almost hear the calculation.

"Or," Merauve said, "I can duel Cassius tomorrow, and you inherit every complication at once." He spread his hands. "This is the narrow path. The only one I see."

The Major's fingers stilled. He stood for a long time in the doorway, the guards' silhouettes framing him from behind.

"What do you need?"

"I need to speak with Elenden—to confirm he still agrees, and to learn what he requires." He paused. "Armaments. Proper ones—not training gear. If Pakonaskow is to be satisfied this is a legitimate Virtue Duel and not a staged execution, the blood-stead must be equipped for a genuine contest."

Thorne considered this. "Done." He turned toward the door, then stopped. "I will escort you to the tower myself."

The walk through the keep felt longer than it was. Soldiers lined the corridors—more than usual, posted at junctions and stairwells where Merauve had rarely seen sentries. They pressed against walls to let the party pass—Thorne in front, Merauve behind, two guards at the rear. Faces turned and looked away. Voices died in corridors and resumed after. The fortress had already learned its new vocabulary: the Inquisitor, arrested. Merauve caught the word *traitor* twice at his back.

He kept his eyes forward and his hands at his sides.

Then the same stairs he had climbed every morning for weeks. Thorne climbed ahead of him, the guards' boots rang behind, and the door at the top opened to admit him one last time.

Thorne gestured for Merauve to enter first. Then followed. The door remained open.

Elenden sat at the small table by the window, the last of the day's light falling across his hands. The satchel was not visible.

The blue eyes lifted.

"Hello, Elenden. I have come to accept your offer," Merauve said as he took his usual chair. The familiarity of it—the worn arms, the angle to the window—was almost unbearable.

Elenden studied him. Studied Major Thorne. Whatever he read there, he did not name.

"I have appealed to Justice. Will you stand as my blood-stead tomorrow at first bell? A Virtue Duel on the charge of conspiracy against the Empire." He kept his voice flat. "The Major requires that the duel be properly conducted to satisfy our northern guest."

Thorne stood near the door, arms folded, watching them both.

"I watched from the window." Elenden's voice was quiet. "Must you always reason your own way? You put such faith in your plans and schemes."

"I have a mind," Merauve said. "It seems only right that I use it."

Elenden's gaze had not left his face. "It was freely given, and I won't rescind it. I will stand for you."

Merauve held the look longer than he intended. Then turned to business.

"What do you require?" Merauve asked. "Weapons. Armor. Name it."

Elenden was quiet for a moment. Then: "Loose robes and wrappings. Belt, wrist and foot bindings—wool, not cotton. Long enough to cover from knuckle to mid-forearm, and from foot to calf." He demonstrated on his arms and legs. "If wool is not available, linen will do. Nothing dyed if possible."

Merauve waited for the rest. The traditional choice for a Justice Duel would be a blade—but he suspected Elenden might select a staff. The reach would be advantageous.

Nothing came.

"That is all?"

"I have everything I need."

Merauve turned to Thorne. "Wrappings as described. And I need my blade—Tachet—returned."

"Your blade stays in the armory until the duel."

"Then it goes to the field with me tomorrow. Not before—but not without."

Thorne considered this. "Done." He turned to one of the guards filling the door. "You heard. Have the quartermaster cut them tonight and deliver to this room before dawn." The guard departed.

Thorne turned back to Merauve. "On your feet, Inquisitor."

Merauve rose. The chair scraped against stone. He stood over Elenden for a moment—this young man had offered to die for him—*would* die for him, he corrected himself.

"Thank you," he said.

Elenden looked up at him.

"Be at peace, Inquisitor."

Thorne escorted him back to the cell himself. The same walk in reverse—soldiers at junctions, voices dying. At the cell door, the Major paused.

"If this holds, I will get you out of this fortress alive. Beyond that—" He extended his hand.

Merauve took it.

"Get some sleep. Dawn comes early."

The door closed. The bolt found its housing. Merauve stood in the center of the room and listened to Thorne's boots fade.

He sat on the edge of the cot. The absence of Tachet ached like a severed nerve. He unlaced his boots. Set them beside the frame. Lay back.

The cell was dark. The window admitted nothing but the cold.

Above him, Pakonaskow slept—a man who had traded his freedom for a prisoner. Above them both, Elenden slept—a prisoner who had offered to die for his captor.

A chain of irrational sacrifices, with himself as the beneficiary.

He did not sleep well.

Chapter 77

The Duel

Lightning split the dark.

Merauve's eyes opened to its afterimage—a white burst already fading. Thunder broke an instant later, close enough to rattle the stones of the keep. The sound rolled outward across the fortress like a declaration, and before its echo died, rain arrived: a downpour, thick and relentless, hammering the courtyard stones with the beat of a thousand drums.

At least it wasn't snow. He lay still. The cell was black. There was no hint of dawn behind the storm.

The hours since Thorne's departure had passed in a kind of restless inventory—more of accounts than of plans, for there were no plans left to make. Debts tallied and found unpayable. Faces cataloged and released. The mind, stripped of agency, had circled back to the only utility that remained: memory. Merauve had lain in the dark and let it spend itself.

Now rain filled the silence where thought had been. He listened to it strike the stone, the field, the window—each surface returning a different pitch.

He rose and dressed in the dark.

By the time Major Thorne's knock came, Merauve was standing at the window. The rain had not relented. Beyond the keep, the courtyard was a sheet of moving water, its flagstones submerged beneath a shallow river that caught each flash of lightning and threw it back in broken silver. The fortress walls were reduced to outlines.

Thorne filled the doorway.

"It's time."

Two guards flanked him, their cloaks darkened to black with the wet. One carried an umbrella. The corridor lamp threw long shapes across the stone.

Merauve adjusted his cuffs and followed him out the door.

The rain struck him as he stepped outside. Not just cold but *heavy*, pressing against his shoulders with the weight of something deliberate. One of the guards wrestled an umbrella over Thorne's head; neither man offered Merauve the same courtesy. Within ten strides his coat was drenched. Within twenty, it ceased to matter. The world contracted to the ground beneath his boots and the shape of Thorne's back moving ahead through the grey.

They crossed the yard at an angle, skirting the deeper water where the drainage channels had surrendered. Lightning split again—nearer now—and in its flash, Merauve caught the shape of the tent at the eastern end of the dueling field: canvas snapping taut between its poles, its sides lashed down against the gale. Two guards flanked the entrance, rain streaming from the brims of their hoods. They parted without a word.

Inside: lamplight. The stale scent of oilcloth and the live scent of wet earth. And warmth—not much, but enough to make the rain's absence register against the skin.

Thorne relieved the guards, turned at the entrance, and drew something from beneath his cloak. Tachet. The stiletto rested across his palm, handle toward Merauve.

Merauve accepted it without a word—sliding it into his belt—and felt the world rebalance by a fraction.

The tent was full. Elenden was already there.

His garments were plain, if practical, and to Merauve's eye, absurdly insufficient for a man about to face a Lightbringer's blade. He looked less like a duelist than a body being dressed for the ground.

Fitting.

Brendan and Maudalia were just withdrawing from the table when Merauve entered. The chef carried an empty tray; the kitchen girl balanced a covered basket against her hip. Their eyes met Merauve's—Brendan with a nod, Maudalia dropping her eyes to study the ground. Then they were past him and through the tent's flap, gone into the rain.

On the table between two lamps: a meal laid like a final offering. Sliced cold meats, dark and lean. A round of hard cheese with a dulled rind knife beside it. Ship's biscuit broken into quarters. Dried apricot and fig pressed into cakes. A pot of honey, unstoppered. Two cups, and between them a clay pitcher.

Nothing that would sit heavy. Nothing that would slow a man who needed to move.

If he made it out of this fortress alive, Merauve would miss Brendan's art.

He lowered himself into the empty chair.

"You haven't eaten," he observed.

"I was waiting for you."

Elenden poured water for both of them. The gesture was unhurried, his hand steady. He placed Merauve's cup at his right and bowed his head. His lips moved without sound.

Merauve watched and said nothing. Outside, the rain hammered on.

When Elenden lifted his head, Merauve reached for the cheese and cut a wedge. The cheese broke clean. He ate mechanically, tasting nothing.

Elenden cut a strip of meat and folded it around a piece of cheese. He ate slowly.

"You are going to die for me," Merauve said. He had not intended to say it aloud.

Elenden chewed. Swallowed. Took a sip of water.

"If the Spirit wills it," he allowed, "but I hope not today."

Merauve set down his cup. "I've seen what Cassius can do. Whatever dark compact gives him power, it is real." He heard the rawness in his own voice and did not modulate it. "And Ember—the Fire Monastery's location is known. Sirius has the intelligence now. He has no reason to spare you."

Elenden reached for a biscuit. His blue eyes held Merauve's across the small table.

"I am not worried about Ember. It is harder to find than a set of coordinates on a map." A trace of—was that confidence?—something adjacent to it. "And better defended than you might expect."

Merauve had no time to pursue the comment.

"And what about you?" he asked.

Elenden did not answer immediately. He folded his hands on the table and was still for a moment. Then he pushed back from the chair and crossed to where the satchel rested against the tent's rear pole.

Merauve saw it before he understood it.

No hitch at the hip where the deepest bruising had been. No compensating lean to favor the ribs. Elenden bent, gathered the leather satchel by its strap, and rose—and every joint answered the one before it without hesitation. This was not the movement of a man recovering. His body moved as a single thing.

Elenden set the satchel on the table between them.

Merauve did not touch it. He was staring at Elenden's legs—at the ease in them, at the way Elenden returned to his seat smoothly. He had watched those ankles buckle. He had noted the injury switching sides and accounted it fatigue. He had explained it away.

"Forgive the misdirection, Inquisitor." Elenden folded his hands on the table. "While my injuries were real, I may have been... selective in what I revealed about the recovery."

Merauve stared at him. The weeks of careful observation—every halting step, every wince as Elenden lowered himself into his chair, the way he favored his right side when he thought no one was watching. The guards' logs noted only "stretching exercises" through the viewport; *would they have known the difference*?

"You have been lying to me."

"I have been telling you the truth, Inquisitor. All of it." A pause. "Perhaps not all at the same speed."

"You used my own estimation of your weakness to shape my strategy," Merauve said. "To shape everyone's strategy."

"I used what I had." Elenden held his gaze. "I am not lying, Inquisitor. I am telling you now. When you need to know. Not a moment before." His eyes dropped to his hands—the wrappings at his wrists. "I was protecting something important."

He looked up.

"You."

Thunder rolled again outside—distant now, the heart of the storm beginning its long retreat southward. The rain continued, but lighter. Steady.

"You could not stand against the Lightbringer." Elenden's voice was quiet. "And none would let *me* if they believed I could win."

Merauve leaned back in his chair and pressed his palms against his eyes. Behind the darkness of his hands, the implications rearranged themselves.

If Elenden could move like that—genuinely, fully, with the command of his body unexaggerated from his testimony—then this duel was not the execution Merauve had resigned himself to. This was not a lamb walking toward a wolf.

This was something else entirely.

"You could win?" Merauve asked.

Elenden said nothing.

Merauve's fingers found the edge of the table. The board had changed. Every piece he'd resigned in the dark hours was back in play—but on squares he hadn't mapped.

Merauve dropped his hands. "Have you considered what *happens* if you win?"

Elenden tilted his head.

"The verdict falls in my favor. *My* charges are annulled." Merauve's words quickened as the implications assembled themselves. "But you—you are still a prisoner of the Empire. You will have humiliated the Inquisition's chosen champion. Sirius will not simply release you into the courtyard with a handshake. Especially with what you claim to know."

The tent flap shuddered in a gust. One of the outside guards coughed.

"I can only share the truth, Inquisitor. I can't control what other people do with it." He turned the fig cake in his fingers. "Besides. I came here for you, not for Cassius."

"He will be the one standing across from you with a sword."

"I am not fighting *him*." Elenden broke the fig cake in half and offered the larger piece to Merauve. "I am bearing witness."

Before Merauve could respond, a bell rang through the rain—a single, clear stroke that opened the storm like a seam. First bell. The note sustained itself, carried by the rain.

Elenden rose. Again that clean, unbroken motion. He drew his hood up and tightened the wrapping at his left wrist.

The tent flap opened. A guard leaned in, rain cascading from his hood.

"Sirs. They're ready."

The dueling field was drowned.

Rain had beaten the dry turf to mud. The stands sat empty—not worth braving the storm for, or the garrison had been discouraged from attendance. A ring of standing torches fought the downpour, their iron posts capped with shallow hoods meant to shed the rain—though the gusts drove water sideways beneath them, and the flames guttered and leaned, throwing shapes across the mud that made the field seem to move.

Merauve led. His satchel hung across his shoulder. Elenden walked a pace behind, the hood of his robes drawn forward against the rain. In the downpour, with his head covered and his frame folded against the weather, he could have been anyone—a scribe, an orderly, a man not worth a second look.

They passed the eastern boundary where Scout Corbin and Scout Naman held position. Corbin's face was set like a man standing watch at a funeral. Naman had knelt to press one palm flat against the muddy earth, his eyes closed, his lips barely moving. Neither man spoke as they passed, though Corbin's chin dipped a fraction.

To the right, Pakonaskow stood at the field's northern edge, motionless as the stone behind him. The elder's dark eyes tracked their approach from the tent. Rain ran from his braids and beard and pooled at his feet. He did not seek shelter.

Beside him, Scout Alena stood with her hands clasped at the small of her back. Thorne's doing. If the elder required a voice today, he would have one. Under the oilskin hood, a coil of auburn hair had wound itself tight with the moisture. Her grey eyes moved across the field's perimeter—reading the ground, the positions, the distances between them.

On the left, Major Thorne walked to the southern edge, flanked by the two guards whose names Merauve did not know. Thorne stood with his hands clasped behind his back, watching no one. Rain streamed from the brim of an umbrella one of his guards held over him, though the Major showed no awareness of the courtesy.

The High Inquisitor had claimed the west.

Sirius stood beneath a canvas awning that a cloaked orderly worked to stake against the gale—the squares of grey fabric snapped and billowed like sails fighting their rigging. He wore the Inquisition's formal black—the purple edging at his sleeves was barely visible in the dark. Beside him, a camp table bore a bottle and a half-filled cup that the mist of rain was slowly diluting. He had dressed for a verdict, not a contest.

Near the kitchen entrance, sheltered beneath an overhang, Brendan stood with Maudalia at his side. The chef's thick arms were crossed over his apron. Maudalia gripped the basket she had carried from the tent. Her knuckles looked white against the woven reed.

They had stayed. That made twelve witnesses.

Merauve stopped at the edge of the field's center. Elenden halted beside him, hooded, still.

From the base of the tower awning, Cassius emerged.

The Lightbringer crossed the field with long splashing strides. His white robes—pristine through some art or vanity Merauve could not determine. He moved through the grey like something luminous. The pearl-hilted sword hung at his hip. His left hand rested on its pommel. His right swung free.

He was smiling.

High Inquisitor Sirius stepped forward to the edge of his canopy. He did not invite anyone in. His orderly held out a scroll, its seal already broken. Sirius accepted it without acknowledgment and unrolled the parchment. The wind caught its edges.

His voice cut through the weather—not raised, but hardened to carry.

"By the ancient right of appeal to Virtue, and by the authority vested in the office of High Inquisitor, I declare these proceedings sanctioned under Imperial law."

The rain hammered on.

"The accused: Inquisitor Merauve, formerly of this garrison, charged with conspiracy against the Empire, trafficking of Imperial intelligence, and corruption by the heresy of the Truth." He did not look at Merauve. "The accused shall face the champion of Justice in trial by combat. Should—"

"I claim the right to name a blood-stead."

Sirius' scroll dipped. The parchment edge reached the wall of rain before the High Inquisitor caught it. He looked at Merauve for the first time.

"Well then," Sirius said. The words came through his teeth. "Let the accused present him."

Merauve turned to the figure beside him.

Elenden reached up and drew back his hood.

The rain struck his face and he did not flinch. His blue eyes blinked around the drops. The water ran through his hair and down his jaw, and then he was smiling toward the sky like a man greeting an old friend.

High Inquisitor Sirius' gaze locked on Elenden. Disbelief first—parted lips, a lifted brow. Then the nostrils narrowed and the upper lip curled back a fraction. Hatred. His eyes shifted to Merauve—and the lip settled. The brow smoothed. He lifted his cup and drank.

Across the field, Cassius had stopped walking.

The Lightbringer stood perhaps ten paces from the center, rain streaming down the white robes. His brown eyes found Elenden and did not blink. His tongue passed across his lower lip. His hand tightened on the pearl pommel.

Sirius recovered. His voice came clipped, each word bitten short.

"Good. Yes. Elenden deArthis. Do you stand freely, without bribe or burden, as blood-stead for the accused?"

"I do."

Merauve's gaze found the northern edge.

Pakonaskow was still rooted there, rain running from his beard. But as Elenden's hood fell and the young man's face turned toward the storm, Alena had leaned close. Her lips moved near the elder's ear—quick, low.

Pakonaskow's dark eyes rested on Elenden across the distance of the field. He was still for a long moment. Then he raised one hand—open, palm forward—and held it there.

Elenden turned. Across the mud and the rain and the torchlight, Elenden's right hand rose—index and middle fingers pressed together over his heart. He held it there for one breath. Two.

Pakonaskow's hand lowered. The elder's expression did not change.

"I, as accuser and witness for the Empire, witness the blood-stead." Sirius rolled the scroll with a single sharp motion and thrust it toward the hooded orderly. The parchment struck the man's chest before his hands found it. "I will not read every article in this weather. Sir Cassius, Lightbringer of the Order of the Morning Star, will stand as my blood-stead to deliver justice."

Sirius turned from the field and seized the bottle from his camp table. The diluted wine went into the mud. He poured a fresh measure without looking at it, then waved a dismissive hand.

"May Truth be divined by these combatants."

Cassius' laugh cut across the rain—bright, genuine, the sound of a man handed a gift he did not dare expect. "Oh, this was well done, Inquisitor." His eyes had not left Elenden. "I cannot guess how you managed it. I misjudged you."

The combatants took the field.

Cassius' white robes trailed through the mud without seeming to touch it. He claimed the western half and turned, planting his boots wide.

Elenden walked to the center. Barefoot, slow. The mud grabbed at his feet and he let it. He carried no weapon.

Cassius drew his sword.

The blade emerged with a sound that was not a ring but a hum, low and sustained, like the steel was savoring the moment.

He held the weapon before him, point skyward, in formal salute. The rain ran down the blade and dripped from its guard. His smile had not dimmed. If anything, it had deepened—wider now, showing teeth.

"I have waited"—he leveled the blade at Elenden's chest—"a long time for this."

His eyes found Elenden's across the rain. They burned.

Elenden regarded him. The rain ran between them.

"I'm sorry for what was done to you," he said.

Cassius' smirk lost its footing.

Five paces of mud and rain separated them.

Cassius moved first. Three long strides carried him to striking distance, the pearl-hilted sword describing a low arc that tested the air between them. A question.

Elenden stepped aside.

The blade passed through the space where his ribs had been. Rain hissed along its edge. Cassius recovered, turned, and drove in—a probing backhand into a thrust. His boots found purchase in the mud where others would have slid.

Elenden was no longer there.

He had moved perhaps a hand's width—no more than the distance required for steel to miss skin. His bare feet shifted in the mud and held. His hands stayed at his sides.

Merauve had watched duels at Waterfall, attended exhibitions in the capital, even stood across from several blades himself throughout the years. But this—this belonged to no school he recognized.

Art.

Cassius cut again. A lateral slash, chest-height, fast enough that the rain parted in its wake. Elenden dropped beneath it. The blade sang over his head. He rose as it passed.

Remarkable, what you've accomplished.

The thought arrived clean and fully formed, and Merauve accepted it without question.

Cassius lunged. A committed thrust aimed at the center of Elenden's belt. Elenden turned sideways—the blade passing so close that rain spattered his robes—and Cassius' momentum carried him a stride past. The Lightbringer wheeled, boots cutting furrows in the mud.

A stroke of genius, really—convincing the prisoner to stand as your blood-stead. I had thought the arrangement a closed door. But this—this shows depth.

Merauve's fingers found the edge of the satchel strap at his shoulder. The thoughts felt warm. Familiar. He agreed.

On the field, Cassius had reset. He circled now, sword extended, reading Elenden's stance. Elenden turned with him, keeping his chest toward the blade, barefoot in the mud, his hands now raised, ready.

"The deArthis name carried weight once. Before you soiled it with *treason*." The Lightbringer's voice was pitched for the witnesses.

"I serve the Emperor," Elenden answered. "Do you?"

Cassius' eyes narrowed. He feinted left—a half-step that would have drawn a lesser fighter's weight—and struck right. The blade came in high, aimed at the junction of neck and shoulder. Elenden's left hand rose and slapped the flat of the blade aside with the back of his forearm. Not catching. Not blocking. Redirecting. The sword slid past his shoulder and Cassius stumbled a half-step.

He lies. The thought was sharper now, edged with certainty. *He has been lying to you from the first day. Every word, every prayer, every show of meekness—performances, Merauve. You of all people should see it.*

Merauve's jaw tightened. Yes. He had always suspected. The entire testimony. Those eyes that never flinched. What kind of man endured captivity with that impossible serenity unless it was rehearsed?

Cassius pressed. Three quick cuts—low, high, low—each a flowing circuit as he spun, each faster than the last. Elenden's bare feet found the mud and released it, found it and released it, each step placed where a swordsman would not think to look.

"Stand still," Cassius hissed.

"You're the one who's moving."

Coward. The word settled into Merauve's mind as a conclusion. *Too afraid to acknowledge the truth. But when it costs something, they run.*

Elenden stepped between them.

He was twenty paces away, circling with Cassius on the muddy field. But the angle of his movement carried him across Merauve's line of sight to the Lightbringer, and for a moment Cassius' brown eyes were hidden behind Elenden's turning shoulder.

The warmth vanished.

Merauve blinked. His hands were shaking. The rain struck his face and he felt it for the first time in—how long? The echo of thought rang hollow in the sudden absence. He looked at the field and saw what was actually before him: an unarmed man facing a blade. Whatever name one gave that, it was not cowardice. Fool, but not a coward.

Cassius attacked again. A diagonal slash that would have opened Elenden from collarbone to hip. Elenden stepped inside the arc—*inside*, where the blade had no edge, only hilt and hand—and for one breath the two men stood close enough to share the rain running down their faces.

"You can be free of it," Elenden said. Close. Almost gentle. "The dark that holds you. Forsake it. Turn your back on it; renounce—"

Cassius' off-hand cracked across Elenden's jaw.

The blow sent Elenden back a step, his bare foot sliding in the mud. He caught himself. A thread of blood ran from his lip into the rain.

Cassius' face had gone white—not pale, *white*, the color of something drained from within. His teeth bared like an animal. The sword came up in a furious overhead strike and Elenden stepped clear, and it came again, and again—hacking now, the fencer's precision abandoned for something that looked more like murder.

"MINE!"

Elenden moved between the blows. His body turned and settled and turned again with each stroke, his feet finding ground that should not have held. When Cassius pressed close, Elenden's hands found the fulcrums—a palm to the shoulder, a strike to the elbow, fingers at the wrist, a heel driven against the pommel—redirecting the blade at every joint between its edge and the man who held it. Proximity should have favored the swordsman. It didn't. Rain streamed down his face and he did not wipe it.

One slash came wide. Cassius' boot stamped the flooded ground and a sheet of muddy water caught Elenden full across the face.

Elenden blinked his eyes closed.

The next thrust came instantly—a killing stroke aimed mid-body, right under Elenden's ribs. Merauve's breath stopped.

Elenden moved. Eyes shut, face streaming mud and rain, he turned his shoulder and let the blade pass beside him. Cassius recovered, slashed backhand. Elenden dropped beneath it. Rose. A third strike came high—and Elenden's bare foot rose to meet the pommel. His heel connected with the pearl grip and drove it sideways. The sword spun from Cassius' fingers and turned twice in the air before burying itself in the mud ten paces away, hilt up, the pearl slick with rain.

His eyes remained closed.

The rain did its work. Mud ran in dark rivulets down his cheeks and throat. When his eyes opened again, the sea-blue had gone dark as deep water.

Cassius had recovered his blade and now stood ten paces back, breathing hard. His white robes had begun to darken at the hems, the mud's persistence finally defeating whatever art kept them clean. The pearl sword trembled in his grip.

Cassius raised his blade with both hands.

Warmth fled the field—drawn out like frozen iron on bare skin. The rain thickened: each drop *colder*, half-crystallized, striking skin like grit. Merauve's breath came short. Beside him the satchel strap stiffened against his shoulder. The torches along the perimeter guttered and died, each flame pinching out as though pressed between wet fingers, until the field held no light but the diffused grey of the morning storm and the occasional crack of distant lightning.

Then fire leapt along Cassius' sword—the same unnatural flame Merauve remembered from his quarters. Blue chased silver up the steel, hissing where rain met it, illuminating Cassius' face from below. His brown eyes reflected the light in blue pinpricks.

"Try turning this blade again," Cassius said.

Elenden stood still. The rain ran between them. The fire on the blade threw shadows that writhed across the mud like living things.

"That isn't yours," Elenden said.

He made a cutting motion toward the blade.

The fire went out.

It simply ceased. One moment the blade burned; the next it was steel, dark and wet, still steaming from its edge.

Cassius stared at the weapon in his hand. His lips parted. For the first time in Merauve's observation, the Lightbringer's features read naked bewilderment.

He will kill you. The voice was back, and it was no longer warm. No longer brotherly. It pressed against the back of Merauve's skull. *He has already brought you to this. He would destroy the Inquisition's authority. He will bring the Empire to ruin. He will undo everything you have built, everything you are. You know this.*

Merauve's hand drifted to his belt. Tachet's hilt met his fingers.

The True has his back to you. One throw. You have made harder throws in the dark. When the body falls, we shall discuss your future. I will remember this, Merauve. I reward loyalty.

On the field, Cassius attacked again—savage now, all craft stripped away. He swung and Elenden moved and Cassius swung and Elenden moved and the rain fell between each stroke.

He lied to you about everything. He used you. He's using you now. Why defend him? He hates you.

The lies were beautiful. They arrived wearing truth's clothes—Elenden *had* deceived him about his recovery, *had* shaped the strategy—and each one carried just enough weight to tilt the floor beneath Merauve's feet. He could feel himself leaning. Could feel the logic assembling itself: Elenden was the threat, Cassius was the ally, the blade in his belt was the answer to every question.

Elenden stepped between them again. The line of sight broke.

Cold clarity. Rain on his face. The smell of mud and petrichor.

Merauve had drawn Tachet. He did not remember doing it.

On the field, Cassius was panting. His hair clung to his skull. The white robes hung heavy now with rain and mud, and the man inside them looked diminished, as though the fire that had left his blade had taken something with it. He held the sword in both hands now, its point wavering.

Elenden had not attacked. Not once. In the entire exchange he had not struck, kicked, nor grappled beyond what was necessary to deflect the blade. He had only moved, and redirected, and refused.

"Yield," Elenden said. He was breathing hard too, but his voice held. "Why fight for them? They hate you. You can be free."

Cassius' answer was a scream—wordless, raw, the sound of something cracking behind a wall that had held too long. He charged.

The strikes came without pattern. Overhead, lateral, thrust, slash—each one thrown with the full weight of a body that had abandoned defense. Elenden retreated for the first time, his bare feet moving fast over the flooded ground, his hands rising and falling to redirect occasional blows. One slash caught the upper sleeve of his robe and tore it. Another grazed his forearm—a thin line of red, bright against the rain, through his wrappings.

Cassius lunged. Overcommitted. Elenden stepped inside the arc, caught the Lightbringer's sword-wrist, and planted his bare foot against Cassius' chest. He pushed. Not a strike—a dismissal. Cassius left the ground. His back hit the mud three paces away, the pearl sword jarring loose from his grip. He scrambled for it, gasping, and came up spitting rainwater.

Elenden stopped retreating.

He planted his left foot in the mud and it held. His breathing deepened, each inhale drawing longer than the last. His arms wheeled outward, then swept rapidly inward—two fingers of his left hand drawing a line from between his eyes down to his sternum, his right arm pulling to tension. His right knee bent and lifted. He balanced on a single foot in the mud with a stillness that had no business existing on a battlefield.

Merauve recognized it.

The *kon-dah*. The spirit-scattering strike. One leg, weight gathered, the body coiled around its center. Elenden's eyes were open and clear, fixed on Cassius, and in them was something that had nothing to do with violence.

He is not looking.

The thought arrived kind, paternal. Fond, even.

Merauve's thumb found the neck of the blade where it emerged from the hilt.

Think, Inquisitor. You are a practical man. Your hand. Your blade. Your reward. Your choice.

The warmth pressed closer.

Then Elenden's preparation straightened him across Merauve's line of sight to Cassius. For one breath, the young man's shoulder blocked those brown eyes.

The warmth dimmed. Not gone—not the sharp severance of before—but quieter. Distant. As though the voice had said its piece and was content to wait.

The silence that remained in that void was worse.

Merauve had spent a career watching men mistake sentiment for strategy. The practical path was rarely the comfortable one. And the logic held on its own merits, cold and clean.

Whatever truth the boy had spoken, this remained: Elenden had decided what Merauve needed to know and when he needed to know it. He had made Merauve's choices for him.

Not this one.

His hand closed around the hilt. Not because a voice commanded it. Because every board he had ever played on had been someone else's—Sirius', Cassius', and now this barefoot boy's. The throw was the only move on the field that belonged to him alone.

It was regrettable. He had come, against his better judgment, to value Elenden's life. That made it harder. It did not make it wrong.

Forgive me, he thought, and did not know who he was asking.

Cassius charged. The gap closed fast, the white robes streaking through the rain. Elenden's planted foot turned a degree inward as his body wound tighter, his right arm drew back, his fingers straightened and fused to a blade.

Tachet left Merauve's hand spinning end over end—aimed at the center of Elenden's unguarded back.

Then Elenden's left foot shifted.

Not much. A fraction of a fraction. The mud beneath his instep surrendered to the rain, his ankle buckled, and his weight slipped a hand's breadth to the left. His body followed, his left shoulder dropping, his right arm sweeping wide to recover his balance.

Tachet passed through the space where his spine had been.

Cassius was mid-charge. Sword raised, mouth open, the gap between them closing with each stride. He did not see the blade. He was looking at Elenden's eyes.

The stiletto took the Lightbringer in the chest.

Serpent steel met whatever lay beneath those white robes, and for one instant—half a breath, less—the blade sang. That same clear note from the forge, from the grinding wheel. It rang across the muddy field and the rain carried it upward and outward, and the torches that had died rekindled—every one—their flames burning steady and orange in defiance of the storm.

Cassius stopped.

His sword lowered. His hands found the hilt of Tachet where it stood from his chest, the ironwood grip dark with rain. He touched it tentatively.

His brown eyes found Merauve across the field.

The voice was gone. The warmth, the whispers, the beautiful lies—all of it. The silence it left behind was vast.

Cassius' knees found the mud.

The pearl pommel of his sword caught the renewed torchlight as the weapon fell from his fingers and slipped to the mud beside him. Both hands cradled around the blade in his chest, and the white robes darkened—not with rain this time, but with something the rain could not wash clean.

His lips moved. No sound came.

Elenden turned. The failed *kon-dah* abandoned, his left ankle half-buried in the mud that had betrayed his balance. Rain ran down his face. His eyes found Cassius—then Merauve—then Cassius again.

He crossed the field, limping slightly.

Merauve watched him go. His right hand hung at his side; his fingers were still curved.

Elenden knelt before Cassius in the mud. He did not reach for the blade. He placed his hands—open, empty—on either side of the Lightbringer's face.

Cassius flinched. Whatever passed between them, Merauve could not hear. Elenden's lips moved near the dying man's ear, close enough that the rain could not steal the words. Cassius' hands fell from the hilt.

Then the Lightbringer's eyes went wide.

Not wider—*wrong*. The pupils swallowed the brown whole, iris drowning in black, and the black kept spreading until nothing remained but white rims around twin voids. His mouth opened and what came out was not his voice.

"HE'S LYING!"

The sound struck the field like a physical thing. Not loud—*total.* It filled the space between the rain and the ground, between heartbeat and heartbeat. The torches that had just rekindled shrank to blue points, fighting for their lives against a cold that had nothing to do with weather.

Cassius' body convulsed. His back arched, his hands clawing at the mud, and from the wound in his chest—from the space around Tachet's buried blade—something began to seep. Darker than blood; the color of nothing. It pooled at his knees, then spread outward, pressing against the rain-soaked earth as if testing the ground's willingness to receive it.

"HE'S MINE."

The voice wore Cassius' throat but nothing else. It came from deeper than lungs, deeper than bone. Merauve heard it in his own ears, felt it in his feet.

Elenden pulled back from Cassius' face. Grief spread across his features. As his hands withdrew, blackness poured from Cassius' eyes—thick, slow, pooling in the hollows of his face.

Elenden rose. His left ankle gave and he caught himself, one knee in the mud. He stood again, set his jaw, and began to drag the heel of his other foot through the earth.

A circle. Elenden was drawing a circle. And singing?

The dark pool reached the arc his heel had carved—and recoiled. Where the line met the spreading shadow, the shadow threw itself back like water thrown against hot iron, hissing, steaming. The rain in the circle's groove seemed to glow faintly where it gathered—almost silver.

Cassius—or what remained of Cassius—screamed.

"SHE LEFT YOU FOR RIVEN!"

The words hit Merauve like a fist to the sternum. He staggered. He could see it—Aerellyn in the courtyard, turning away. The image burned with the vividness of memory, though it was not his memory. It was not anyone's memory. It was a wound made from whole cloth and driven into sound.

Across the field, Maudalia dropped the basket she had been clutching. Her hands flew to her mouth.

"MASTER CHEN IS DEAD—YOU FAILED HIM."

Merauve's knees buckled. The rain-soaked earth met his palms and he was kneeling, gasping, the words lodged in him like splinters because they were close—*close enough*. Not this. No.

Elenden's heel kept moving. The arc widened. Half the circle now.

The darkness surged—tendrils reaching, probing, pressing against the groove in the mud and finding no purchase. Each time it touched the line, light flared along the carved earth and the shadow fell back.

"THE STARS LIE!"

At the field's northern edge, Pakonaskow's head snapped back as though struck. Alena reached for his arm. The elder shook her off. He stepped forward—one pace, two—his boots compressing the mud, his dark eyes fixed on the thing that writhed within the closing circle. He raised his right fist toward it. Not a gesture of threat. An act of resistance. Refusal. The fist held steady, knuckles forward, arm extended, the way a man holds a torch against the dark.

"YOUR FAMILY HATES YOU."

The screams came faster now, overlapping. Merauve could not sort through them all. He felt them pass through the field like concussive waves—some striking him, some finding others. Brendan had turned his back. Thorne stood rigid, both hands locked at his sides, his jaw working against sounds no one else could hear. The guard beside him had dropped the umbrella. It lay overturned in the mud at Thorne's feet, rain pooling in its bowl. Neither man reached for it.

"THIS FORTRESS WILL FALL."

Elenden's circle was nearly complete. His heel was carving the final quarter through mud that had gone black beneath him. His foot left a clean groove, and where the groove passed, the darkness could not follow.

The thing in Cassius' body saw the gap closing. Its head—his head, still his head, still bearing Cassius' face, though with black eyes and bared teeth—whipped toward Pakonaskow. The elder stood closest to the circle's edge, fist raised, immovable.

Cassius' hand found Tachet's hilt.

The blade came free from his own chest with a sucking sound. Blood—real blood, bright red—followed it. The stiletto spun across the broken circle and flew at Pakonaskow with force no dying arm should have possessed.

"YOUR CHILDREN WILL FORGET YOUR NAME."

The steel flashed as it crossed the distance.

Elenden's bare foot completed the circle.

The line closed. Merauve saw light flare along its circumference—bright, clean—and the darkness had no way out. It still screamed, but the sound broke against the ring of the circle and reached him muted, distant, as though from behind thick glass. The shadow collapsed inward, wrenched back through Cassius' eyes and the wound in his chest—drawn into whatever void had spawned it—and the white robes were shredded, and the thrashing stopped, and the body settled.

Outside the circle, Tachet stood buried to the hilt in Pakonaskow's chest.

The elder looked down at the blade. Looked up.

His fist dropped.

Alena reached him first. Her hands found his shoulders as his knees gave, easing him down.

Elenden was already running. He crossed the field barefoot and limping. The distance between the circle and the northern edge could not have been more than twenty paces. It took a lifetime.

He dropped beside the elder and took his face in both hands—the same way he had held Cassius, but the hands were different now. They trembled.

"Papa." The word cut through the rain. "*Papa.*"

Pakonaskow's eyes found Elenden's face. They blinked. Lost focus. Found it again. His lips moved. The sound that emerged was barely breath.

Alena leaned close. Her ear near the elder's mouth.

"He says—" Her voice splintered. She pressed her lips together. Tried again. " 'Thank you.' "

Elenden's thumbs moved across the old man's rain-soaked cheeks. "I know," he whispered. "Ka."

Pakonaskow's gaze drifted from Elenden's face. Upward. Past the young man's shoulder, past the fortress walls, past the tower, up to the storm. His dark eyes blinked against the falling rain—once, slowly—and then widened.

Whatever he saw there, it was not the clouds.

He smiled.

The storm broke open.

The overcast split along a seam that ran from the east, and morning light poured through the gap. The rain continued to fall—lit from within—and the sun struck the dueling field in a single broad shaft that turned the standing water to gold and the mud to bronze and the rain to falling fire.

Pakonaskow lay still in the arms of the man he had come to save. The light held his face. The rain washed him clean. The wind accepted his last breath.

Merauve stood at the field's edge, empty-handed, empty.

The rain fell on.

Chapter 78

Merauve

"Treachery!"

The word split the thinning rain. High Inquisitor Sirius had risen from beneath his canopy, one arm rigid, finger aimed at Merauve like a blade.

"Arrest that man!"

On the field, inside the circle, Cassius lay still. His white robes had gone the color of the dead grass around him. Steam rose from the body—thin, acrid—curling where the break in the clouds spilled light. The air above the circle shimmered like air above a forge.

Merauve's boots carried him forward. He was not certain he had told them to. The mud pulled at each step, and the field tilted. There was nothing left to hold his world level.

Across the field, Thorne was already moving. The Major crossed toward Sirius' pavilion in long strides that splashed through the mud. His voice arrived in fragments—blown thin by the weather, landing in pieces.

"Your *champion* just killed a diplomat!" Thorne was growling. "What in the name of stone and storm—"

Sirius' reply came clipped. Merauve caught the cadence—defensive, brittle—but the words dissolved before they reached him. The High Inquisitor's hands had found his sleeves again.

"—do not presume to lecture me on—"

"—three hundred riders, Your Justice, and their elder is lying on my field with a blade in his chest—"

"—broke the rules of conduct—" Sirius' voice broke the surface, sharp and clear.

Thorne's answer was too low to hear. But Merauve saw the Major's hand rise toward the circle—toward the body that steamed in the clearing weather. Sirius made a dismissive gesture.

Merauve staggered on. His coat hung heavy with rain. The field stretched before him, scored with the evidence of violence—furrows where boots had torn the turf. The dark ring of the circle still held its shape in the mud—and beyond it, at the northern edge, Elenden.

He was kneeling. Pakonaskow's head rested in his arms.

Alena stood three paces behind. Her hands were at her sides, her grey eyes glazed with rain or tears. She breathed through her nose. When she saw Merauve, she stepped back another pace. Her gaze found his empty hand and stayed there.

Elenden did not look up. His thumbs moved across the elder's rain-soaked cheeks. His lips were moving—not words Merauve could hear. His shoulders shook once. Stilled. Shook again.

Merauve stopped beside him. Silence became more unbearable than inadequacy.

"I don't know what to say."

Elenden's hands withdrew from the old man's face. He sat back on his right heel. The sun found the welt where Cassius' fist had landed—already darkening to a bruise against the mud-streaked skin. His eyes were red. Tears had carved clean tracks down his cheeks.

He breathed. Steadied. When he spoke, the rawness was still there, but beneath it, something load-bearing.

"Can you get us out of here, Inquisitor?"

Merauve met his eyes. Nodded.

Purpose. He turned and crossed the field toward the pavilion.

Sirius saw him coming. The High Inquisitor stepped out from beneath the canopy, and his composure—already frayed—tore open.

"*You.*" He thrust a finger toward Merauve. "You made a grave mistake. You will answer for every—"

Merauve raised his hand. Open palm, chest height.

Sirius stopped.

Merauve looked past him. Found Thorne.

"I will go with the prisoner north to the Val'dren." He spoke to the Major as though Sirius were furniture. "Alone, or with an escort of your choosing. As proof that Pakonaskow's blood-stead was accepted and the man goes free."

Sirius' face went scarlet. "*Absolutely* not. You killed my champion outside the bounds of the duel. You violated the sanctity of—"

"Agreed."

Thorne spoke from behind him. No louder than Sirius, but heavier. He stepped forward, past the table with its wine bottle and half-filled cup, and turned to the High Inquisitor.

"I do not know what *that* was." His arm swept toward the circle. "But it was *not* normal." His jaw set. "I have a fortress to consider."

Sirius' mouth opened. Nothing came.

Thorne turned to the nearest guard. "Show him to his things. Ensure he's equipped." A pause. His eyes flicked to Sirius once, then back. "Keep them safe on the way out."

To Merauve: "You leave, alone and on foot, in five minutes."

Merauve nodded. The guard—the one who held, and dropped, the umbrella—stepped forward. Merauve fell in beside him.

They crossed the field. As they neared the circle's edge, the pearl-hilted sword caught the corner of his vision—lying in the mud beyond Cassius' outstretched hand. He stepped wide to avoid the circle's groove and lifted it by the pommel.

The guard raised an eyebrow, but led him to the storehouse adjacent to the keep's north wall—a low stone building with a heavy door that the guard shouldered open. Inside: the scent of damp wool. Merauve's effects waited in a canvas roll beside the entrance. He unrolled it on the nearest bench and took stock. Pack. Waterskins. A wool coat—imperial issue, but unmarked, chosen for the northern parley weeks ago because it would not announce its owner. It was the warmest he had, and it would have to do.

He stripped off his dress coat. The purple threading caught the storehouse light one last time. He held it a moment—the weight of it, the cut. Then he laid it across the bench, folded the sleeve over the pearl-hilted blade, and drew the fabric along the steel. Mud came away in long streaks. The threading snagged once on the crossguard. He worked it free and kept wiping until the blade was clean.

He left the coat where it lay and pulled the wool one on. It sat heavier across the shoulders, cut for weather rather than theatre. From the roll he drew a second pair of boots—riding boots, sturdy, a size smaller than his own. He had packed them for the parley as spares. They would fit Elenden well enough.

He checked his belt. The gap where Tachet should be stared back at him like an empty socket.

He turned back to the roll. His riding coat—leather, better than nothing. He pulled it out, held it a moment, and set it with the spare boots. A leather sword belt hung from a peg near the door—plain, unadorned, the scabbard scratched from use. He slid the pearl-hilted blade into it. The fit was loose but it held.

The guard coughed from the doorway.

Merauve slung the pack over one shoulder, gathered the sword belt and spare boots, and followed him out.

When he returned to the northern edge, Elenden had risen. He stood over Pakonaskow's body, handing a knife back to Alena—hers, by the look of it. A braid hung from his right fist, heavy and dark, threaded with beads. Near its end, a falcon feather turned slowly.

Elenden looked up. Looked Merauve in the face.

Merauve stopped.

Sirius' shrill condemnations and accusing fingers, he could ignore; this was different.

He set his shoulders. Focused his eyes over Elenden's shoulder. The spare boots and riding coat hung from one arm, the pearl-hilted sword from the other, and he stood with all of it—chin level, spine straight. And waited for what he deserved.

"It's a good thing you are a bad throw, Inquisitor."

The words arrived around a faint smile—exhausted, strained and half-broken. His eyes were still clearing. The bruise on his jaw had gone the color of an overripe plum. Mud, blood, the braid clutched in his fist, and still that smile—extended across a chasm that had no business being bridged.

"Good thing you are clumsy."

Elenden's smile reached his eyes and held for a breath.

"Papa would have laughed at that." The smile faded. He looked down at the body. Exhaled a full breath that came slow and heavy and hitched near the end. "He was a good man."

"I...am not."

Merauve extended the pearl-hilted sword.

Elenden looked at it. Something moved behind his eyes—a decision made faster than Merauve could follow. He pushed the belt back toward Merauve's chest.

"Keep it. You'll need a replacement." His gaze dropped to Merauve's belt.

"You mean I can't—"

Elenden's head snapped toward him. The exhaustion vanished. What replaced it was sharp, immediate—the same look from the tower room, the morning after Cassius' first visit.

"No." Final. "By the five, **no**. That blade escaped the circle as the last act of a Dark spirit. All of its thought, all its power, all its hate, all of its cruelty, everything it *hungered for*—it spent on that blade and that throw." He looked at Pakonaskow's chest. "Leave it."

Elenden turned to Alena. They spoke in low voices. Burn both bodies, outside the walls. Alena nodded once and moved toward the eastern edge of the field where Corbin and Naman kept counsel.

Merauve looked toward where Tachet's ironwood hilt rose from Pakonaskow's chest. The serpent steel that had been his companion, his instrument, his morning and his evening. He could feel it.

Not hear it. Not see it. *Feel* it—just there. His hand had simply forgotten to pick it up. To close around it.

He knelt. Pretended to adjust the spare boots under his arm. He was so close.

The weight of years was magnetic, drawing him toward the only companion that had never disappointed him, never judged him, never required explanation. How could he leave his only friend?

A hand entered his vision.

Elenden stood over him, arm extended, palm open. The braid with its falcon feather hung from his other fist. His sky-blue eyes held steady.

"Come, Inquisitor." Gentle. The way one speaks to a man standing at a ledge. "I'll not leave without you."

Merauve looked at the offered hand. At Tachet. At the hand.

He took it.

Elenden's grip was firm, calloused, warm. The contact did not sever anything, but the feeling went quiet. Not gone. Quieted to an ache.

Merauve rose. Handed Elenden the spare boots. Buckled the sword belt at his hip and cinched it.

"How's the ankle?"

"Sprained. Bruised." Elenden turned one foot against the mud. "It'll hold."

Merauve turned to the guard.

"Lead on."

The guard started toward the north gate. Merauve fell into step beside Elenden. Ahead, the gate stood open—the iron lattice drawn back, the passage clear, the northern road visible beyond as a pale line winding into hills still remembering the retreating storm.

As they passed through the gate, the guard stopped at the threshold.

"This is as far as I go." He looked at Merauve. Then at Elenden.

"May your ways be true," Elenden said.

The guard stepped back. He was shaking his head as he walked away.

The road was mud. The sky was clearing from the north—the storm retreating southward in a long dark mass, surrendering the horizon by degrees. The air smelled of pine and the sharpness that follows lightning: clean, scoured.

Elenden walked beside him. Barefoot and silent—he carried the boots tied and slung over one shoulder rather than wear them.

After fifty paces, Merauve exhaled. After a hundred, he spoke.

"Did the wall open?"

Elenden glanced at him. "Wall?"

"The *Azurath* wall. In the library at Ember." Merauve kept his eyes on the road. "When Adam—when Emperor Vaylen spoke. Did the wall open?"

A pause. "Yes."

"What was inside?"

Elenden was quiet long enough that Merauve thought he might not answer. Then the pastoral register returned.

"A room. Small—barely wider than my arms could span. The *Shiranath* were lit when we entered. The stone inside was older than anything else in the library. You could smell it." A breath. "You could feel it."

"What was in the room?"

"At the center, a pedestal. Waist-high, carved from a single piece of dark stone—basalt, Jonathan thought. The top was slotted. A narrow groove, perhaps two fingers wide and a handsbreadth deep, lined with what looked like beaten gold. Shaped to hold something specific."

"The slot was empty. The item had been removed. The lining was undamaged." He made no effort to avoid stepping into a deep puddle. "But someone had left a note in its place. Folded once, tucked into the groove. Heavy paper—the kind that outlasts the hand that writes on it. The ink had been purple once, but browned at the edges."

"What did it say?"

"Jonathan translated it. Old formal Thamarian. *By order of His Imperial Majesty Alaster, in this, the ninety-first year of the Second Founding, with solemn conviction—the key is hereby removed to Imperial custody. May it serve us in our time of need.*"

The road was theirs. The only sounds were their feet and the last of the wind nosing through the trees—shaking loose the rain that the season-stripped branches had kept, so that drops fell around them in irregular percussion, striking dirt and stone and the standing water in the wheel ruts. Somewhere to the east, a stream had found its voice in the storm's runoff, threading through rocks they could not see.

Merauve opened his mouth.

Elenden raised his hand.

"Please." His voice was very quiet. "Our freedom was purchased at a great cost, and I am glad for it." A deep breath. "But I have lost a friend today, and I would hold his memory a little longer before I continue my story." Elenden's thumb moved over the beads in his other hand.

Merauve closed his mouth. And walked. His hand drifted to his belt and found the cold pearl pommel where the ironwood should have been.

He managed to last until the fortress sank behind the final hill. "I feared we were at the end."

Elenden was quiet for a step. Then: "The end?" He shook his head. "Perhaps *an* end."

A glance, sidelong. The faintest brightness glowed behind his eyes. "I've not told you the half of it, Inquisitor."

The road bent north through low hills, and the sky opened further with more and more blue. The wintered fields thinned, stubble giving way to stone and scrub, and the bare hardwoods yielded to pine—dark green and indifferent to the season.

Merauve shifted the pack on his shoulder. The satchel's strap dug at his collarbone, and he adjusted it—then paused. His fingers moved to the flap.

The ring was where he'd left it, wrapped in a square of doeskin at the bottom of the inner pocket. The rice paper beside it, fragile with age. He drew them both out.

He unfolded the rice paper.

Chen's brushwork had faded unevenly—some marks darker where the ink had pooled at the base of each stroke, others thinned to ghosts. Tally marks. He had counted them before. He counted them again. The refugees they had saved together. The last thing Master Chen handed him. One of those marks was an emperor. *The* Emperor?

He looked at Elenden. At the bruise on his jaw, the mud on his bare feet, the braid in his hand. At the man who had stood over him with an open hand.

I'll not leave without you.

He held out the ring.

Elenden saw it and stopped walking. His eyes moved from the ring to Merauve's face. He did not reach for it.

"Yours, I believe," Merauve said.

Elenden's hand opened slowly. Merauve set the ring in his palm—the leather cord uncoiling in leaps and starts, the stone catching light like the open sky. Elenden's fingers closed around it. He lifted the ring to his face with cupped hands. His eyes closed. He inhaled once, long and slow. After a moment, he slipped it over his head.

"Thank you, Inquisitor."

Merauve folded the rice paper along its original creases, careful not to tear it where the years had worn the fibers thin. He slipped it back into the satchel's inner pocket, pressing the flap closed with his thumb.

He adjusted the strap on his shoulder.

"Call me Merauve."

Elenden looked at him. He inclined his head.

They walked north.

Encore

Shemah needed to find shade.

He had walked through the night, which was the only way left to him. Two days ago the wadi had been dry stone and dust. He had made camp in its bed because the walls offered shelter from the wind, and because his grandfather had camped in wadis, and his grandfather's grandfather before that, all the way back to the first of his people, who had pitched their tents west of the Cindrel Vale and never found sufficient reason to cross it.

The rain came without warning. Not the slow grey veils of the southern lands—he had heard of those, could not imagine them—but a wall of brown water that arrived with a sound like tearing cloth, and then like thunder, and then like nothing at all because there was only the water and the dark and the desperate scrabbling of his hands against stone that was suddenly slick and alive beneath him.

His camel was gone. His packs, his food, the rolled hide that served as tent and blanket and prayer mat—all of it swept into the torrent's throat. He had saved himself by climbing, fingers splitting against the wadi's lip. He escaped with his waterskins because they tangled in the roots of a ghost-brush that clung to the rim. He escaped with his knife, because his people slept with blade and water within reach. He escaped with his life, because the Spirit had not finished with him.

Or so he had believed.

He had water—the skin was still half-full, and the flood had left standing pools in the wadi's stone pockets, clear enough to drink if he strained them through cloth. Water was not the thing that would kill him.

It was the salt.

Two days of sweating under the desert's hand, drinking water that replaced what left his skin but not what left with it. The cramps had started last night—his calves first, then his fingers, seizing into claws around the waterskin as though his body was trying to hold itself still by force. His thoughts had begun to fray at the edges. He would be walking and then he would not be walking, and the distance between those two states had no memory in it, only a gap, like a word rubbed from a page.

Now the third morning opened its eye above the eastern ridge, and the desert laid its judgment bare. According to the stars and his memory, the nearest edge of green—the place where the sand surrendered to scrub grass and the air began to taste of living things—was a full day's walk to the north and east.

One day. He could walk another day without food.

But not without shade. Not without salt.

He sat in the lee of a rust-colored ridge where the shadows still held, his back against stone that the night had cooled but the morning was already reclaiming. His waterskin rested across his knees. He allowed himself two mouthfuls—warm, tasting like leather. He held both on his tongue before swallowing.

He was the second son. Not the heir, not the keeper of the herds, not the one whose name was carved into the family's tent-pole alongside the names of ancestors. He was the one the elders could spare when the stars spoke and someone had to answer. His mother had wept. His father had not, though his hands had lingered when they clasped his son's shoulders. His brother had given him the camel—the good one, the one with the easy gait. He loved his brother. His brother was the better man. He was glad his brother would live.

The stars had spoken of a great turning in the north. Something had shifted in the heavens, and his people—who had watched the sky since the first ancestors—had seen it and understood that someone must go. Must witness. Must carry word back, or die in the attempt.

He was beginning to suspect which it would be.

The shadows shortened. The ridge that sheltered him was low, and the sun climbed with steady malice. Within the hour he would be exposed. He could move—follow the ridge north, hope for an overhang, a cave, anything that might hold shadow through the killing hours—but movement spent sweat, and sweat meant salt.

He closed his eyes. The heat pressed against his lids like a thumb.

He opened his eyes in a panic. How long had it been?

The wadi stretched north beneath the ridge—a dry channel of pale gravel and smooth stone, carved by the same waters that had nearly killed him. He had followed it since, because wadis led somewhere, and somewhere was better than nowhere. But now, fifty paces ahead, the channel bent east around a shoulder of rock, and above the bend, a stone overhang jutted from the ridge like a shelf.

He had not noticed that before.

He rose. His legs protested, but they held. The fifty paces cost him in the sun's angle against his neck, in the sweat that left his skin and vanished before it could cool him.

The overhang was deeper than it looked. The stone shelf extended back three body-lengths into cool shadow, and the wadi's curve had deposited a bed of gravel beneath it—dry, shaded, sheltered from the wind. He lowered himself to the ground and let his head rest against the stone.

Then he saw the bundle.

It sat against the back wall where the overhang met the ridge. A leather roll, cinched with cord. It had not been hidden. It had been placed—deliberately, recently. The cord was still supple. The leather bore no dust.

His hands found his knife before his mind finished the thought. He waited. Listened. Alert. The desert spoke only wind and the distant cry of a hawk looking for its morning meal.

He crawled forward. Cut the cord. Unrolled the leather.

Dried meat, dark and dense. Hard cheese sealed in wax. Some baked flatbread—four rounds, pale and hard as stones. A small clay pot, stoppered with wax: honey, by the color that wept from the seal. A twist of cloth holding six white tablets he knew at a glance: salt.

Shemah stared at it. His throat worked once, dry and tight.

No note. No marker. No explanation. Just food, left beneath a stone overhang in a dry wash at the edge of the world.

He took the nearest piece of dried meat and bit. The salt and smoke of it bloomed across his tongue—dense, almost too rich after days of nothing, and his jaw ached with the sudden effort of chewing and making spit. His eyes burned, and he blinked.

He was going to make it.

He chewed slowly, carefully, the way his grandmother had taught him to eat after a fast: small pieces, patience, gratitude before greed. The shade held. The food was good.

Who places bread in the wilderness and walks away? Surely the storm had washed it here. But the gravel beside the bundle held the print of a boot—clear-edged, recent, undisturbed by wind. No, someone had left it here on purpose. But why? Who would do such a thing?

He owed this person a life-debt.

Shemah took another bite. The hawk cried once more, high and thin, and turned east toward better hunting.

Physick Grendle was not happy.

The cold season always brought the usual harvest—ague cycling through the garrison, chilblains among the wall sentries, a flux in the lower barracks he'd traced to a contaminated cistern. Routine. Manageable. Now there was this business with the duel. First forbidden from attending, now handed the aftermath.

The Imperial Academy had been thorough in its dismissals. Every term, one folk tradition after another held up for examination, displayed for spectacle—laying on of hands, humoral balancing, prayer healing—each discussed, disassembled, and dispatched as superstition. Grendle had nodded along with the rest of them. Had even written a creditable paper on placebo mechanisms underlying faith-based recovery. Then came his station at the borders. Years of watching people heal when they shouldn't. Live when they shouldn't. Die when they shouldn't.

Die *how* they shouldn't.

He lowered the sheet on the second body.

The elder had been straightforward—penetrating blade wound to the thorax. He'd been advised to leave the blade in place; he was happy to comply. No sense unplugging what the steel had sealed. The certificate wrote itself.

This one refused to cooperate.

Scorch marks radiated from the wound in the solar plexus—blackened lines spreading outward in a pattern that was not random. Symmetrical. A dark star drawn to follow the body's meridian lines. The flesh along each line had gone rigid, the tissue sealed and calloused—it looked cauterized, but not by heat. The chest wound hadn't punctured either lung.

And the head. The eyes had sunk too deep into their sockets. The blackened eyelids were drawn tight over the hollows. No external head wound, no fracture he could find. But the bone at the crown had gone soft under his fingers, as if the structure had been crushed from within.

Dead was dead. He pulled the form toward him. Dipped his pen.

Cause of death: chest wound.

Vague. Not his finest work.

Not like the body in the cold room beneath the infirmary. *That* was his finest work—or close to it. A near-perfect match for the Inquisitor's description. He'd prepared it at Merauve's request. The same man who had, apparently, been stripped of rank earlier this morning and escorted from the fortress alongside the prisoner. He'd barely had to doctor it. Some mountain fellow the scouting patrols had brought in two days prior—killed by a wild animal, which was odd. Most predators large enough to take a grown man would be denning this time of year, not hunting. And this one had killed without consuming. He had considered it a stroke of luck.

He removed his gloves and dropped them in the bin.

"Plague protocol," he called after the departing guards. "We know, we know," came the reply, already halfway down the corridor.

He was tired. Maybe, when this was sorted, he would take some time. Visit his family. Remember what it felt like to attend to someone who was still breathing.

Inquisitor Jerome.

He tested it again, silently, letting the shape of it fill his mouth. *Inquisitor.* Not junior. Not provisional. The word had weight to it, a gravity that pulled the world into a different arrangement around the man who wore it.

Sirius had barely looked at him when he said it. The High Inquisitor's face was the color of old brick, his composure in ruins, his finger still jabbing toward the north gate through which Merauve and the prisoner had disappeared. "Cassius mentioned you. *Someone* must maintain Inquisition authority at this post until I return with a tribunal." His lip curled. "Do try not to embarrass the office further."

The seal had been pressed into Jerome's palm—still warm from Sirius' hand, still slick with the wax he'd heated over the candle in Thorne's quarters. Purple wax.

Jerome had closed his fist around it and said nothing. Saying nothing, he had learned, was almost always the right choice. Merauve had taught him that much, at least. Merauve would have found something clever to say. Something devastating. Jerome didn't have his gift. He had the discipline to keep his mouth shut, though, which was the next best thing.

Sirius rode south before noon, his escort kicking mud from the road. The fortress exhaled.

Now Jerome stood at the back of a cart watching two soldiers wrestle a body wrapped in canvas onto the bed beside the one already loaded. The soldiers worked without speaking. The first bundle was heavy. The elder. Blood had soaked through in a wide dark crescent where the blade had entered. The canvas on the second bundle—Cassius—had gone grey-brown where fluids seeped through.

"Downwind, downstream, separately. Burn them both. Don't touch anything."

The soldiers knew. The scouts knew. Everyone knew.

Especially those who stood on that field. He shuddered.

Jerome climbed onto the cart bench. He could have ordered one of the soldiers to drive, but the task gave him something to do with his hands, and he wanted distance from the fortress. Besides—he was Inquisitor now. Time to take the reins. He snorted.

The carthorse leaned into its collar. The gate passed overhead.

The road south was rutted and still soft from the storm, but he turned the cart east after half a mile, following a sheep track that wound along the ridge above the river. Downwind. Downstream. He would find a place far away where the ground had not yet frozen through—the season was turning, but slowly, and south-facing slopes still yielded to a spade.

The cart rocked and lurched. Behind him, the bodies shifted with each rut, canvas scraping against the cart bed. Jerome kept his eyes forward.

All things considered, it was a good day.

One month ago, he had begged the Inquisitor for help with a Virtue Duel he couldn't win, and had traded his dignity for survival. He'd told Merauve he had a family—a wife, a child, the whole pitiful tableau, thinking it would make him more sympathetic. Sympathy hadn't worked, but the flattery had.

There was no wife. No child. There was only Jerome, who had learned early that the world sorted people into those who used and those who were used, and had chosen his side accordingly. Merauve believed him, or hadn't cared enough to check. Either way, the lie had held for a full month, which meant Jerome had managed his caseload, avoided the worst attention, and survived to stand at Sirius' elbow under the pavilion, mostly dry, while other men bled in the mud.

Sirius said Cassius had spoken of his potential. Jerome did not examine what that meant too closely. The Lightbringer was dead, which closed the only mouth that might have elaborated on exactly what "potential" he had recognized. Clean. Neat. Unlike Cassius' death. He shuddered again.

He found a spot where the ridge dipped and the river bent away—a south-facing shelf of earth above the flood line, soft enough that the spade bit without ringing off frost. He set the soldiers to digging. Two graves, thirty paces apart. The wind came from the west and carried the river smell with it—cold water, pine, stone.

They unloaded Cassius first. The canvas peeled back around the face where the seepage had glued it to the body, and Jerome kept his gloves on and his breathing shallow. The Lightbringer's eyes were black; the rest of his face looked slack and waxy. Jerome watched them roll him into the shallow trench.

The elder was heavier, and the blood had dried the canvas stiff around the wound. Jerome and the nearer soldier tilted him from the cart, and the body landed in the second trench with a sound that Jerome decided not to remember.

That was when he saw it.

Merauve's blade. Its ironwood hilt rose from the elder's chest where the canvas had torn, the serpent steel catching what was left of the afternoon light. Someone had bundled cloth around the point of entry, but the wrapping had shifted in transit, and now the blade stood exposed, angled slightly from the body like a sundial's gnomon.

Jerome paused.

Merauve had left it behind. Superstitious. That was the word. Merauve had gone superstitious at the end, soft in a way Jerome had not anticipated and did not respect. Some men believed it was ill luck to rob the dead. Jerome was not some men. You wiped it clean and found a new sheath.

It really was a beautiful thing. That kind of steel held an edge that Jerome's own blade—standard Imperial issue—would never match. The ironwood hilt was dark with years of use. A tool like that was worth more than Jerome's quarterly wages. Might be worth more than the seal in his pocket, if he was being honest.

Jerome looked at the soldiers. They were thirty paces away, shoveling loose earth over Cassius, their backs turned. The wind covered small sounds.

He knelt beside the trench. His gloved hand found the hilt.

The blade came free with less resistance than he expected—a wet, grinding release, and then it was in his hand, surprisingly light. He turned it once, watching the steel catch light along its edge.

He wiped it on the loose cloth that had covered the wound, then he kicked a pile of earth over the elder's body, tamped it down with his boot, and called for the soldiers to bring the firewood.

The smoke rose in two pale columns against the darkening sky. Downwind. Downstream. Separately. Jerome watched from the cart bench, legs dangling, the blade resting safe under the cart seat.

He would need a sheath. Something plain, nothing that would draw attention. And he would need to practice with it. But these were practical problems, and Jerome was good at practical problems.

The soldiers gathered river stones and stacked them. After the fires died down, they stamped the embers flat and piled the stones over the ashes.

Inquisitor Jerome gathered the reins and turned the cart toward Fortress Kestrel.

It was a good day.

Author's Note

When I was a child, I dreamt I stepped outside into the night and gathered a stone. With it, I carved letters into the earth. As I wrote, the words caught fire—rising bright into the dark sky, shining against the clouds for all to read.

I've carried that dream ever since, wondering what it meant.

C.S. Lewis once wrote that myth is "at its best, a real though unfocused gleam of divine truth falling on human imagination." I have tried to write toward that gleam—to let the Truth beneath all stories shine through without explaining it, without diminishing it by dragging it into the open and naming all its parts.

Perhaps this story is for you—compelled by the Spirit of Truth from my youth. To reveal through a myth of magic and mystery, a *glimpse* of the True myth.

If *The Truth Dancer* moved you, **would you consider leaving a brief review on Amazon or Goodreads** or even better: **tell a friend**? Even a sentence or two helps other readers discover this story. Thank you for being part of this journey.

Should you notice any errors—you may be blessed with True sight—please let me know. Note that I have used American English spelling throughout, excepting the word *grey*, which I thoroughly believe to be correct. I am stubborn about this (though I apologize if you found it distracting).

If you enjoyed this story, I suspect you'd also love Jonathan Renshaw's work—and if you happen to know him, I'd be delighted if you'd introduce us. Likewise, if you have any connection to the good people at Rabbit Room Press, I wouldn't mind a nudge in their direction. I, unlike the Val'dren, have no qualms with saying thank you (or repaying).

For updates on the Spirit of Truth series or to share feedback, drop me a line over at https://thetruth.dance.

For press or business inquiries: inquiries@thetruth.dance

May your ways be true,

L.R. Merriman

Books in the

Spirit of Truth

series

Movement I

The Truth Dancer

Stave I · Earth

Stave II · Water

Stave III · Air

Stave IV · Spirit

Stave V · Fire

Movement II

The Wilds Girl · forthcoming

Sign up for updates on the Spirit of Truth series at

thetruth.dance

ALSO IN THIS MOVEMENT

The Truth Dancer is also available as a single-volume ebook.

Made in the USA
Coppell, TX
10 August 2026

86193636R00169